# Lord Firebird
# A Novel

# J.F. MacCrimmon

Wolf Moon Press
Tombstone, AZ

ISBN-10: 1494285169
ISBN-13: 978-1494285166

Dedicated to all who encouraged me through the years. Far too many to mention, but you know who you are!

Special thanks to Professor Charles Burm, Dr. Lori Muntz & the English Dept. at IWC, The Society of Great River Poets, and especially to Mrs. Hull and Ms. Byrd who first introduced me to the joy of the written word all those years ago.

Of course dedicated to my family who encouraged me to pursue my passion.

Also dedicated to the memory of a wonderful poet and friend, Corinne Davis-Kahl. May your memory and legacy endure.

# Part I

"The young always have the same problem – how to rebel and conform at the same time. They have solved this by defying their parents and copying one another."

-Quentin Crisp-
(The Naked Civil Servant, 1968)

# Chapter One
## In the Beginning There is an End…

"The young have aspirations that never
Come to pass, the old have reminiscences of
What never happened.  It's only the middle-aged
Who are really conscious of their limitations.
[Saki (Hector Hugh Munro) 1904]

As I glided along Charleston Road, a preternatural knot embedded itself deep within my chest as I gazed off the side of the Tombstone Hills to the vast, high desert below.  The hum of the *Indian's* engine reverberated through my body, accentuated by the haunting beauty and lingering malevolence, I had learned of late never to ignore – overwhelmed by the serenity of the road ahead.  As I looked over one last time at the looming hills, tall, magnificent, and majestic, a dark figure wandered through the arid sands of the high desert to disappear into the waves of rising afternoon heat.

As I cruised along the lonely desert highway, I gazed across the scarlet sands at the dark clouds of an approaching monsoon.  Patches of blue, white, and grey tinged with pink, consumed the horizon beyond, and swallowed the sun like a Southwestern Cronos to hover above the Dragoons in the distance.  The static hum electrified the heavy air and raised the fine hairs on my forearms as cool winds began to gather strength from the east.

A frightened stallion's cry echoed from nearby barns to the looming hills beyond, leaving me to shutter as involuntarily as the slight miss in the *Indian's* engine beneath me.  I felt I was being warned of something – something dark, ominous, and inevitable.  I felt a page was being torn from my life and the cover was about to be closed. I tried to clear my head of worry as I gently felt the pocket of my leather vest, but the feeling of glass beneath leather did little to comfort me or steady the irrational shutter of my heart.

I eventually parked behind the *S*tate *T*rooper *O*n *P*ot sign at Fourth and Allen streets. As the first hints of thunder rattled the mountains, I wandered past the OK Corral. Throughout town I was reminded of my namesake. Locals referred to me as "Doc" (although the only PhD I held was from the School of Hard Knocks). John Henry's eyes, followed me, the cold gaze that had been the last thing so many had seen, always captivated me as I passed by the shop windows that lined the plank sidewalks.

Worn and weathered blue jeans ripped out at the knees tightly cradled my legs and concealed silver-buckled bush boots. A beaten tank top and bandages covered the freshly scored scarlet and gold phoenix across my shoulders that ran down my muscled back. A white bone-bead choker, with a hand-carved stone phoenix, formed to my neck and set off the tanned skin and high-set, protruding cheek bones that sat just visible under mirrored lenses to betray what the subtle blend of London boarding school and Midwest redneck in my voice couldn't – my Lakota heritage.

I crossed Allen Street and made my way towards my usual haunt to escape the afternoon storm. The heels of my bush boots echoed across the wooden floor as I entered the swinging gates of the saloon. The saloon, like most of town, held the aura of the town's lawless past. The days of tough-as-nails lawmen and frontier justice were kept alive, to my chagrin, only in memory and daily gunfights on Allen Street.

Gus sat at the far end of the bar, separated from the rest of the patrons that congregated just inside the door by the large picture window. At the sound of my steps, a toothy grin adorned his dusty Lakota face. Fresh bruises and rope burns were evident on my youthful great-uncle's lanky, weathered arms. Compared to the cowboys and western aficionados that surrounded him, Gus appeared to be an oil stain on a white dress shirt – suspiciously out of place. He was literally the Indian in a cowboy bar holding two cigars.

"Still fighting that damned colt?" I questioned as he waved a cigar at me. "I think you should just put a .45 in him and call it a day!"

"I've still got one last trick up my sleeve," Gus replied as he handed me a cigar and proceeded to light mine, then his. "The little bastard ain't got me licked yet!" He laughed as he rubbed a large bruise on his right forearm. "Troy Three Feathers is arriving tomorrow. If anyone can break him, Troy can!"

As I sat down on the barstool next to Gus, he cried out, "Great Caesar's Ghost! What happened to your back?"

"Just a little ink work I had done in Scary Vista," I replied.

"Are you crazy?" he continued to rant as he pulled the neck of my tank top to look at the bandages that ran the width of my shoulders and the length of my back.

I'd certainly been accused of it enough. Gus shook a head of blue-black hair with just a wisp of grey to allude ominously to the fact that he had turned the tide past sixty. My mood always lightened as soon as I was in the presence of my great-uncle. It was impossible to be in a bad mood with Gus around. I was, however, surprised at how shocked he was by the new tattoo. It wasn't like it was the first I had ever had done. My left shoulder was adorned with an aging image of a black knight on a midnight steed adorned with the epitaph, "Requiescat In Pace '85".

The rope burned hand of my youthful great-uncle shakily poured the remnants of a pitcher of Bud Light into a once frosty, but now hot mug before asking the question, "Have you thought about the chances of infection?"

"Oh, mother," I dismissed.

"Hey, Doc," the bartender chimed as he placed a fresh pitcher of beer before Gus. "The usual?"

"Course. Thanks, Jim," I replied.

Jim threw a white bar towel over his turn of the century shoulder as he reached for the bottle of Scotch behind him. I spun lazily around to face the doorway and the equally empty floor and tables. I never did like to leave my back exposed – call it an old habit, mingled with a good dose of cover-my-ass and just a hint of paranoia. True, I could have just looked through the vast mirror before me and seen the breadth of the bar, but there was something comforting about keeping a true eye on the doorway. Besides, I knew Gus was already watching the mirror.

As I took my first long sip, the question of the hour was posed, "Does Sarah know you mutilated your back simply to get another Firebird?"

I involuntarily choked as I swallowed, causing me to shoot scotch from my nose. Gus laughed uncontrollably as I pinched my burning nose and turned red.

"Piss on you, Gus!" I coughed, remembering it was just the kind of asinine stunt that made him everyone's favourite asshole.

"You know I'm serious," Gus attempted to catch his breath as he continued his scolding. "You know she's going to have a all-out fit when she finds out."

"How would you know?" I queried as Gus raised his eyebrows in reply. "As a matter of fact, I've nearly got her convinced to get a tattoo around that pudgy little belly button of h…"

Just then, I looked up to see Sarah step into the doorway. Her silhouette shadowed the doorway and stretched across the scuffed wooden floor below. Her brown eyes widened with shock and disappointment from behind a few scarlet wisps that hung loose from the ponytail atop her heart shaped head before she turned the other way and left. Gus turned his head and emanated a brief whistle reminiscent of Donald Sutherland's "Hawkeye." It was a whistle that had become a standard sarcastic standoff for when he wanted to make a point to leave him out of it, or just to point out how much of a selfish ass I could be.

"Get off it, Gus!" I snapped at my great-uncle as I jumped from my seat to chase down my irate wife as she crossed the street.

Sarah had always been self-conscious of her weight. At a size fourteen, she thought herself less attractive than other women. When in fact, nothing was farther from the truth. She was extremely sexy. Sarah was a muscular farm girl who never would have looked right skinny. It seemed no matter how many times I tried to tell her that, she would never believe me. She never understood my jealousy. I never felt I deserved a woman like Sarah. I knew she was too beautiful, too perfect for me, and it tore at me like an Inquisitor's poker each time I gazed at her. Long before we met, I had resigned myself to a destiny of melancholy and loneliness.

I raced across the street to catch her. Instead, I caught a mouthful of dust as I called to her speeding car, "Sarah, wait! You don't understand!"

With a clenched jaw and doubled fist, I turned to the awning post, issued a firm blow, and returned to the saloon. Dead silence filled the bar as I walked in – a silence that was only broken by anther of Gus' "Hawkeye" whistles. Two glasses of Scotch awaited me on the bar. As I reached into my pocket, I was informed, "Your money's no good for those."

I nodded, pulled my hand from my pocket, and swung my leg over the barstool to sit.

"Not a bloody word, Gus!" I warned, my unique blend of Redneck and London boarding school more evident than usual in my voice.

Silence choked the room as the two of us, along with a handful other patrons, tried to forget that anything had transpired and returned to drinking. It was only after several, unsettling minutes that Gus ventured to speak to me about what happened.

"You two do this all the time," he observed.

"Do what?" I sulked.

"Don't play coy with me, boy!" he demanded. "You know what? You both try to be the first to drive the other away, like you're doing each other a favour. You're both too damned jealous."

"So, who are you now, Sigmund bloody Freud?"

"I've stood by and watched you try to throw the best thing to ever happen to you away. Do you really think she's going to find someone younger and stronger?"

"Wait a shaggin' minute! I'm only thirty-five and strong as a bloody ox!" I disputed.

"I know a few doctors that would beg to differ the fact with you. Besides, she thinks that you're going to run off with Miss September."

Gus stared me down with his dark, ominous eyes. He knew that comment would rub salt into an already long festered wound in my side. My mind dwelled on the image of my mother, Gus' niece, standing at the airport with her hand to a plate glass window; her eyes awash in tears.

"Now wait a God damned minute!" I spewed. "I am NOT James MacIntyre!"

"Nobody said you were," Gus responded, his dark eyes piercing through me.

"I'll thank you not to mention it again!"

"The point is…"

"About time!"

"…she loves you. And I know you love her."

He was right. There had always been something about Gus that I respected. It ran beyond the fact that he was my mother's uncle and they had been raised like sister and brother, or the fact that he was the one male figure in my family that ever really cared about me. It was a comradery that I had shared with only one other person. Gus had been more of a father to me growing up, than my own. He would shrug it off as fulfilling his "Injin" duty as an uncle, but there was more to it than that. He was trying to keep the family together. He had already given up hope on my older brother, Benton, by the time I was born and he was determined not to lose mother and I.

"What you need to do, boy," he concluded, "is to put your past behind you before you no longer have a future. I know you've been through hell."

From the dust and first sprinkles of the storm, Admiral Albert Cavelli stepped through the saloon's open doorway. The Admiral was a forceful man; forged in the heat of battle from two tours as a Navy pilot in Viet Nam and having been raised an orphan on mean Brooklyn streets. His salt and pepper hair was strewn with streaks of gold from the mid afternoon sun. A flashy western shirt and blinding metallic tie hung loosely over his thin five-foot-seven frame. He was dwarfed as he sat next to Gus and motioned for a beer.

"I'll get Al's" I commented as I pulled a ten from my pocket.

"He's right you know," the Admiral directed towards me. "I've got a string of ex-wives to prove it."

It was a real comforting thought coming from my stepfather. I took a long draw from the glass of Scotch before me and tried to clear the disturbing image from my mind. I found myself unable to envision Al with anyone other than my mother. In a way, I didn't want to be reminded that she wasn't the first.

"Not you, too, Al!" I sighed.

"Nice one with Sarah, Ace," the Admiral snided at my latest marital spat.

"Word travels fast, I see," I observed.

The Admiral shook his head as he did an amateurish, at best, John Wayne impersonation, "The women folk went to rustle up some grub and a picture show in Scary Vista."

"Why aren't you with them?" Gus enquired of his nephew-in-law.

"What and spend the evening with the estrogen committee? No thanks! I'd rather take my chances in that hole of a VC camp again! Sarah came barging in yelling that men are pigs and I took that to be my cue to leave. I had a feeling it had something to do with the other half. It was no big surprise when I found you two assholes sitting here."

"No lectures, Admiral," I warned.

"Wouldn't dream of it," he replied. "Anything you want to talk about?"

"Not particularly."

"It won't leave this bar."

I glared at my stepfather as Gus pursed his lips and turned his head the other way, uttering yet another "Hawkeye" whistle. He knew where Al was going and he also knew all too well the reception that I was about to take towards digging up old bones.

"No lectures, Al!" I snapped.

"So fatherly advice isn't my strong suit, son," he relented.

*If only he knew how many times I'd wished he had been my father…*

# Chapter Two
## The Brash Yank

**"The atrocious crime of being a young man...
I shall neither palliate nor deny."
[William Pitt, First Earl of Chatham, 1741]**

My entire childhood was spent in constant battle with a man who thought he was a mix between John Steed, James Bond, and Hugh Heffner. When my parents met, mother was barely of age and infatuated. She was taken by what could be loosely termed, father's James Bondish side. He was British, handsome, and worked for the government. What she failed to see was his romantic government job was nothing more than an entry-level desk job with the consulate. His sharp suits and romantic side entranced her. Unfortunately, it was a side that would barely survive the *I do's*.

Father saw opportunity in my mother. She worshipped him and he found it fashionable to have an exotic Lakota wife at a time when half the world was playing Indian. When he found that many of his socialite friends didn't approve of mother's bubbly personality and sometimes brash, country ways, the novelty wore off. That was when his eyes began to wander.

For years, mother kept his liaisons a secret from my brother and I. During one fight, when I was fourteen, I heard mother's voice carried down the staircase with anger, "Where did you find this one? The University! Do you ever once think of our sons?"

"For one thing, Ian is YOUR son! I only gave you him to keep you quiet so you wouldn't run off to that insane uncle of yours!" father bellowed.

"Don't you dare talk about our son like that!" Mother's voice was reaching a crescendo.

"I will talk however I like! It's the truth! He's more like that mad Indian than any son of mine!"

My blood was acid forced through my veins by a maddened jackhammer as I began to climb the steps, my hands shaking in fists at my side. I intended to force my way through the door at the top of the stairs, grab my father by the throat, toss him down the stairs, and personally kick him out the front door and my life. I was stopped mere steps from my target when the door burst open, father barged out, and stared me down as mother yelled, "You'll have the papers by Friday, James!" He just stood before me, twisting and contorting his bowler in his hands, as he looked at me like he was about to step on a cockroach.

Eventually, he sneered, "Pack your bags. Its time you were off to a proper school."

\*\*\*\*\*\*\*

My breath hung in silver clouds that chilled August evening. An early winter sun blinded my dark brown eyes. Rogue, prematurely fallen leaves swirled ominously across the dull concrete runway. As I passed the large line of windows that hazily covered the image of my parents, I paused as I boarded the plane that would usher me from the only life I had ever known.

Mother stood with her hand on the windowpane in longing. Her long, dark hair was braided with flowers that matched the print on her flowing lace shirt and bell-bottomed jeans. Father was reticent beside, always the epitome of the British gentleman. He held his bowler in one hand and leaned on his umbrella with the other, his latest liaison, skinny as the straw that broke my mother's spirit, at his side to spite mother. With a shaking hand, mother sprawled the words, "I love you" as her dark eyes welled with tears.

I trembled at the sight of mother so hurt. Father's eyes rolled in arrogance as I fought back the resentment, fury, and betrayal that threatened to consume me. I thought of Gus and wondered if this was how generations of my ancestors felt. I couldn't help but feel connected to the scores of the disenfranchised, stolen, and lonely generations that emerged from reservations, Indian schools, and assimilation, as I wandered towards the belly of an unfriendly steel, fiberglass, and polyester monster.

Father's belittling taunts of, "Dear god, Madeline! Do restrain yourself," echoed through my mind as I turned to enter the plane and exit existence, as I knew it.

I arrived in London what seemed ages later. Even a direct flight from New York seemed to drag. The cramped, narrow seats pressed against my knees and made my feet numb. It seemed that each time I was just about fall to sleep, the old man in the seat next to me would begin to, not so much snore, as whistle and snort in his sleep. I would nudge him in the arm just to have him jostle a bit, reposition, and repeat. By the time I arrived, I felt like a dead man walking. It was the longest trip of my life.

My mind drifted through uncertainty as I pondered what lay ahead of me. The English side of me was excited to experience my homeland, while the Lakota made me feel like a traitor. *Is this how all half-bloods feel?* I pondered. It was as though my mind, body, and identity were at war.

I knew my brother hadn't the crisis I had. He was always father's favourite because he denied his Lakota heritage and nearly everything American. His more golden skin let him blend in much easier than my darker skin. While Benton and I were nearly identical in features, we were worlds apart in identity.

I wondered if this was the fate that all mixed-bloods had – to assimilate or implode. Where Benton gladly assimilated by embracing his British side, part of me simultaneously envied and resented him for it. Gus had always tried to make me feel accepted. Even though I was naive, I wasn't so naive to believe that all people were as accepting. I was aware of those who called mother a "city Indian" and felt my family were traitors for leaving the reservation to pursue a life in the wide, white world. While my ancestors had left the Rez, the Rez never really left my family. Gus and mother at their core were always connected to the people the family had left behind.

The school's car awaited my arrival at the terminal to whisk me to my prison. The school with its gated drives and vast, immaculately cultivated lawns even resembled a prison. The stone buildings, complete with towers, made it seem a bit more like Sing-Sing than I cared for. I kept expecting razor wire and basketball hoops to emerge in the vast, open courtyard at the centre of the compound. As I overlooked the ancient Public School, I wondered if the worms of excitement and dread that consumed me were the same ones generations of my ancestors had felt, those who left or were taken to the Indian Schools. Like them, I was being thrust into the ultimate culture shock a world away. I, too, was torn from my family and my culture to be re-trained in a proper, white way. But unlike the generations before, I would not have the one comfort of being surrounded by those like me. I was truly alone.

The car gently pulled to a stop before a set of wide glass doors. The driver unloaded my luggage and tipped his hat as I began towards the entrance. My footsteps echoed through the vacant corridors as I approached my fate. Well-shined floors glimmered beneath my feet as golden walls drifted along side. Ahead, loomed a sign that simply read "Office". With a shaking hand and pounding heart, I reached for the door. Slowly, I turned the knob and reluctantly entered. Along the walls hung portraits of Headmasters past, the Queen, and Prime Minister. Beneath, along the far wall, were rows of antique, well polished filing cabinets. I felt as though I was being drowned in this sea of order. The only island of chaos that existed was a conspicuously over cluttered desk in the centre of the room.

An aged secretary was perched behind and snapped, "Can I help you?" I dropped my weighty bags then cleared my throat. "Spit it out, lad!" she snapped again. "I haven't all day."

"My name is Ian MacIntyre," I explained with a wavering voice. "I was told you'd be expecting me."

"Go wait in the lounge. I'll send someone around as soon as your paperwork is in order." I thanked her, lifted my bags, and hesitated before the door, intending to ask directions. "You expect a royal invite! Off with you!" the secretary howled before I was able to speak. Dejected, I opened the door and wandered lost through the corridors that lead to the hell's mouth.

Fifteen weary minutes later I found myself at a small first floor lounge. By the time I arrived, I was too exhausted to care if it was the right room or not. I dropped my bags with a weighty slam and melted onto the nearest couch. Being a good week before the beginning of the term, there were few students to be found. (Most parents actually enjoyed having their sons at home, unlike my father.) Having the entire room, if not the majority of the school to myself, I stretched onto the couch and into a fitful, dreamless sleep.

I awoke to find that I was no longer alone. Above me loomed chubby cheeks and ashen hair, clad in the school uniform: a yellow striped tie, white shirt and blue blazer embossed with the school crest, black slacks, and spit shined loafers. He just gazed down at me with a smug grin that left his dark eyes sparkling with childish wonder. At first I thought I was dreaming, but after stretching and rubbing my eyes the vision remained – motionless with that overwhelming, idiotic grin.

"You must be the Ham Shank," he stated. "Is it true you're Benton's brother?"

"Don't call me a Ham Shank!" I growled. I always did take offense to the cockney term for an American. "How do you know my brother?"

"Everyone's heard of him from McKnight," the boy explained.

*McKnight*? I rolled the name over in my head. It sounded familiar, but I couldn't place from where. Wherever I had heard it, I knew it meant everything was about to go all pear shaped.

"McKnight?" I finally ventured to ask.

"Of course. The Fencing Master."

*Fencing*! I wanted to scream at the word. I had often attributed the skill to some genetic mutation I, thankfully, did not inherit. My father and brother were both champion fencers. The pair of them, for my not following the family tradition, often belittled me. As a young boy, I was forced to endure stories of glories past over opponents otherwise long forgotten. Benton and father had driven any desire for the sport from me with their endless barrage of insults and obsession. Whenever the two of them were together all that mattered was fencing. Consequently, due to my disinterest in the sport, that meant, I wasn't important.

"A MacIntyre that doesn't fence!" the boy laughed when I informed him of my disgust of fencing. "That'll be the day!"

I had already heard those exact same words uttered by the Headmaster via the telephone the week prior. Everyone refused to believe that I was the one MacIntyre that hated fencing. It seemed the more I pleaded my case, the funnier it became to everyone around me. Most simply told me I was jesting or just being modest.

"That's what the Head said!" I enlightened.

"Don't be associating ME with the Head!"

The words no more than passed his lips when none other than the infamous Headmaster bellowed, "William!"

"Coming Uncle Francis!" the boy replied only to correct himself with, "I mean Headmaster Peters!"

William "Mouse" Jones, I was to become aware, was nephew to the Headmaster, a stern, overbearing man named Francis Peters. Then again, I'd be overbearing, too, if I were forced to go through life with a girl's name. Mouse was more or less an errand boy and all around school joke. He kept to himself and knew almost everything about everyone, which was why the bullies tended to leave "the mouse in the wall" alone. He had the Headmaster in one pocket and a phantom in the other. Mouse had the power to make an enemy's life unbearable, but never possessed the common sense to realize it.

After tripping over three chairs, knocking over one table, and nearly receiving a concussion in the doorway, Mouse stumbled from the room. I slowly wandered along the deserted hallway on my way to (I still hate the word) Fencing practice. Some boys were able to choose football or rugby, but being a MacIntyre, I was assigned to fencing. I always felt like a pompous Frenchman, holding a wimpy foil, dressed like some effeminate skydiver in that ridiculous jumpsuit, yelling things like "on guard" or the dainty, "parry," and of course I can't forget the ever so masculine, "thrust." I wished someone would have simply shot me and put me out of my misery.

I only made it halfway down the corridor before I was met by elephantine steps from behind. As I turned to see what the racket was, I found a winded Mouse raced to catch up to me.

"MacIntyre!" Mouse called desperately. "Wait up!"

I stopped and waited for my out of shape friend to catch up. Sweat dripped from the pale brow that hung below his cropped ashen hair. His childish eyes still sparkled as he began to toddle beside me. "The Head wants me to show you to practice," Mouse stated.

I knew it was futile to argue. The whole of London had

their minds made up at that point. So, together, we walked to my inevitable doom. My disgust of fencing crippled me a in a shock wave of terror and the thought of entering the gym filled me with such dread as to cause my mind to momentarily go AWOL. I hesitated uncomfortably at the doorway while Mouse stared bewildered at me. Then with a stern shove, I stopped once more to see the group assembled at the far end of the gymnasium and became immediately aware…I was late.

My mind was drowning in fear as I gazed at the group that might as well been halfway around the globe. They were too far away for me to simply blend in as if I had been there the entire time. Yet, as far away as they were, I was sure they could hear my struggled breaths, the nervous pounding of my heart against my ribs, the sweat that dripped from my nose and impacted the floor with the force of a grenade…

Then like a sundog on a hazy plains horizon, came a tall broad shouldered yet lanky, youth with dark curly hair, cut short at the sides and back that tapered to a mass of curls at the top. He was a phantom as he approached from behind and floated past as though I didn't exist. I seized my opportunity as I hid myself behind his tall frame and followed him into the gym. As if sensing my presence, my shield briefly turned his head to look over his shoulder through the corner of his eye, gave a cockeyed smile, then turned away as we stopped before the group.

"I see you finally decided to grace us with your presence," McKnight commented.

McKnight was a young man, close to my brother's age, and an alumnus of the school (which was probably how he knew Benton). All accounts given had to place him in his mid to late twenties. His dark hair strikingly contrasted the gunfighter grey of the school's fencing uniform and gave him the appearance of a disembodied head as grey blended with grey along the walls. There was a sadistic glint in his eye, the kind found in old photos of gunfighters, which added to my apprehension – a distant, piercing gaze, filled with mania that always made me shudder. It was a look that attested to greatness as well as insanity.

"I don't suppose you happened to have seen the new chap?" he queried.

Before my shield could utter a single syllable, I piped up,

"I'm here, sir!" I figured it was best to incriminate myself before someone else did.

"Yes, I know you are," McKnight remarked. "I saw you walk in. Tell you what, since you are the new chap…and late, perhaps you'd care to help with today's demonstration."

He wanted me to help with the demonstration! I knew it was useless to argue. No one to date had taken me serious, McKnight certainly wouldn't. I knew I was condemned to look a fool. Could my day possibly have gotten any worse? I was soon to wish I had never asked…

My knees trembled beneath me as I stated, "I can't fence, sir."

"A MacIntyre that doesn't fence?" he mocked. "That'll be the day!"

*I do wish people would quit saying that,* I thought reluctantly. I slid past my human shield and resigned myself to fate as the clock knocked off the seconds slowly. At my approach, the disembodied head leaned nonchalantly against his foil and held his face shield under one arm. The muffled sound of whispers and my own resounding footsteps filled my ringing ears. My face burned as the blood raced through my body, forced by the panicked pounding of my heart. Sweat began to fall nervously down my brow to sting my eyes.

Desperately, I tried to think of a way to save face, and quite possibly my life, before I died of humiliation. Perhaps a fire drill would be called, or a freak storm would rip the roof off, or maybe, just maybe, it was all some horrid nightmare and I would awaken in my own room in Vermont, screaming at any moment. But alas, none of these would come to pass.

I stood before the Master of the Foil with hunched shoulders, rounded back, and a rapidly churning stomach. Every molecule of my body screamed to simply flee. I felt as though my arms and legs were being torn in separate directions as I prayed to the god of fencing to grace me with his presence, or better yet, fence for me.

McKnight raised a dark eyebrow and snapped, "Straighten up, lad!"

With some hesitation, I rolled my shoulders back, sighed, and entrusted myself to the hereafter. Just as I reached a trembling hand for the rack of foils, McKnight thrust his rapier of doom. I tried to dodge his brutal attack, only to trip, and fall backwards into the unshaken arms of my former shield. As I lay hovering only inches above certain oblivion, and the wooden floor, I pulled my head back to catch a brief look at the mocking grey eyes and dark face of my unholy saviour.

With a wink, he stated in a cold, Scottish accent, "I'm sorry, lad." Then released his grip and allowed me to fall to the hard floor with a dull thud as he concluded, "But you're not me type."

I rolled over to push myself from the floor only to find my way hindered by a large, dusty shoe at my right. I looked to my left to find the mate. Suddenly, I was grasped by the nap of the neck like a dog and raised from the ground. I sensed the intense pressure from constricted fingers send shivers down my spine. But, the physical pain paled in comparison to the humiliation I endured from the riotous laughter of the student body. Slowly, my assailant released his grip then taunted me with those eerie eyes. I had no more than turned my gaze for a moment and he was gone, leaving me at the mercy of the pack of hyenas and their demented leader.

Later that day, I entered the cafeteria with Mouse. I had the distinct feeling from the start it was a summarily bad idea to emerge from hiding. Those fears were only confirmed when the entire student body, lead by a blonde boy named Davies, rose, pantomimed raising a sword and tripped back into their seats. I dejectedly made my way through the din, tray in hand, and my ears still burning with laughter. Even with my head hung low, I could hear various students state, "Bloody Ham Shanks!" or "He's no MacIntyre. Benton and him may look alike, but they caun't be related!" At least they hadn't started whooping and pantomiming feathers behind their heads at me yet. I had enough of that when I went to school in Vermont.

I quickly learned in London, Public School boys were far worse than any Nazi death squad. I am still convinced that if Hitler had enlisted British Public School boys, he would have won the war, hands down. There was no end to their capacity for evil and deceit, especially if you were a "Ham Shank".

Upon arriving at the only free table, the boys that were

seated there rose and promptly left. I dropped my tray with a crash across from Mouse and sat down, disgusted. With my chin in hand, I stared at my rapidly cooling food. I summoned the courage to poke it once or twice with a fork, but never dared eat it. It had long been my established practice to avoid the consumption of toxic waste. Besides, I couldn't eat, even if I wanted to. My stomach was twisted into a thousand knots and the rest of me wanted to run far, far away.

"You going to eat that?" Mouse asked of my untouched food.

"Help yourself," I offered. "Maybe I can starve myself to death."

"Don't get morbid on me, mate!" Mouse exclaimed. "It's just your first day. Things'll get worse…promise."

"Your vote of confidence is overwhelming."

I knew that no matter what, I couldn't kill myself (regardless to how badly I may have wanted at that point). I was dead and thus said, you can only die once. The school was my hell, except I couldn't figure out who the devil was. I knew it had to be, the Headmaster (I had long suspected the devil to be a cross dresser), McKnight (he enjoyed the incident in Fencing a bit too much for my liking), or perhaps even myself (I long attended that Heaven didn't want me and Hell was afraid I would take over). Maybe this was my punishment for a life of wasted afternoons and general unruliness.

My forlorn eyes scanned the crowded, belittling scene until they fell upon my former shield. He sat alone in a corner of the room with his back against the wall. Nearly emaciated legs were folded beneath the body of a man twice his age. Physically, he looked like a starved, middle-aged man that was too stubborn to lie down and die. His face, on the other hand, held a childish stubbornness and sense of curiosity – even adventure run amok. His ghostly eyes were closed in concentration as his chest heaved in rhythmic sighs, giving him the appearance of a demonic Dalai Lama. The colour had drained from a face that mere hours ago was tanned a few shades lighter than my own. It appeared after a few moments of his odd ritual, colour had begun to return to his cheeks.

"Who is that?" I whispered to Mouse.

17

LORD FIREBIRD

"Who?" Mouse questioned as he forced down the last few remnants of my lunch.

"The bloke in the corner," I explained.

After finishing a last piece of bread, Mouse looked wide-eyed and immediately returned his gaze to his empty tray. "You don't want to know him!" he cried, a tinge of fear evident in his wavering voice.

"Why?" I egged.

"That there is Kingston. You'd be wise to keep your distance!"

That was going to be a bit hard to do. I had only found out before lunch that we were roommates. There was a certain amount of relief in finally being able to place not only a face to the name "Kingston" on our door, but a name to the source of my morning humiliation.

"He doesn't look so dangerous to me," I stated idly.

"You don't know him!" Mouse announced. "Not that you'd want to, mind you. He's older than almost every other student. This is his last year here. He's been here two and half years and no one knows a thing about him. No one but the Head, McKnight, and Doctor Michaels – and they aren't talking. The bloke's a savage! I heard he got in a knife fight in Inverness and killed four men!"

"Four men!" I laughed. "Just who did you hear this from?"

"Everyone in town talks…"

"Idle gossip! If everyone in town jumped from the Brooklyn Bridge would you?" Nausea fell upon me as I remembered the thousands of times I had heard those words uttered by my mother and wished once again that someone would just shoot me.

"Why are you taking his side all of a sudden?" Mouse demanded.

I wasn't exactly sure why I took Kingston's side. It may have been initially nothing more than compassion for a fellow outsider. I had just received a crash course in what it was like not to fit in, courtesy of London's future elite. Their tolerance wasn't much more advanced than that of the enlightened students of the Vermont public education system I had left behind. Besides, Kingston didn't look like a killer. Having spent a good part of my childhood pinballing between New York, Vermont, and the winding Mississippi River valley, I grew to be a fairly strong judge of character, if by nothing else than sheer survival.

True, he was steely and had an unusual sense of humour, but he surely couldn't be all that dangerous, at least my peace of mind demanded as much. I couldn't fathom the idea of boarding with a psychopath. Still, I was cautious in my dealings with Kingston. I would watch night after night as he did his Houdini act, disappearing somewhere between supper and lights out, not to return until just before morning Cricket practice. This went on for nearly a week and a half before I dared make a move…

"You're going to do what?" Mouse exclaimed when I informed him of my plan. "Have you gone completely balmy?"

"Why? Because I'm going to do something no one else in this godforsaken hole has ever dared do?"

"Do you have any idea what he could do to that scrawny little body of yours?"

"I'm willing to take my chances. You know, I'm going to do this, with or without you!"

"That's what I'm afraid of."

Actually, I had absolutely no intention of going alone, but I wasn't about to tell Mouse that. Somewhere in the back of my mind, I wanted one of two things: either for Mouse to jump at the opportunity to accompany me or to seriously talk me out of it. However, neither uttered from Mouse's lips and my stubborn pride wouldn't let me back down. If there was one thing I had been raised to be, it was a man of my word. Now that I had said it, I had committed myself. There was no turning back now. I would have to trail Kingston.

"Does insanity run in your family?" Mouse accused.

"No," I replied. "It gallops!"

That night after lights out, Kingston rose from his bed and made his way to the door. I feigned sleep as I observed him glide through the door and out into the darkened hallway. When I was sure he was out of sight, I emerged from the bed and began to follow the elusive wraith. From atop the stairs, I saw Kingston slip past McKnight into the silhouetted student lounge. I was intent as I awaited my opportunity to arise. After a few moments, McKnight left his watch, allowing me to enter the lounge undetected. I cautiously scanned the shaded room to find the only trace of Kingston that remained was a lace curtain that flapped in the breeze from an opened window. As I crouched, poised at the window's edge, debating my decision, I became aware of approaching footsteps on the marble floor outside. With less than my usual grace, I leaned forward, fell through the window, and onto the sticky bushes below.

"Thank God, no one saw that!" I breathed as I rose, cradling my backside.

For hours, I wandered the streets in search of the ever-elusive Kingston. In that time, I continued to pick thorns from my pride, was nearly hit by a bus, and assaulted by some little old lady I offered to help across the street. People think Americans are rough; they have nothing on the British geriatric crowd. I thought I had fallen into a *Monty Python* sketch. I half expected to find a naked pianist around the next corner.

After the assault, I realized the phantom had outwitted me and I returned to the school a miserable failure. I entered my dormitory room dejected to find none other than the wraith lounged in bed reading a *Sherlock Holmes* collection with a Cheshire cat grin across his wicked face, perched ominously below a *Black Sabbath* poster.

He looked over the book with his ghostly eyes and asked, "Where 'ere hae ye been all night? Don't ye know it's against the rules to leave school grounds after dark?"

With a disgusted grunt, I flopped onto the mattress only to be pricked by one last thorn. With a yell, I bounded to my feet and pinched the slacks away from my pride. Out of frustration, I tore them off and threw them at Kingston who ducked behind the book and began to laugh heartily. Out of despair, I sank onto the mattress and, for what it was worth, tried to go to sleep. I laid bug eyed with the sound of Kingston's laughter echoing through my mind. God only knew what the others would say when they saw my beaten, bruised, and sore form the next morning. I may have been dead, but I certainly wasn't Ol' Clootie. That honour belonged to Kingston and his childish trickery.

When I was finally able to drift to sleep, I was startled from my bed by a dull thud that echoed from the outer wall. As my pounding heart clogged my throat, I raced to the door to find out what the matter was. As I swung the door open, Kingston met me. He stood holding Davies by the neck. Reddened eyes bulged from their sockets and stared at Kingston, filled with terror. Ashen eyes stared back at the jiggled heap with sheer contempt as the boy hung there, his feet inches above the floor as Davies babbled inaudible sounds that couldn't even be called words from behind a tear stained face and reddened cheeks. Davies' terror only seemed to delight the phantom more and before I could say a word, the enraged spectre turned his head, looked at me with macabre eyes, cocked his head, and released his grip. The heap crashed to the floor as Kingston walked off.

As he paused by me, he whispered, "I dona think he'll be bothering ya again."

Cautiously, I approached the boy who looked at me with dread deep in his eyes. I offered my hand, but he just brushed it away. In mock arrogance, he rose, straightened his tie and blazer, and then shifted his neck in disdain. Even after being terrified and humiliated, Davies still tried to exude absolute control.

"I wonder what got into him?" he queried as he waddled down the hallway with conspicuously saggy trousers.

With a twisted smile, I remembered the lunchtime taunt and commented, "Serves the bastard right!"

I turned and walked back to the room. As I gazed down the length of hallway, all I could see were heads craning from doorways. The muffled sound of whispers and the desperate looks of each craned neck left me in fear for Kingston. If the Headmaster caught word that he had instigated a fight, he'd be expelled.

Somehow, it was my fault and I couldn't let Kingston take the blame. It was more than pity or a sense of obligation that drove me. I had never been a squealer, but beyond that, I had a sense that Kingston was looking after me. There was a connection we had that was an unspoken brotherly bond that I hadn't felt even with my own brother. I couldn't then and I still can't articulate it, but I knew there was more to Kingston – that no matter what, I could trust him absolutely. We had to look after each other.

I slowly entered the room to find Kingston sitting on his bed with his head cradled in his hands. He gazed briefly at me as I shut the door, and then returned his, once again drained, head to shaking hands. All I could bring myself to do was sit at the other side of the room and watch. I had no idea what I could say or do to help. I would have made myself a fool to say anything at all. I saved face with silence and hoped that Kingston's aggressions weren't turned on me.

Nervously, I opened the door to a hallway full of students and the petrifying sight of McKnight. The Headmaster stood stone faced behind with a look of absolute disapproval. Mouse looked at me with large, sympathetic eyes from under his uncle's arm. I turned to look at Kingston who cast me an apprehensive gaze and a worried smile. I purposely left the door open as I walked over to where Kingston sat. As secretively as I could, I cast him a reassuring wink, then turned to sit next to him.

"Mr. Davies tells me that he was assaulted in the corridor this morning," the Headmaster accused. "Is this true, Mr. Kingston?"

Kingston looked momentarily at me then turned his gaze shamefully to the floor. His ghostly eyes were fixed on the gold coloured carpet at his feet. His hands were still in his lap as he breathed in through his nose and out through his mouth.

"Do you know any of this, Mr. MacIntyre?" he continued to interrogate.

I let the white man in me take hold. For a few moments I envisioned myself at a treaty signing with a handful of beads. With all the confidence of a politician, I did as a politician…I lied. "I'm not aware of anything of the sort, sir. You can ask anyone here."

"Mr. Davies said that you were in the corridor with Mr. Kingston," McKnight stated.

"Then Mr. Davies, with all due respect, sir, is a pathological liar," I condemned. "It just happens that Mr. Kingston and I were discussing last week's episode of the good Doctor's adventures."

"*Doctor Who*?" the Headmaster asked.

"Exactly," I cynically snided. Although, I didn't truly enjoy it again until Peter Davison. "Now, if you don't mind…"

Ok, so I went overboard, just a bit, but it worked. An excitement came over the shocked gathering of students outside. My words had been like TNT to the Hoover Dam. Soon everyone was speaking out.

"He's telling the truth, sir," one boy surprisingly aired from the open doorway. One by one, the others agreed, forcing the Headmaster to leave in a whirlwind with the tails of his robe smacking innocent bystanders in the wake. Like a lost puppy, McKnight followed in the Headmaster's steps so close if the Head were to trip, McKnight would have found himself with a rather nasty case of anal optilitis by proxi. With the excitement at an end, we were left to the incoming wave of animated students as they flooded our already crowded room.

"I caun't believe you stood up to the Head like that!" one exclaimed.

"I canna either," Kingston agreed, a look of genuine shock on his face.

For the first time since I arrived at that isolated place, I was respected. To think, it only took sticking my neck out to do; who would have known? I felt as though I had finally proved that I was someone other than simply some "Ham Shank." It was also the day that I earned the admiration of Kingston. Something that I never truly appreciated until it was too late...

# Chapter Three
## Young Sherlock Holmes and Mr. MacIntyre

"Green be the turf above thee,
Friend of my better days!
None knew thee but to love thee,
Nor named thee but to praise."
{Fitz-Greene Halleck, 1790-1867}

Kingston and I became close friends over the following months. He spent a considerable amount of his days conspiring new and more creative ways to torment our fellow students. Most of his schemes fizzled out prior to fruition, but at least it kept Kingston's mind busy and made for devious enjoyment for me.

Then out of the blue, Davies opened his mouth and stuck the noose around his own neck.

Kingston sat across the room, his usual arrogant self. Nothing seemed to bother him until Davies began ranting about the day's assignment. Kingston's eyes seemed to glow when Davies began to air his know-it-all ideas. I was never to know a thicker-skulled individual. He never seemed to learn that he couldn't win against the phantom. The confrontation in the hallway had only temporarily shocked reason into him. Soon enough, he was his usually overbearing, unreasoned self.

"I don't see why we have to be submitted to such rubbish!" he boasted. "The entire premise that someone could be haunted by the pounding of a heart is completely preposterous!"

"Poe is regarded as one of the finest American writers," I protested, much to Kingston's delight. "Not to mention one of my personal favourites. Just because you don't care for the story doesn't mean we should have to endure your dribble!"

"I'm shocked you'd like it. I figured you'd complain we should be reading *Crazy Horse*. In fact, I'm shocked you can read at all. Isn't your Indian name *Walks-into-walls*?"

This really piqued Kingston's attention. If he wasn't listening before, he was now. He sat low in his seat with his arms crossed at his chest. His eyes glowed with fury as he sized Davies up and down before speaking, "I'd watch what you say. He isn't the one who needs to worry about walls, ye arrogant elitist!"

Davies face was afire at Kingston's allusion to the incident in the corridor. Yet it seemed to do nothing to cool Davies temperament as he spouted, "So what are you now, his protector?"

One of Davies' friends whispered over his shoulder, "Maybe he thinks he's his medicine man."

Davies laughed, only because his friends surrounded him. If there was one thing I had figured out about Davies, it was that he was essentially a coward unless he had his friends to impress. Kingston glared at Davies in silence before asking, "So are ye sayin' ye don't believe in things beyond human comprehension?"

"Tell me, since you seem to know so much, do you?" Davies countered.

"Oh, aye. And if I were ye, I would watch what you say. Ye have no idea what lurks in the shadows," Kingston alluded.

"And you do? Was Van Helsing your great-grandfather?" Davies smugly asked.

"Of course not…Dracula was," the phantom laughed as he hissed at Davies.

The class erupted in a pandemonium of laughter. With a grin of pure evil satisfaction, Kingston sank comfortably farther into his chair. The gleam in his villainous eyes told me that he was plotting. To Kingston, simply calling out Davies in class wouldn't be near enough retribution.

The following morning began spring break. Most of the students and faculty had left to be with their families; all that remained were Mouse, Kingston, the ever-tireless Headmaster, a handful of forgotten students, Davies, and of course, me. I found the break to be the perfect time to catch up on some well-deserved sleep. I was awakened from a dream in which Linda Carter was tying me up with her golden rope, by the sound of mortal terror from down the hallway. I dashed groggily from my room to find Kingston leaning against the wall cross-armed with that all to familiar look of satisfaction in his ghostly eyes. A cockeyed grin crossed his lips as he looked down the hallway as Mouse ran from Davies' room looking like the living dead. He wore upon his roundish body something that may have once been a fine custom tailored suit, but now was nothing more than tattered, filthy rags.

"The look on his face!" Mouse squeaked in joy.

"I don't want to know!" I asserted irritably. Had I been awakened for a legitimate reason, I wouldn't have been near as upset. I was always crankiest when wakened unnecessarily from a perfectly good wet dream.

"You should have seen it! Pure bloody genius! The bloke was white as a sheet!" Mouse continued.

"I said, 'I don't want to know!'"

Half drunk from sleep depravation, I wove my way down the hall to my bed with Kingston at my heels like some hyperactive terrier, a childish grin still upon his tanned face.

"Where are ye going?" he asked.

"Back to bed! Wake me in three weeks!" I snapped as I slammed the door to a torrent of laughter from Kingston and Mouse.

Later, I was informed of the devious plot. Kingston had planned and re-planned all night the perfect way to get at Davies. He desired public humiliation. Literature class had fuelled a fire that already raged well out of control. When Davies started on one of his know-it-all lectures, Kingston was determined to change his mind about the existence of the supernatural.

It seemed Kingston's plan worked. Davies was scared shit-less. All Kingston would have to do was look at Davies and pantomime nailing a nail. His crooked, evil smile seemed to say, "Ah, another one in the box," and Davies would dash the other way in mortal dread of the fearsome creature of the night.

Late that night, I awoke to find Kingston restlessly pacing the room as if he wrestled with his conscience. I watched Kingston's lanky silhouette cast in the blue light of the window.

"What's wrong?" I wearily asked.

"Nothing," he replied as his sunken eyes turned in my

general direction. There was a strain in his brow that told me he was lying. "I just need a wee bit of fresh air, that's all." I knew what was coming next – the window was closed. "I'm going for a walk."

"This isn't another of your wild schemes, is it?" I questioned.

"May me poor heart fail me if it 'tis."

Cautiously, we made our escape. I felt like Steve McQueen, minus the motorbike, as we sneaked past the snores of the teacher on night duty. Around daybreak, we arrived at an abandoned section of the docks. It was a section of rotted planks and cracked concrete that hadn't been used since the days of Sherlock Holmes.

We stood upon the dilapidated surface and watched the reflected streetlights as they danced a jig upon the meringue waves of the Thames. The water softly caressed the rotted legs of the pier as the waves bounced against it and gurgled some long forgotten tune. Even though the planks creaked and bent under foot, I felt ominously safe. I stared across the river at the row of streetlights along Broad Street. Beyond, stood the blackened silhouette of the tower of London and Big Ben. Between rose black lines of emptiness where during the day houses and shops sat. The void was accented only with the haunting yellow glow emanated by the numerous streetlights. The unearthly serenity of the place made me momentarily forget about the trials of life and I began to understand why Kingston brought me there.

Kingston stated unsure, almost as if he were afraid he would sound weak, even human, "I come here when...Well, I'm sure you've figured out by now."

I had learned enough about Kingston to realize when he was being open and sincere. It was something he wasn't very good at. I knew it killed him to have me know that he was actually human and indulged in nostalgic things. He prided himself on his cold exterior and mysterious ways. Most saw only the distant, cold youth – the prankster. Only I knew the other Kingston, the Kingston he kept locked deep within the abyss of his heart.

"Its even more beautiful when the sun rises o'er the buildings...But I suppose we should be making our way back before morning roll," he resolved.

Kingston stood, arched his lanky back and then started towards the security of land. I sat a moment longer and took in the stillness of the river. I can remember the delightfully acrid scent of the river mixed with car exhaust and a subtle hint of urban decay that hung in the thickening fog.

The air brought back memories of summer street fairs and open-air concerts along the banks of the Ol' Muddy when I was a child. The image of brown splashing waters, driftwood, a winding brick alley, and an aged green iron bridge flooded my memories along with the drifting tugboats that hovered in the open channel. As my mind returned to the present, I rose to get a better look of the sunrise through the gathering mist when I felt the planks creak and give way beneath my feet.

*******

I paused and looked at the scar on my forearm. The wound had long since healed, but in that moment, the pain remained. I placed the glass to my temple and closed my eyes to the resurrected memories. I wanted to stop. I wanted to tell Gus and Al it was none of their business, but the ache in my heart told me I had to go on.

I lowered the glass and opened my eyes. As I swirled the remnants of my scotch absently, Gus took a deep swig of beer, finishing his glass, then poured himself and the Admiral another.

The Admiral looked at me wide-eyed and asked, "So, then what happened?"

*******

I was awakened by the trickle of water on my forehead. Slowly, my eyes focused on the sight of Kingston. His hair hung in dripping ringlets as he hovered concerned over me. At my sudden awakening, he jumped back.

"Ye scared ten years off me, lad!" he cried. "I thought I'd lost ye for a while there."

I strained for breath as searing pain shot through my chest and shoulders like a 4th Calvary bullet. It seemed the deeper I tried to breathe, the worse the pain became. I arched on the ground in a feeble attempt to subside the torment. Slowly, it dulled to nothing more than an ache entrenched over my panicked heart.

"What happened?" I rasped.

"Ye nearly drowned! That's what happened!" Kingston responded. "Don't try ta move just yet. I wouldn't be surprised if you've got a couple of broken ribs."

I slowly rolled over to find my shirt lying in tatters at my side as if it had been ripped from my body. I looked more closely over Kingston as I lay on my side and tried to cough the last remnants of the Thames from my lungs. His face was ashen and he was shivering not so much from the chilly air, as from shock. From every piece of clothing water ran in streams. He had even jumped in with his shoes on. Kingston cautiously slipped a finger to my shaking wrist. Satisfied, he took me by the arm and helped me to my feet as blood drained from a long gash across the top of my forearm.

"How do ye feel?" he questioned as he began to tear at the tail of his shirt to form a bandage.

"Like I've been hit by a truck," I coughed. "How do you think I feel, mate?"

Later I awoke to find myself back in the dorms. Doctor Michaels smiled down at me as he rose to leave the room. Kingston stood in the doorway and gazed like a mother cat. Nervously, he twirled a pencil thorough his fingers only to fumble and drop it at his feet. Never had I known Kingston to crack under pressure. As the doctor left, Kingston leaned back and banged his head against the wall in desperation.

"You boys really should be more careful," the doctor recommended as he disappeared down the hallway.

"MacIntyre!" the Headmaster's bellow rattled the dormitory walls as he approached.

I could see the smoke emerge from reddened ears as he stood in the doorway. Kingston sulked away in shame as I lay upon my bed and trembled in cold terror. I knew this was the final straw. If I weren't already dead, I soon would be. And no glass of ice water to carry.

"I've had enough of these midnight raids!" he continued to rant. "You could have killed yourself tonight!"

"But I didn't," I simply pointed out.

In the background Kingston muffled a whisper of, "That's debatable."

"Ian James MacIntyre!" a voice thundered through the halls.

"God, don't let it be," I prayed for what good it was.

The immense figure of my father entered the room. He was in town checking up on my progress. *Wouldn't want anything to tarnish the MacIntyre name, now.* I had picked the wrong time to mess up. His blue eyes were afire with anger as he stood at the foot of the bed twisting and contorting his favourite bowler. His white-hot glare seared through my tremulous form like an Inquisitor's poker.

He fumed, "Tomorrow, you're packing your things! I'm sending you to live with your brother!"

"In Australia?" I gasped, scarcely able to fathom what I was hearing.

Benton, after college, went to work as a conservation officer somewhere in No-Man's Land, Australia. I had often half-heartedly hoped he would mysteriously be dragged off into the desert by a dingo.

Twice that year, my life was turned upside down only to leave me hopeless, desperate, and alone a world away. The thought of being uprooted again left me in a black hole, a void of despair that ripped apart the best parts of me and left only a shell behind. It seemed each move took me farther and farther from home. My father could never let me be happy. He had sent me to London to be miserable. My happiness and acceptance thwarted him. That was the only reason I was being sent to Benton. Father knew my brother would ensure my misery and ultimate submission.

"No arguments!" my father continued to rant. "If you're not at Heathrow tomorrow afternoon, I'll send every Bob in London to track you down. Who knows maybe a night in jail would straighten you out! God knows something has to. You are too much like you're damned mother!"

The following morning was spent searching for Kingston. It appeared as if he had fallen off the edge of the world. No one at school had seen him; least of all knew where he might be. I checked all his favourite haunts: the tower of London, Hyde Park, even the docks (though the sight sent chills down my spine and left me thinking that someone had just walked over my grave), all to no avail. As I stood at the gates awaiting the taxi that would whisk me from London forever, Mouse slowly approached with a look of disbelief on his face.

"Have you seen Kingston?" I desperately enquired.

"I only just heard," Mouse whispered. His eyes were large with shock and his voice quavered with a sadness I thought as jolly a soul as Mouse incapable of. "I overheard Dr. Michaels and my uncle talking. Kingston's in the hospital. It seems when your father arrived he took off…"

"AND?" I demanded, scarcely able to believe what I was hearing.

"Some Bobby found him half dead on Waterloo Bridge."

My heart sank in my chest. I threw my bags at Mouse; called, "Hold these!" then dashed off for the hospital.

I looked like a prep school Jim Thorpe as I dodged my way along crowded London streets. I had never been so determined in all my life. I ran until I could run no more, but still found the strength to keep running. My sides ached, my lungs burned, my heart pounded against my ribs to the point that I thought I would catch it in my hands. Yet, I still kept running. Sheer determination kept me going.

When I arrived at the hospital, I stood breathless at the information desk and was met by an unconcerned look from the nurse as I feebly attempted to steady my breath and calm my heart. I wanted to speak, to yell even, but lacked the physical ability.

"Can I help you?" she asked, though her tone said otherwise.

I stood straining to get the words past my burning lips and parched throat. "I'm here to see Mr. Kingston," I eventually rasped in between gasps for air.

"And your name is…" she interrogated.

"Ian. Ian MacIntyre."

As she flipped through a stack of papers, she would occasionally look at me over her wire-rimmed spectacles.

"I'm afraid you caun't," she flatly stated. "Family only in critical care."

She shook her head, as she looked suspiciously once more over my shoulder. Rage welled within me. I pounded my fist upon the desk and screamed, "He is by best friend and I WILL

NOT leave without knowing that he is all right!"

"I thought I might find you here!" my father bellowed behind me.

I turned to find my father, accompanied by two of London's finest. As I tried to run the other way, I found police also blocked it. Filled with frustration, I stood with my mind racing for another way out when I stopped, faced my father, and stated, "I'll not go freely. You'll have to arrest me, father."

So, they did.

Even as I was dragged down the walkway, I would strain my neck backwards in the hope that I would see Kingston gazing from a window or he would step from the lobby. I had absolutely no intention of leaving without knowing what happened the night before on the bridge.

I had to say goodbye to Kingston. Its one thing to loose a friend because you drift apart as you grow older, but I was being forcibly removed from the one real friend I had ever had. I was hurt, angry, and desperate as I thrust my elbow into one policeman's stomach and then pushed a surprised second to the ground. Frantically, I raced for the lobby only to have my father grab me around the waist.

"Enough!" he called as the surprised policemen lifted themselves from the pavement.

Reluctantly, I collapsed onto the curb. In the distance Big Ben loomed ominously over the mad, mindless scene. All I could do was gaze empty at my feet. Every ounce of strength had vanished. I lost the will to fight and with it my entire reason for staying.

# Part II

"So the two brothers and their
murder'd man
Rode past fair Florence…"

-Jack Keats-
(1795-1821)

# Chapter Four
## Dead Man's Party

"Most people wouldn't know music
if it came up and bit them on the ass."
{Frank Zappa (60's rock icon)}

Eight years had passed since I left London. Surprisingly, at the end of that section of highway called life, I was at the intersection of Irony and Karma's-a-bitch. I found myself drawn farther away from the future of unappreciative adolescents – an existence locked behind an oak desk and chained to a chalkboard - that I had been nearly hard-handed into submission for.

After London I focused on my studies, became a Dean's List student, and was almost content to do whatever Benton and our father wanted. I had resigned myself to become the obedient British Gentleman father wanted. In short, I relented.

Then one day, I was lying under Outback stars surrounded by red sand. A dingo howled like a wolf off in the distance and I felt a knot tighten around my throat like a vigilance committee's noose. I realized the man my father and brother were grooming me to be, wasn't who or what I was or what I was meant to be. I knew then, I should have run back to America and jumped headlong into the Mississippi. I was intent to do just that when I saw my grandfather's guitar. That was the moment all my plans changed – grad school, America, and most importantly, the plans of others.

Instead, I was entering into uncertainty. I left behind a blueprinted future in Sydney academia for the unpredictability of life with a six string. My father and brother accused me of throwing my English degree away on nothing more than sheer silliness. But it seemed the more they objected, the more intent I was to leave. The past years of torment flooded back and filled me with resolve. Some might say it was simply rebellion, but I knew it was more. It was about being true to myself and creating my own destiny instead of being content with the one that was crafted for me. More importantly, it was about finding who I was.

So it was, that I left with nothing more than a degree that was essentially useless to me, the clothes on my back, a worn out guitar, and enough money to keep one foot out of the gutter for a couple of weeks.

I left for London at the height of what was beginning to be termed "The Second British Invasion." There was a revival in British musical artists in America and I saw London as the lyric heart of the New Romantic movement.

Immediately upon arrival, I rented a room at the Youth Hostel. It was little more than a bed, but it was a roof over my head. Soon, I found a job in the music store down the street. True, it wasn't the glamorous dream job in the music industry that I had envisioned, but it paid enough to keep the rain off my head for a while and one meal a day in my belly.

Whenever I would begin to feel deprived and starving, I would think of Gus and the stories of fry bread and potatoes on the Rez that he would use to get me to finish my dinner. Most Americans had starving kids in Africa as their incentive to eat brussel sprouts. I had "cousins" on the Rez and somehow, I always envied the other kids who could shrug off the kids in Africa. I was always humbled to know how far my family had come in a couple of generations and suddenly, one cheap meal a day and a crappy record store job in London didn't seem worth complaining about anymore.

I soon made the acquaintance of a rather strange young man named Styles. His name stemmed from the fact that his hair changed on a semi-daily basis. It was so over treated, coloured, and abused that I expected it to either fall out or burst into flames like he was in a Pepsi commercial. He worked most of the same hours as I did at the store. He was a strange mix of 70's punk and 90's grunge at a time when neither was essentially mainstream. In fact, grunge wouldn't become mainstream until Nirvana released "Nevermind" a few years later, and even then, London couldn't have cared less. Falco, Duran Duran, Adam Ant, and Madonna were the reigning royalties of the airwaves and the English Beat were pleading, "Stand Down, Margaret!"

In the idle time at the shop, we would pass the lonely hours by discussing the top twenty lists or about how close Styles got to the band at the club the night before. Styles had tried for weeks to get me into the clubs. He was an all right guy, just not the type I would normally associate with outside of work. He obviously had much more to say about me.

It was on one of those days that had become routine when I would stare at the park across the street. I wondered how the store stayed in business with no more customers than they tended to have. When the mail came and went, it at least provided a change to the monotony and it seemed, even though Styles had the day off, he still wouldn't go away.

I found myself idly passing the time. I had even been ambitious enough to wash the windows and re-alphabetized the vinyl section just to have something to do. Styles and I were engaged in a round of *name that top 40* when I was shocked by the presence of an actual customer. A man dressed in leather walked in. His purple and blue flamed *Elmer's Glue* Mohawk brushed the doorway as he approached. He scanned the racks in disinterest as he approached the counter. He seemed a man with a purpose and I hoped that purpose didn't involve robbing me.

"Are you Ian MacIntyre?" he rasped. Shocked, I nodded. I closed my eyes and waited for the beating I knew was to come. Styles sat on the glass with his usual vacant stare. "I was told to deliver this," he continued.

I squeezed open my left eye and braced for the pummelling to come. Instead, he handed me a black envelope with scarlet lettering, then left as abruptly as he appeared. My adrenaline was in overload as I sank onto the floor in relief.

Styles just continued his vacant grin as I stared at the envelope for a while before he questioned, "Well, you going to open it?"

I looked wide-eyed up at Styles as I turned the envelope over and over in my hand. The thick, obviously expensive, paper was embossed with a seal of a black knight on a midnight steed. I wondered who could possibly have sent such an unusual letter.

The only people I knew in London were Styles, the other record store employees, a handful of regular customers, and a very few Hostel residents. None of them could afford such lavish paper. Slowly, I pulled open the flap and pulled a matching invitation embossed with Aries on his chariot. The only writing was a time, date, and address. Styles began to drool as he gazed at the invitation.

"Bloody hell!" he cried excitedly. "I'll take it if you don't want it! Do you know what that is?"

"Some junk mail?" I joked as I slowly rose to my feet.

"Jesus! It's an invitation from the God of War, mate! The Dead Man's Party!" I looked bewildered at Styles as he continued on his rant, acting as though I were Simple Simon for not knowing, least of all caring, about this common knowledge. "It's just the most coveted invitation in town. People wait years to meet the Dead Man. You cheeky bastard! You haven't even set foot in a club! I can't get within ten miles of the bloke…and YOU get invited to his bloody house!"

"I'm not going," I decided. "I don't even know who this guy is."

"Come on mate! You've got to go. It's the Dead Man's Party, the hottest ticket in town. When they say, 'Burn down the house!' they mean burn down the house! Anybody that's anybody is there. I've even heard rumours that record execs and mainstream bands go there. Elvis Costello and Adam Ant have played the party. You have to go! This could be your big break."

Reluctantly, I decided to take Styles advice. God knows, I could use any chance at making a break in the industry and if the rumours were true, this was it. Fear of rejection had kept me from sending out demo tapes and every pub I had spoken to either already had regular performers or wanted an ensemble.

It did still bother me though, that if I was being summoned to a club party, why was the invitation for five in the afternoon? Besides, anyone calling himself *the God of War* or *the Dead Man* made me nervous. Then there was the all too important issue of, what do you wear to meet a god?

At the established time, I paid the cabbie and began my approach to the lavish estate. I crept up a set of marble steps past a pair of stone lions as they held their eternal vigil. With some degree of apprehension, I knocked upon the bronze Rococo double doors. I nervously adjusted the collar on my leather jacket, tugged on the tail of my *English Beat* tee, and smoothed the creases in my best jeans as I rocked on the heels of a pair of crocodile skin boots I brought from Sydney. Slowly, the doors inched open and I was met by a quivering, elderly voice.

"Can I help you?"

"Yes," I replied. "My name is Ian MacIntyre."

"The after party does not begin until four in the morning and has been cancelled for the remainder of the week. Good day."

But, just as the doors began to close to me, a voice echoed from deep within the manor, "Let him in." Then just as suddenly as they were closed to me, the doors were opened to reveal an elderly butler who by my reckoning had to be older than Methuselah and as Gus would say, "So goddamned tight you couldn't drive a flax seed up his ass with a moll." The shuffle in his gait left me thinking, *definitely gives new meaning to the term "tight-ass-Brit"*.

The butler led me to a lavish base floor study off the west wing that vaguely resembled a dungeon in its blinding darkness. After my eyes adjusted, I became aware of the vast array of antique weapons and medieval tapestries that lined the shadowed walls. Across from me stood an impressive suit of armour that glistened the reflected firelight into my eyes as I approached the plush scarlet couch. Cautiously, I sat down to face the back of an antique leather chair in front of the ornate hearth.

"Can I offer you a drink?" my mysterious host enquired with a slight accent.

"No, thank you," I politely replied. "I don't drink."

We sat in unbearable silence for what seemed an eternity. The longer the silence persisted, the greater my paranoia grew. I scanned the walls nervously. Swords and glass from a display case of muzzle-loaded handguns shimmered with the feigning firelight. Axes and an assortment of bludgeoning weapons hung menacingly from the dim panels. I began to feel as if I had walked straight into the Bates Motel and at any moment "Mother" would appear brandishing an axe as objects began to levitate around the room. I even expected to see my host's head begin to spin like a top, leaving me with an inexplicable hunger for pea soup. These feelings of apprehension were only increased when I summoned the courage to introduce myself.

"My name is…" I began to be cut off by the stranger's comment of, "I know."

A long arm holding a remote control emerged from behind the chair to adjust the volume on a built in stereo. The only sound that filled the heavy air was the playing of Falco's *Rock Me Amadeus*, a song I had heard given considerable airtime in the past couple of weeks. I continued to survey the eccentric scene to be lulled back to reality by the slamming of the bronze doors.

"Harrison!" a distinctly English voice called from within the great hall.

"Damn!" my host expounded as he rose from his seat.

At first, all I could see was the back of a scarlet smoking jacket and a head of dark curls. It was only as he turned to leave that I saw the beaming grey eyes. I suppose I never put two and two together, or if I had, I got seven. The thought that Kingston, a man I assumed to be a born Scotsman, could be the son of a wealthy English aristocrat made as much sense to me as Lady Godiva riding through town fully dressed.

His appearance had changed over the years. The skinny youth that had a body twice his age had become a strapping man. His physique told of hard-earned hours at the gym. His arms, legs, chest, and shoulders were three times the size they had been in school; leaving me to feel out manned and out gunned.

Kingston left the study to face the irate Englishman. As he approached the barely shorter, fairer haired man, his face tensed. The man seemed so frailly built next to the brick-walled Kingston that the first good wind might just blow him right over. I know I must have had a cocky smirk on my face as I stood watching from the doorway to the dungeonesque study.

"Early start, Andrew?" Kingston enquired.

"Not nearly as early as you, I see," the man retorted. "I can smell it from here."

"Somehow, I didn't expect to see you about before midnight. Aren't vampires afraid of daylight?"

"I'll leave the bloodletting to you, big brother," the Englishman alluded.

With that final comment, the Englishman left for the east

wing of the estate.

Andrew Kingston was the youngest of the Kingston men – a Kingston only in name – and stepbrother to my friend. He spent his days buried in studies and his nights as an intern at the hospital.

Cautiously, I approached Kingston, as he stood alone in the great hall. He ran one hand through his coal curls while rubbing his chest with the other.

"E'er sae fair, grey-nick quill, Lallan carlin! How I'd like ta stick me gully ta 'im!" he muttered in Gaelic.

He then turned on one heel, brushed past me, and raced towards the back of the mansion like it was the Royal Ascot. I followed behind as he ran farther and farther ahead. I was led to a lavish garden complete with a statue of Athena on an island in the centre of a cobalt lake. Just as I began to think that I would catch up to him, he dove off the dock and disappeared into the depths. I watched intently for him to surface only to see him reappear on the statue.

"Would ye care ta dance?" he propositioned the grey-eyed goddess as he threw an arm over her stone shoulder.

I stood shaking my head in disbelief at my obviously disturbed friend as he dove from the statue. I scanned the lake and waited for him to resurface. Slowly, a crimson jacket and coal curls floated to the surface. I reached down into what would have surely been a watery grave, to have an icy hand pull me into the frigid, spring depths. Stricken by a sudden, macabre terror, I grasped the dock with such force as to turn my knuckles white. Pain shot through my chest and left me scarcely able to breathe…

"Ian," a distant voice called.

When I finally came to my senses, I found Kingston gazing down at me. His hair hung in dripping ringlets around his ghostly eyes. The pain in my chest had subsided, but the trembling hadn't as I desperately gripped the dock.

"I'm sorry, lad," he apologized. "It was in poor taste. Gie me yer hand."

As he reached to lift me to my feet, I doubled my fist and knocked him back into the water. "Stupid son-of-a-bitch!" I ranted as Kingston pulled himself onto the dock behind me. "Don't ever do that again!"

"I suppose I have that coming," he admitted as he rose to

his feet. "I should have realized that the body believes what the mind tells it."

"What the bloody hell are you babbling about?" I was beginning to grow irritated and confused by the moment.

Kingston was talking in riddles and I wasn't in the mood to play games. In many ways, he reminded me of a quote by Percy Bysshe Shelly I was forced to read in college, "Although a subtler Sphinx renew Riddles of death Thebes never knew." To be perfectly honest, Kingston was making just as much sense to me.

"You just relived falling from the docks," Kingston finally explained, matter-of-factly. "The panic attack was a natural reaction to the memory."

"Memory? What memory?" I corrected, "I don't remember anything."

"Of course not, you were dead."

Before my befuddled form could speak, Kingston raised a hand to silence me as he stared blindly at the mansion.

"He's back!" he exclaimed like a thrilled child as he tore off towards the house.

As we entered the great hall, Kingston suddenly stopped.

"You all right?" I questioned as I nearly bowled him over. Although the thought did occur to me that he was never all right, least of all, all with it. I was beginning to think Kingston had let a few bats loose in the belfry and they had begun to overrun the place.

"I haven't seen him in eleven years," Kingston solemnly stated.

We stood side by side, as we began our tremulous approach. The squishing from my boots echoed through the marbled room and caught the attention of a man in his mid sixties that stood just inside the Rococo doors. He held a look of aristocracy about him, a look that only comes from centuries of blue blood. Sir Charles Edward Stuart Kingston was everything my father attempted to be and I hated him from the first moment I met him. He spent his life sealed behind the walls of Parliament and pining the globe for new archaeological finds. His son spent his life pining for him.

"Well," the man exclaimed in disapproval, "isn't this a sight? You didn't get upset with Andrew again, did you, Deos?"

"Aye, father," Kingston soberly stated.

"Well, at least the walls are intact this time," the man concluded. "Get my bags, Andrew. I have quite a bit of catching up to do."

"I can get them," Kingston adamantly protested.

"That's not necessary. Andrew is quite capable."

I had a cold shiver run down my spine as Andrew passed by toting the bags. "I'm more of a servant than a son," he muttered as he climbed the stairs with a sneer.

I stood pondering my saturated situation as Kingston followed his father to the library. Almost in answer to my prayers, Jonesie approached holding a stack of dry clothes. I quickly changed in Deos' study then re-joined the other in the library. Upon entering I became aware of Sir Charles' questioning glare.

"Father," Kingston announced. "This is Ian MacIntyre."

"The pleasure is all mine," I commented as I offered my hand.

"It generally is," Sir Charles dryly replied. "Weren't you the one labelled *Young Doctor Watson*?"

"I'd rather not discuss that right now," Kingston interrupted.

There was urgency in his voice that left me ill at ease. It was almost as if he were trying to hide things. I was beginning to grow tired of Kingston's little games already. I never knew what demons might emerge from one. Part of me wanted to call a cab and return to my unhappy life at the record store, but curiosity and old memories kept me at Kingston's side.

"Sir Charles," Andrew interjected from the doorway. "The PM is on the line."

"Excuse me, Deos...Mr. MacIntyre," Sir Charles voiced with an air of condemnation at my name as he left the room.

Having summoned what courage remained me, I ventured to ask, "Why did Andrew call you *Harrison* and your father call you *Deos*?"

"Elementary, my dear Watson!" Kingston jibed as I furled my nose in disgust. "It just happens to be my name: Harrison Ian Amadeus Kingston. Hence Deos. Call me Harrison and I'll rip your heart out." There was a glimmer in his eye that told me he was kidding about the ripping my heart out, but I knew the warning was serious.

"I never knew that," I replied, feeling like a simpleton.

A smug smile adorned Kingston's weathered face as he informed me, "You never did ask."

He was right. Back in school it never seemed to matter much what anyone's Christian name was. Everyone was referred to by their surnames or a nickname and at the time that was good enough for a Yank like me. I was MacIntyre, Mouse was Jones to all but his friends… and I thought Kingston would forever be, Kingston.

"Not to change the subject, Kingston," I began.

"Bloody hell!" Deos interrupted. "Don't be so bloody formal. Call me Deos. There do happen to be three Kingstons in this draftee auld place."

Once night had fallen and brought with it socialites, dignitaries, their tag-alongs, and the like, I felt as though had died and gone to stiff-collar hell! It was like being at the funeral of your least favourite relative, having to sit in front of the casket, and all the while knowing that you're missing the Super Bowl.

Deos seemed to wander preoccupied through the house in an attempt to avoid the main party. Andrew on the other hand, spent most of the night with what Deos termed, "John Barleycorn." It seemed Sir Charles was the one really enjoying himself.

Deos and I eventually ended up in front of his study miserably sipping Krystal. Actually, I was sipping; Deos was guzzling like a dying man at a desert oasis. I scanned the crowd in vain hoping to see a familiar, or at least friendly, face. Deos simply stared at his feet and kicked the immaculate marble floor with a well-shined shoe. He looked at the crowd a couple of times, but always returned his gaze to the floor. I was shocked that something as simple as a crowd would intimidate the usually overconfident Deos.

"Ye know," he stated, "ye don't have to hang around me if don't want to."

"Who else am I supposed to talk to?" I glibbed. "It doesn't look like Venus is in the room."

Then the impossible happened. A blonde angel in a silver evening gown approached me. Deos had stepped away for what seemed to be his hundredth refill, leaving me uncomfortably alone.

She glided across the floor with a glass in each hand and held a satin-gloved champagne-laden hand towards me on her approach.

"Hello," she stated as I took the glass. "I don't believe we've met. My name is Katherine James."

As I raised her gloved hand to my lips, I turned on the charm. She gazed over my shoulder at the figure of Andrew, looming like a vulture atop the stairs. He raised his glass to her and she returned her eyes to me.

"Ian MacIntyre," I introduced. "I find it awfully crowded in here. Would you care to join me for a walk...I know just the place."

I led Katherine to the garden behind the estate. We walked along the brick paths for the majority of an hour. Her emerald eyes and dainty, petite nose captivated me. It was as if I could have been lost in a sea of green forever as we sat upon a marble bench to talk and gaze at the carnival coloured fountain.

"I'd like to see you again," I stated nervously.

"I'd like that," she was equally as nervous as she handed me her business card. "It has my home and work numbers, call."

As we rose, I realized the unnatural quiet that gripped the estate. The music had stopped, thankfully. There was only so much Baroque, a broke guy can handle in one evening. With the silence ended the dancing, incessant talking, everything. It was as if we had entered a graveyard. Not even the crickets were chirping. The dead quiet left me ill at ease as I made my approach to the great hall.

Inside, I found Sir Charles laying face down at the base of the stairs. A broken wineglass still gripped in a motionless hand, a look of pain and horror adorned his face. His free hand lay perfectly still at his side. I gazed captivated at his unmoving chest and back wishing for any sign of life. His eyes stared blindly towards the crowd. I knew he was dead.

Andrew approached slowly from his perch atop the stairs. He drew the coat from his back with unnatural calm as he met the final step. Kneeling before his stepfather, he placed a finger to a limp wrist, then an ear to a motionless back before covering the head with his jacket.

"I'm sorry," he voiced calmly, almost with calculation, "he's dead."

Unconsciously, I rushed to where I had last seen Deos. I eventually found him gripping the doorframe to the kitchen for support. His face was pale and drenched in sweat, revealing a pulsating artery in the middle of his forehead. Grey eyes stared from behind widened lids. He opened his mouth, but couldn't form words. I watched his neck throb chaotically as I reached to help as he finally collapsed onto the marble floor.

"Help me take Harrison to his study!" Andrew ordered as he nonchalantly approached his afflicted stepbrother.

With Andrew holding Deos' feet and me at his head and shoulders, we made our way through the crowded sea of people to the darkened study. Andrew fumbled his way through the darkness to the couch.

"I will never understand why he insists on living like some Victorian horror novel," Andrew complained as we set Deos upon the couch.

Andrew stretched over his afflicted brother to a desk lamp behind. Enough light was emanated to allow me to find the main switch by the door. In adequate lighting, the room lost its sinister appearance and held a romantic charm. The antique weaponry, armour, and books led you to believe you had passed into another century, an ancient, forgotten time, a time of knights and sorcerers – a time Deos would have belonged in.

"Leave us!" Andrew barked before I could even ask what was happening.

I did what I was told, no matter how reluctant I was to leave my friend's side. There was something malevolent about Andrew that I didn't trust. I could sense it about him the first time I met him and I suspected there was something to the brothers' relationship that transgressed simple sibling rivalry. Andrew seemed too calm to me. There was a distant, sinister lack of emotion in his eyes that added to my dread. I began to wonder what I had walked into. I prayed this was all some twisted nightmare and I would awake safe in my lumpy, cheap bed in the Hostel, late for work again. But as the minutes turned to hours, I realized it was no dream.

# Chapter Five
## Monsters of the Abyss

"The prince of darkness is a gentleman."
{Shakespeare, *King Lear*, III.iv}

Police routed the mansion like a plague of locusts. Where you saw one, you saw three. Outside the media were entrenched around the perimeter of the estate. As a guest was questioned and allowed to leave, they were bombarded by a frenzy of questions and accusations by the press stalking outside. I knew it was only a matter of time before I was the inquisitioned. With each person I heard subjected to their line of defamation, the deeper the pit grew in my stomach.

I stood anxiously pacing the great hall. I had been passed by, I know not how many times, unacknowledged by the detectives. Perhaps the fact that I failed to hold a title placed me at the bottom of their waiting list. Not that it mattered to me; I was perfectly content to remain where I was for the meantime. It saved me from, or at least, postponed my turn with the Inquisition. I know I shouldn't have felt that way, but I'd had more of the circus than my stressed state could stand. Besides, I had more on my mind than the sideshow outside; I was deathly worried about Deos.

Twice I had decided to confront Andrew and demand an explanation and twice just as I was about to barge through that door, I choked. Finally, I collapsed against the wall and slid wearily to the floor. As I sat there with my arms around my knees, Andrew emerged from the study.

"How is he?" I demanded as I jumped to my feet.

"Fine, unfortunately!" Andrew replied in a smug tone as he made hi2s way through the throng of police.

"Mr. Kingston," one policeman addressed Andrew. "May I

have a word with you?"

I entered the study to find Deos propped on one elbow upon the couch. He lazily turned over and placed his hand behind his head. Slowly, I rolled a desk chair over and sat with my arms draped across the back. His eyes were encased in dark circles and his weathered face was drawn, weary, and pale as he stared at the oak panelled ceiling.

"I assume half of New Scotland yard is here," he commented.

Just as I was about to answer, a tall impressive man in a tan trench coat and fedora entered the room. He smiled kindly at my afflicted friend then briefly glanced at me. I smiled the sincerest smile I could muster under the current circumstances, but to be honest, my heart wasn't in it. In return, all I received was a snide smirk from the stranger.

"Look who's re-joined the land of the living," the stranger commented.

"I had to return to torment ye, didn't I?" Deos smirked. "Ceud Mile Failte to ye, John!"

"I do wish you wouldn't speak in the mongrel dialect!" the stranger lamented. "I take it you're firing on all cylinders again."

Deos put on one of his grins of pure satisfaction then laid back and stared at the ceiling, some colour once again returning to his face. "Like a fine tuned Bentley...I take it Price has assigned only the best," he solemnly stated.

"Of course. He's handling this one himself," the stranger acknowledged.

Deos raised his head, stared in disbelief for a moment, then regained his composure. I felt this man Price was someone to be reckoned with. Not to mention, someone Deos didn't particularly care for. The look of shock and horror in my usually fearless friend left me filled with apprehension and dread. I wondered what new demons awaited revelation at the hands of this man Price. Very little of what I had encountered fit my memories of Deos and certainly did nothing to instill morale in me. I thought of the desert and the dingo, and wished I hadn't changed my mind about going home.

"Out for blood, no doubt," Deos remarked with an air of mock arrogance. "The carlin never did like me much."

I sat confused as the stranger moved aside to make room for the forceful, well-dressed man that opened the door. I knew in an instant that this was the infamous Price. The room fell silent as the man strode across the Charles Edward Stuart tartan rug to where Deos lay. The forceful eyes of Deos met the equal gaze of Price. Each held a cold look of determination as they studied one another. Two warlords preparing for battle could not have been a more harrowed sight.

"As always, it not a pleasure to see ye, again, Johnny!" Deos voiced. His tongue as well as his eyes shot ice-sickles at the formidable man.

"That's Chief Inspector Price to you, Kingston!" Price retorted with equal coldness.

"I'm sorry, Cheap Inspector. What ever brings ye to me humble abode?"

With each insulting gesture, the Chief Inspector tensed. There was hatred between the two men that I found appealed to my darkest curiosities. Deos' courage, perhaps even his arrogance, shocked and inspired me. He had a courage I had often tried to emulate, but never truly possessed.

I wondered what could have transpired to instill such a mutual hatred. There seemed such a personal nature to the dislike between them that I found it incomprehensible. I knew there was more to the story than a general mistrust of the law or Deos' usual flippancy. There had to be a history.

"I'm here over the matter of your father's death," the Inspector explained.

"That's right, isn't it," Deos retorted, a little too confidently for my liking.

Even though I found Deos' brash ways admirable, I couldn't always bring myself to sanction them. Perhaps I was too much of an emotional fool for my own good. God knows, I'd often been betrayed by the trait. Still, I found Deos' seemingly callous attitude to his father's death horrifying. I knew enough of Deos to understand that he dealt with things unusual ways at best, but this seemed to be a stretch, even for him. I thought that maybe he had placed a front for the Inspector. However, the front remained long after the Inspector had gone.

As I gazed upon Deos' cold exterior, I felt as though I had

gazed into a wide abyss, an arctic pit devoid of life, a place where only death awaited the weary passer by. A place from which any man that dares wander its expanse can never return. I pondered what could have turned Deos so cold, so distant. Much of the childish prankster was lost. What replaced it was more of a phantom than I had ever known before. There was an empty void in Deos that was vaguely masked under the flippant comments and eccentric behaviour.

"Don't get any foolish ideas," Price cautioned as he prepared to leave. "If you try and interfere with the investigation, I'll have you locked up faster than you can say 'Bonnie Prince Charlie'. Clear?"

"Crystal," Deos seemingly surrendered.

As Price left the room, I observed Deos rub his left arm as he opened and closed his fist. His eyes took a brief glassy haze as his face ran pale. Then as suddenly as his appearance had changed, he returned to normal. Slowly, he rose from the couch and proceeded towards the doorway. I followed anxiously behind, knowing full well under the circumstances, he could have been a very dangerous man. Armed with this knowledge, I questioned what good I would be should he rage out of control. The thought of being an accessory never did cross my mind.

"Do ye have a place to stay?" Deos turned to ask me.

"Yes," I replied. "I've got a room at the hostel."

"Not anymore. I need someone around I can trust."

Deos led me from the house and down the drive to the garage. In the darkness, it was a large black fortress against a grey landscape. Dots of firefly-like lights wandered the expanses as police waved across the terrain in a vain attempt to find clues.

Just inside the doorway stood a partially restored *Indian* motorcycle and a blue and silver Jaguar. Instead of approaching the Jaguar, Deos walked over to a dilapidated green tarp. With one fell swoop, he jerked the tarp and created a cloud of dust and mildew. Below shined a candy apple red 1929 Mercedes 660 with gold trim. Emblazoned on the illustrious bonnet was the Stuart coat of arms complete with crossed claymores. The impressive sight left me amazed and in awe.

"Twere it only me," Deos chimed, "I'd take the bike."

As I was about to ask about the Jaguar, Andrew flew into

the room, tossed a disapproving look towards his two of us, threw open the door of the Jaguar, slid in, slammed the door in anger, and after starting the engine, left enough rubber to have supplied the allies for a month. Obviously, the Jag was his.

I eased into the passenger seat of the grandiose convertible. Uncomfortably, I laid my arm on the leather-panelled door only to pull it away out of respect. I was afraid to touch anything in the museum on wheels. That is, until Deos idly tossed the cellophane from a fresh pack of cigarettes behind the seat. I slid down in the seat until my head nestled comfortably on the back.

As we glided down the road, I glanced at Deos. The green dash lights glowed off his callous face and enfired the ghostly eyes as he stared blindly over the dead, winding road. For what seemed an eternity, we rode in unbearable silence. The darkened scenery floated forebodingly by. Leaves were swirled and uprooted to create wraiths in the background. Thoughts of the night's events filtered through my mind and left me filled with mortal dread. I tried to suppress the irrational doubts and fears that consumed me concerning my friend's intent. Something deep inside me said to trust him, that he was essentially the same man that had befriended me in school, but I still continually questioned whether I truly ever knew him.

An hour later we eased to a stop in front of a line of middle class housing. The streets seemed to resemble the video to Madness' "Our House". Had I not been in such a sombre mood, I would have tied a handkerchief around my head and bashed it between two bricks *Monty Python* style, just for shits and giggles. It may have been nothing more than the look in Deos' haunting eyes as he stared distressed across at a darkened house that reminded me that it was neither the time nor the place for stupidity of that calibre.

With an ever so slight quiver of dread, Deos voiced, "He said he'd be waitin'."

Not knowing whom the "he" in question was, I began to reconsider my involvement. I watched Deos slowly slide from the car and approach the door. Hesitantly, he motioned for me to join him.

Upon my nervous approach, he rang the bell with a shaking finger. My heart skipped a beat and found a new home in my throat at the howl of neighbour dogs.  After a second pause, Deos nervously began to fumble through a sizable set of keys.  The rattle of pot metal only seemed to enrage the barking further.  I swallowed hard as Deos stifled a curse in Gaelic and I prayed the curse wasn't on me.  Just as he was about to slide a key in the lock, a searing porch light burned my eyes and momentarily blinded me like an interrogation lamp.  With intentional force, the door flew open to reveal a tall, dark haired man resembling Arthur Dent, and I found myself wishing I had brought a towel.

"Ye scared three years off me, lad!" Deos exclaimed.

"I didn't think you had three years left," the man retorted in an Irish brogue.

"I don't now you dumb sot!  Where the bloody hell, were ye?"

The man shrugged as he gave a heavy yawn.  "I went back to bed after you called.  Figured there wasn't any use in both of us not getting any sleep.  The way it sounds I have a full day ahead of me thanks to your father."

I followed hesitantly behind, dwelling on the *full day ahead of me thanks to your father* comment.  My eyes struggled to adjust when the strange young man flipped on the overhead light in the living room.  Deos wandered across the wooden floor to an overstuffed couch and collapsed wearily.

"Danny-boy!" Deos called to the ceiling.  "Put my fiere in the guest room."

"My pleasure, m-lord!" Danny jested.  "Walk this way," as he slid down the hallway like Quasimodo.  After pausing before a door, he straightened his back, whipped around, and presented his hand.

"Where are me manners?" he exclaimed.

"Same place as yer brains, lad!" Deos interjected from the other room.

"You must be *Young Doctor Watson* I presume," he alluded.  A faint look of disapproval undoubtedly passed over my face as he continued with a bow, "Allow me to introduce myself, Daniel J. O'Selle, metro forensics, at your service."

Politely, I replied, "Ian MacIntyre."  When in actuality, I was thinking, *doesn't Deos know any normal people?*  I would soon discover my answer to be infallibly – *no*.  Only to then realize, what did that say about me?

With a dramatic swoop, the forensics assistant propelled open the door and turned on the light to reveal the small, quaint, and very green guest room.

"Now with no more ado," he concluded, "I will bid ye goodnight and fare thee well." Then with a wink and a smile, he disappeared into the darkness of the master bedroom.

I entered the room and slid the door shut behind me. Then, approached the shamrock patterned comforter on the bed and delicately sat down upon the edge. Partially from frustration, but mainly exhaustion, I buried my hands in my hair and stared blindly at the cracks in the wooden floor, remembering how the colour reminded me of my mother's eyes, deep brown, almost chocolate, with a hint of velvet.

I pondered how far away from home I really was and wished I had ran back to the states the day I turned eighteen. I could have happily lived out my days as a farm hand or manual labourer. Anything seemed better than the surreal nightmare I was trapped in.

After some time, I kicked my shoes off, pulled off my shirt and slacks until I was left in nothing but my boxers and socks. I stepped to the window to see rows of darkened windows, parked cars under glistening street-lamps, and empty walks. The desolate scene only echoed the emptiness I felt. I debated picking up the nearest phone, calling for a one-way ticket to Vermont, sneaking out the window, running as fast as I could for Heathrow, and never looking back. But, something stopped me.

As much as my mind screamed to go, my heart held me fast. There was this hollow ache whenever I considered leaving, that left it's weight chained to my ankles and held my feet firm – a lingering sense of loyalty that refused to be silenced.

I sulked the remainder of the night away staring into darkness and the shadows cast by the filtered moon and streetlight. As dawn's warm presence appeared, I became aware of footsteps in the hall outside. With a slow, pounding pulse and wide eyes, I slowly made my way through the darkness to the door. As I braced for attack, I threw open the door to an unsettled Deos.

"I see you couldn't sleep either," he toyed.

With a stifled mutter of, "Jesus!" I made my way to the

window. Deos followed prolonged behind in only a pair of shorts. Around his neck hung a large silver military-style dog tag engraved on the back, and bearing the caduceus and Jolly Roger on the front. As he entered the pale light, his eyes glowed with menacing fury and the scars across his chest became blazing nymphs against his dark skin. I stood my ground near the window and waited for the wraith's course of action. With a shallow sigh, Deos collapsed upon the hard mattress and squeezed his pallid eyes shut.

"You have not to fear from me," he stated coldly.

"I know," I replied.

He seemed to be breathing harder than normal as he laid flat on his back. There was a strained quiver in his voice, as if he had to catch each breath to simply finish his sentences as he continued, "I never did tell you how I earned these." He indicated the scars that nearly covered his chest. I shook my head.

Deos took another deep breath, pursed his lips and slowly released it with a slight whistle as if trying to convince himself to continue. "I was fourteen. I'd been bedridden for a month with a rather nasty case of Rheumatic Fever. Father was in London, as always. My stepmother, Andrew, and I were staying at what had been my great grandparent's estate in Inverness. I remember father and her fighting over my illness. She would say I wasn't her problem. If he was so bloody worried maybe he should hire a nanny. She had Andrew to worry about. I was his. When I finally got to feel a little better, I snuck out for a walk. I hadn't been gone a half an hour when I found this wee old lady being mugged by four carlins. They laughed at me when I first tried to stop them. Then, when they realized I wasn't going to give up and go home, they decided to teach me a lesson. I ended up with this lot of knife wounds and a broken rib that punctured my left lung. I was told that I coded twice on the table... Funny thing is, lad... I still haven't learned that lesson."

It was then that I realized what had kept me there, the source of the loyalty I felt towards Deos. We were the same, he and I. We were the unwanted.

*******

I hesitantly gazed at the captivated pair. Out of the corner of my eye, I could see that most of the saloon had joined the conversation. Even Jim seemed entranced by my tale. A cool breeze full of the scent of rain, a blend of old earth with a mix of acid rain and burnt wiring that is indicative of Arizona monsoons, blew in from the open door and tussled a few stray hairs back in front of my dark glasses. With a nervous hand, I slicked them back before asking, "Where was I?"

"You were telling us about the night of Sir Charles' death," Gus enlightened, much to my dismay…

*******

The morning fared no better than the previous night. Every paper, news programme and scandal sheet in town had something to say about Sir Charles. My day worsened when I entered the door to my Hostel room to find that everything was gone. Anything of value, that was. The stereo I bought just two weeks prior, my vinyl collection and, most heart breaking of all, my guitar. It may not have looked like much (it was held together with stickers from around the globe and a bit of duct tape) but it was all I had left of my Lakota grandfather.

I wasn't quite myself as I emerged from the office of the Hostel. The manager was of absolutely no help and in a fury, I threw the key in his face, grabbed my bags, and raced down the steps in a maraud of anger and disgust. Rage and hatred swelled within me until I feared I would explode. An ire of frustration forced me to face the brick wall and release my vehemence against the course surface until my knuckles were nothing more than swollen, bloodied masses. A meat grinder could not have inflicted as much damage.

Surprisingly, I never felt the effects of my self-inflicted torture until I returned to Dan's with the bloody mess concealed in bloodstained shreds of my shirt. Dan had long since left and Deos sat alone on the sofa smoking a cigarette. Across the top of the end table empty bottles of *New Castle* were strewn. Blinds on both sides of the room were drawn to give the same eerie air as the study at Kingston Hall. He gazed at me through clouded eyes as I entered the shadowed room.

I didn't expect ye back so soon," he slurred on my tremulous approach.

"I had a bad day at the office, dear," I replied with a more than distinct air of sarcasm.

"No doubt!" he cried when he spied the blood-stained cloths around my hands and suddenly sobered.

He rose from his seat and approached me with caution. A raised finger beckoned me to wait as he disappeared down the hall. In a few moments he returned toting a black bag. He motioned me to sit on the edge of the couch as he filled a pan with steaming water. As he squatted before me, he slowly unwrapped the hamburgeresque mess beneath. He took a moment to flick the ash from the cigarette that dangled precariously from his lips before wringing the steaming towel out over the pan.

"This may burn," he stated as he wrapped a hand with the warm, damp towel. He then proceeded to wring out a second towel to wrap the other hand. The heat from the towels was almost more than I could bear. I wondered how he could place his hands into near boiling water and never so much as flinch. He repeated this process two or three more times until he was satisfied that the wound was clean.

He gazed at me with his ghostly eyes as he stated slowly, almost soporific, "What ever ye do…Keep looking at me…don't turn your eyes for a moment…Understood?" I nodded, feeling as though I had just been entranced. "Good. Look at your hands."

"But you said..." I corrected.

"I know what I said, lad. Just look down...Trust me."

So, I did. To my shock (and relief) he had soaked the wounds in rubbing alcohol and wrapped them in new bandages. All without so much as a flinch of pain or my even knowing that it had been done. I wondered, *how could he bandage a wound so quick, painless and precise?* When posed with the query, all Deos would say, "Lots of practice, lad."

"Ye know," he continued, "I thought I was the only one who did stupid things like that to themselves."

"You can rest assured there are people far more stupid than you wandering the world," I stated.

I found myself met by the white-hot glare of Deos. His eyes were afire with a mix of disappointment, melancholy, and respect. He shook his head anxiously as he ran a hand through his dark coals and rose to his feet, pacing in agitation.

"No yer not! And I'll not hear ye call yerself stupid!"

I never dared press the issue. I knew his nature well enough to know what he meant. He was the type of man who rushed blindly into a bad situation with no regard for his own safety. He was the Good Samaritan at a traffic accident; the man who pushed a child from danger only to be injured himself. In short, he was the self-sacrificing knight that many had often thought had gone out of style with King Arthur. His scars alone told a story of a life of altruism, an altruistic nature that had nearly been the death of him.

a non-verbal agreement of, "You don't pry into my sex life and I won't pry into yours."

Both our paths were about to change when Ace came over that afternoon. Deos had been pacing the floor all morning to the point that I feared he would wear a groove in the hard wood floors. There was a nervous determination that hung in the air like the evening fog down by the river. As he paced, he wrung his hands and muttered incoherently. It was uncharacteristic of Deos to be that nervous and even more uncharacteristic for him to leave when he knew Ace was on her way over.

"Where's Deos?" Ace asked as she walked through the Rococo doors.

"Can't say," I replied honestly. "He left about twenty minutes ago. He should be back anytime now, I'd think."

When he finally returned, he had a look of uncharacteristic determination in his eyes. I didn't have to be a psychic to know they had something very private to discuss. I also didn't have to psychic to know that it had nothing to do with me.

"I'll leave you two alone," I excused, uncomfortably as I backed towards the door.

Deos laid a hand on my shoulder and stated, "No, you can stay." With that, he pulled a small black case from his pocket and got down on one knee before Ace. "I know I've asked this more times than I'd care to remember," he stated with unusual sincerity, "but I have to know...Will you marry me?"

Instead of the usual cries of joy, waving arms, and tears of delight, all she did was reach for his hand, raise him to his feet and state, "You know I can't."

"Oh, well," Deos shook off as he tossed the case idly behind him. "Try again in another six months?"

"Sure," she replied with a smile.

I was shocked by their blithe approach to her denial. Deos seeing my shock turned to me and smiled.

"Every six months or so, I propose and just as routinely, she turns me down," he explained. "We've been going through this song and dance for close to three years now, isn't it? The first couple of times really hurt. We even broke up for a while."

"Then why do you keep trying?" I asked, astounded.

"I figure I might eventually wear her down. I'm not getting

any younger, ye know."

I'm not sure if I were prompted by Deos' latest proposal or I was blinded by infatuation, but I ran out and bought the largest bouquet of roses I could find, a bottle of champagne and raced off to Kat's flat. I passed by what looked to be Andrew's Jaguar across the street from her building. The passenger side wheel well was nearly destroyed, as if it had been beaten in. I paused before the building and tried to think of what I was going to say. I had never proposed before and frankly, didn't have much of a clue of how to go about it.

I took in a deep breath and entered the building. My heart began to pound in my ears as I climbed the stairway. I tried to picture what the scene would be like. I'd knock on the door; she'd open it just as I fell to my knees. I wouldn't need to say anything. My eyes would say everything. She would cry with joy. We would honeymoon on a cross-country road trip in America. Everything would be perfect.

As I approached, my perfection began to crumble at the sound of a couple fighting. The closer I drew to Kat's door, the louder the voices became followed by the sound of breaking glass and Kat's demand of, "Get out! I never want to see you again!"

The door flew open to find me face to face with Andrew. His face was red with rage. Kat stood behind him with tear stained eyes, wearing the white lingerie I had bought her. She held her see-through robe close around her as she looked shamefully at the floor. Her arm and left cheek were puffed, blotchy, and patched with red as if she had been beaten. I wanted to grab Andrew and toss him down the steps for laying a hand on her. Then I realized why she didn't want Deos to know about us and why Andrew had been so jealous. She was the girlfriend Deos had alluded to at the Opera. I had been used. Betrayal and shame steadied my hand and turned me to a cigar shop Indian, holding champagne and roses.

Andrew never said a word as he brushed by me and stormed down the stairs. I was sick to my stomach. All I wanted to do was double up and die. I couldn't even look her in the face without wanting to vomit. I threw the flowers and champagne from the balcony and watched as they littered the lobby below, turned, then left without a word.

"Ian," she cried desperately after me. "Ian, please! I tried to tell you so many times!"

"Then why didn't you!" I demanded as I paused midway down the stairs.

"Andrew wanted me to keep tabs on his brother. I never wanted it to go this far. I never meant to hurt you."

"Great job!" I sneered as I left.

# Chapter Thirteen
## The Wane

"Half our days we pass in the shadows of the earth;
And the brother of death exacteth a third part of our lives."{Sir Thomas Browne, 1646}

I returned to Kingston Hall several hours later. Deos was sitting in his chair staring at the fire. All the colour had receded from his face, his eyes were distant. At first I attributed his condition to inebriation over the recent rejection. Then, I saw the small brown glass vial of pills he held loosely in his hand. He appeared to strain for breath as he stated, "My arm hurts."

Immediately, fear and worry filled me. I sensed something was terribly wrong. A cold chill ran through me as I called for Jonesie in a panic, only to receive no answer. It was only then that I remembered that Deos had given him the day off. My stomach knotted as Deos' eyes grew colder and the vial slipped from his weakening fingers. Forgetting my personal hurt and anger I called out to Andrew.

"Andrew, come quickly!" I called desperately. At first I received no answer. I knew Andrew was home. I had passed by his Jaguar when I entered the estate. "Damn it!" I called again. "Put your petty differences aside! There's something wrong with Deos!"

Only then did I hear Andrew race across the marble floor. His shoes slid as he grabbed the doorframe to stop. He entered the room with a look of disquiet in his anxious eyes. He looked at his brother and then at me. By this time, Deos had slumped in his seat and his eyes were glossy and cold. Andrew felt his brother's neck in disbelief then put an ear to his still chest. His worried eyes seemed to peer through me as he addressed me, "Call for an ambulance, quick!"

I did as I was told and stayed on the phone until the ambulance arrived. As they carted Deos off on a gurney, a paramedic forced air into Deos with a black bag as Andrew pounded feverishly on his brother's chest.

"Damn it, Deos!" he cried. "Don't you die on me!"

*Did I just hear what I thought I heard? Did Andrew actually call his brother Deos? Not Harrison, not big brother, but Deos?* I was taken aback by the sincerity in his voice. How petty our squabble seemed to both of us now.

"Follow us in the Mercedes!" Andrew ordered as they rushed out the bronze Rococo doors.

As I followed close behind, my mind was a blur. Thousands of scattered, disconnected thoughts swarmed my brain and left me confused. All I could do was follow behind the ambulance and long for the best. Even my arm seemed to disappear in the din of confusion. I forgot entirely about the severe shoulder wound, as I shifted gears as though nothing was wrong.

By the time the ambulance had reached the hospital, they had successfully revived Deos. I still didn't know exactly what happened and wouldn't for some time. I used the (for lack of a better term) dead time to contact Dan and Ace. Neither one seemed too surprised when I described Deos' condition to them. That's not to say they weren't concerned; both rushed to his side as soon as they heard. They just weren't surprised.

I stood in earnest and awaited the news. After a half-hour, Andrew emerged from the emergency department and approached me. His hands were in his pockets and his eyes were fixed to the ground. Visible lines had formed on his face from distress.

"How is he?" I begged.

"He's alive," Andrew stated matter-of-factly as he sat down across from me and buried his hands in his hair. "We were able to restart his heart, but there's no telling what damage there is until the cardiologist arrives."

"Are trying to tell me he had a heart attack?" I was shocked. People our age didn't have heart attacks.

"Didn't you know?" Andrew questioned. The puzzled look in my eyes gave Andrew his answer. "It started when he had rheumatic fever…"

Before Andrew could finish, another doctor, one I took to be the cardiologist, approached him. Andrew rose and walked to the man. They shook hands, talked a bit and then rushed to Deos. Shortly afterwards, Dan and Ace entered through the automatic doors and rushed to me with distress in their eyes.

"Well, have you heard any more?"

"I just talked to Andrew. Why didn't anyone tell me Deos was sick?" I demanded. Dan and Ace shot each other shifty glances, but would never give definitive answer.

In the days that followed, Deos was subjected to a battery of tests. Everything from X-Rays, ultrasounds, and being continuously monitored by EKG. A knot formed in the pit of my stomach each time I entered the room to find Deos wired like the backstage at an *Aerosmith* concert. For the most part he was in good spirits, but weak. As I entered, I caught Deos and Ace at the end of a conversation.

"Tell you what," she stated. "You get out of here and I will marry you."

"Ye're not just saying that, are ye?" he questioned.

"Scout's honour."

Deos looked at her suspiciously, "Ye were never a scout." He turned his head as I cleared my throat.

"Not interrupting anything, am I?" I joked back to the night of the Opera.

"Not at all," Ace confirmed.

"Damn! I was hoping I was. After all, you never know what can go in those hospital beds."

A brief smile of recognition passed by Deos' grey lips as he held an arm out towards me and I walked closer and sat down at his side.

"I hear I have you to thank for my life," he stated as we shook hands.

"I don't know if I'd say that exactly," I replied modestly.

He ruffled my hair as he stated, "Don't be so damned modest. If it weren't for you walking in when you did, I'd have earned the title *the Dead Man*."

After staying most of the day, I returned to the Hall that night to unsettling quiet. Never had I heard the estate so still before. When Deos was around, there was usually music echoing through the vast expanses. But that night, there was nothing but unearthly silence.

I started a fire in the fireplace; settled onto Deos' scarlet couch, and watched the embers burn to nothing. I was still reeling from the news that Deos had kept such an important part of his life a secret for so long. Then again, had I known, things would have surely been different between us and I would have spent everyday fearing for the worst. I realized Deos kept his health a secret for fear of becoming a condition rather than a person. He felt if everyone knew, he couldn't lead a normal life.

In Deos' study, I lay upon the couch and tended to my burning arm. The wound on my shoulder had reopened from the sheer force of overuse. The rapid gear changes, the movement, and jumping from the car had all combined to break it open. I bandaged it as best I could, but it had continuously seeped blood for the majority of the day. Up to that point, I thought it was progressing nicely and might have been completely healed in another week or so.

Out of desperation and the need for some sleep, I threw four painkillers into my mouth, swallowed them with a large glass of Islay Scotch, and laid down for what I intended to be a short nap.

# Chapter Fourteen
## All Things Must End…

"His flaw'd heart-
Alack, too weak the conflict to support!-
'Twixt two extremes of passion, joy and grief,
Burst smilingly."
{Shakespeare, King Lear, V.iii}

I awoke with a start. Pain seared through my chest and shoulders as I struggled for each essential breath. I lay in a pool of blood that dripped down to the wooden floor below. I jumped from the couch only to have my heart pound itself from my chest. Each fatal moment that passed, I fear it to be my last. With one final, turbulent step, I approached the door only to mortally collapse as I reached for the knob as I heard Deos plead, "Ian…"

My eyes opened wearily as I strained to focus on my surroundings. The fire died long before and the room was left in tomb-like darkness. Slowly, the image of the door filled my vision as I stretched for the knob once more. It took every ounce of strength to pull myself to my feet. As I turned the knob, an image filled my mind. A maniacal, morbid image I wished I had never envisioned. The thought that Deos was dead filled my soul with a dark void.

I pulled the Mercedes to a stop before the Emergency entrance to the hospital. I threw a shirt over my bare back as I jumped over the driver's door. With maddened haste, I bolted through the automatic doors to find that Dan awaited me beyond. He placed his hand on my arm and held out a closed fist. After pausing a moment, he slid his hand down my arm to my hand. Gently, he opened my hand and left me the contents of his. I gazed through a fog at Deos' pocket watch and gold lighter. Embittered, I squeezed my fist closed over the contents. I knew for those items to have found their way to me meant the worst – I was right. Deos was dead.

I brushed past Dan and raced to the elevator. Desperately, Dan called, "Where are ye going?"

"For a walk, don't try and follow!" I hissed as the elevator door shut.

A strange curiosity gripped me as I opened the pocket watch. I have no idea what prompted me to know the time. It was as though I was disconnected from the movement of my hands. An odd sensation like I had gripped a bare power wire filled me and drove my hands to open the watch. My mind didn't want to know what the primal already did. As the doors opened, I gazed at the clock at the end of the hallway. It was a quarter past three. Then, I gazed at the watch, half-past midnight. An unmistakable thought pounded at my mind like a Tommy gun; that was the time I collapsed at Kingston Hall. I tried to dismiss the thought as paranoia, but it nagged at me as I continued on my morbid quest.

I was fortunate enough to find the nurse's station temporarily unmanned as well as the corridor empty. With almost assisted ease, I inched open the door and disappeared into the bemoaned chamber. The only light that filtered through the room came from the dying florescent light that flickered ominously over Deos' bed. As I had begun my macabre endeavour, I became aware of voices beyond the grim door. I quickly squeezed myself into the closet and hid behind Deos' coat as two interns entered with a gurney. I glared as they laughed and made light of the lurid task that awaited them.

Deos lay much as he had when I left, except his arm was draped over the edge of the bed. The once lively lips were now grey and empty. Never more would a sharp phrase or acrid jest be uttered. The ghostly eyes that in life could see all truth were now only dull, sunken orbs. The same eyes that could cut straight through a man and leave cold daggers behind stared aimlessly into the darkness and seemed to cry out to me. My only wish was that I could have been there to answer sooner.

As the door closed behind the grim procession, I collapsed to the floor from sheer frustration. I felt as if I could tear every hair from my head and ripped my eyes from their very sockets. My world had ended, leaving me filled with despair and hatred. I raised my irrational head to see a shimmer of light in the darkness. My quivering hand reached for the faint glow. The closer I drew to it; the more form the object took. Nervously, I gazed at the door expecting to be caught at any moment. I pulled a large handkerchief from my pocket and lifted the shattered, empty needle. Tenderly, I wrapped the sharp tip and jagged edges in the handkerchief before placing it in my breast pocket.

I walked away and left the hospital. I drove for hours through the backstreets of London. I had no desire to return to the Hall and certainly no desire to see Andrew again. I wandered until I found myself down by the docks in the pre-dawn haze.

The cold echo of traffic and the gurgle of the water lulled me to tranquillity. I knew I went there because that was where Deos had felt most at ease. It was the one place he could go where he didn't have to prove himself; the one place he was just a man, not a legend. Reluctantly, I returned to the Hall around daybreak to find Ace sitting in Deos' study.

"I've been waiting for you to return for hours," she called. "Dan just went to make some tea."

As Dan entered the room, he mindlessly asked, "Any word from Ian...Oh, there you are. Where the devil did you get off to last night?"

"Here, there, nowhere," I replied. "I've been thinking."

Dan handed Ace a cup of tea as I made my way to the liquor cabinet. If there was ever a time I needed the hard stuff, this was it. I poured a double shot, or so, of Scotch and threw it down with intentional force. Before I had even recovered my breath, I poured a second and started for the blood soaked couch. As I sat down, Dan looked at me in disbelief as I pulled a cigarette from the wooden box on the end table and lit up.

"I thought you didn't smoke," he stated.

"I do now," I retorted as I stared blindly at the carpet. "I've been thinking, what if Deos' death wasn't an accident."

Dan let out a heavy breath as he shook his head, "It was natural causes. He wouldn't let the doctors do surgery. It was a matter of time. We all knew it."

Dan's demeanour seemed to change as he rose to leave. He

assumed because all of Deos' other friends had found out one way or another over the years, that I automatically would accept their reality. What he failed to see was I rarely found my way to planet reality, especially when it came to Deos.

Ace and I were left alone together in Deos' study. She rose and looked down at me with sympathetic eyes. I was inexplicably drawn and repelled to her at the same time. Part of me wanted to ravish her like a beast and the other wanted to shoot myself for thinking it. The tension between us was unbearable.

"I should be leaving, too," she resolved. "Get some sleep."

The door flew open revealing Andrew's drunken form. He still clutched a partial bottle of wine in his hand as he glared at the two of us together, and then wove drunkenly into the room to confront Ace.

"His body's not even cold yet!" he accused.

I rose in anger and stood face to face with Andrew. Ace pushed between us and snapped a stern order of, "Sit down, Ian! I can handle this!"

Reluctantly, I backed away, but still stood ready to fight. There was a presence and command she held that would have made Crazy Horse quake in his moccasins. She gave an order like an Army Sergeant and demanded the same fearful respect. To get in her way would have been suicide.

"First you take my girl from me," Andrew slurred violently. "Now you're after my brother's!"

Ace looked at me in horror. She hated Andrew as much as me, but she also knew the truth when she heard it.

"Tell me this isn't true?" she sheepishly asked.

"About Katherine?" I questioned. "Yes, Andrew convinced her to date me in order to keep tabs on Deos."

Ace looked at Andrew like she was eyeing a bug she was about to crush under foot. Her fists were clenched at her side as she spat, "Ian and I are friends! A word I doubt ever entered your limited vocabulary because no one can stand you! Least of all, me! I'm leaving!"

With that, she whipped her coat from the back of the chair and stormed from the room. Andrew's hot stare followed her out the front door.

As the slam of the Rococo door echoed through the empty

estate, Andrew threw one last indignity at me, "Do you always let women fight your battles for you, MacIntyre?" Then, he turned green and ran from the room.

I held back the urge to follow Andrew to the bathroom, force his arrogant, drunken head down the toilet, and flush! I lacked the ambition afterwards to even climb the stairs to my room. Instead, I lay down on the same bloodstained spot I had occupied before and gazed at the painting above the fireplace. The morning sun filtered through the heavy curtains and bathed the hauntingly beautiful lady in a hazy light. Deos' mother had been a stubborn Scot, grey-eyed with coal waves that seemed to shimmer like the North Atlantic. She had died of pneumonia when Deos was two weeks old. Less than a year later, Sir Charles married an English military widow with a son not much younger than his own.

With a deep sigh, I lowered my head and drifted to sleep. Not that I slept well. Haunting images cursed my dreams. Images of Deos, Andrew, Price…Anyone and everyone were subject to my paranoid revelations. I saw myself standing before Andrew as he hung by the neck in a jail cell. The grey sweater that was tied around his neck matched the equally grey, lifeless lips as I watched in venomous delight. His body slowly turned and swayed, yet his hallowed eyes followed, taunted, and challenged me. Suddenly, he tore the sleeve from around his neck and reached out to me…

I awoke scarcely able to breathe. The searing pain had returned as I gasped for breath. I desperately tried to stand only to plummet to the floor. With my last reserve of strength, I dragged myself back onto the couch. The fevered pounding of a heart that seemed to steal my breath quickly waned. I hesitantly reached for the half-empty glass of scotch at my feet then fumbled awkwardly to light a cigarette. Impuissant, I sat with my hands in my hair and felt as though I had lost not only my life, but my sanity as well.

My hatred manifested itself in the form of a man. Everywhere I saw Andrew, I saw hate; fiery, white-hot, blinding hate. I saw the cause of all that had happened to me and Deos and I wanted not justice, only cold revenge. I wanted him to suffer as Deos did in his last, turbulent moments. A moment I was convinced that I shared that night, as if Deos had reached out to me at the end – a final act of friendship, true brotherly love. I found revenge to be wicked, manipulative beast, a true devourer of the soul.

With unsteady hands, I reached for a cigarette as I pulled the box of matches from my coat pocket. I flipped the cigarette to my lips and then struck the match. I gazed captivated at the flickering flame as it burst at the end of the cigarette. I held the match at arm's length and watched it slowly burn down.

Then, as it was about to touch my fingers, I closed my fist hard around it to extinguish it with a hiss. I opened my hand and dropped the charcoaled match to the floor. Then, I turned my hand over to examine the blackened palm as I took in a strong drag of smoke. I pulled the cigarette from my cold lips and ground it into the greying flesh without so much as a tinge of pain. I let out a hearty, almost maniacal laugh as I realized, "Damn! I'm bloody dead!"

Dan knocked upon the door at six in the evening. I opened the bronze barrier to reveal his weary face in the twilight. A burst of snow laden autumn air blew disembodied leaves across the marble floor as he entered. He looked numb as he drudged a death march to Deos' study. He dropped like an anchor into Deos' chair before the fire.

"You been ok?" I asked cordially.

"I came to ask you the same question," Dan replied. "The lads and I were getting worried. You haven't been around since Deos died."

"Just haven't felt much like getting out."

Dan tried to be reasonable and understanding with me, but his patience was becoming harder to keep than ice on a ninety-plus July day on the Mississippi. I spent so much time obsessed with revenge that I lost sight of everything else. The shattered group had looked to me for guidance and strength with Deos gone. I was perceived to be the Sergeant at Arms, next in command after Deos. They saw me as the key to a puzzle with a missing piece. Unfortunately, I was a factory error. I was Pinocchio's nose on a puzzle of the Titanic. All I could supply them was hate, chaos and destruction. They didn't need me, no one did.

"What has happened to you?" Dan demanded. "I respected you once. Now I don't think I even know you! Fight your little war if you must, but I'll have no part of it!"

With that, Dan rose and stormed from the Hall. I said, nor

did anything to stop him from leaving. I simply rose and made my way to the liquor cabinet to bury myself in a bottle of red label. I slowly rubbed my aching shoulder to reveal a fine haze of blood across my hand before I passed out.

Upon awakening, I did the only thing I knew to do; I walked and drank. I thought that if I walked far or fast enough, I could outrun it all and the alcohol eliminated the pain and made me invincible to the subtle warnings that had begun to present themselves in the form of panic, light-headedness, general weakness, and the sickly hue my skin had taken. Had I rested, I would have been fine. Instead I pushed myself to the breaking point and beyond. I refused to give into the wound. Stress, infection, and blood loss had begun to take their toll and all I had done was given them a little push.

# Chapter Fifteen
## The Price of Friendship

"From wrong to wrong the exasperated spirit
Proceeds, unless restored by that refining fire
Where you must move in measure, like a
dancer..."
{T.S. Eliot, 1944}

I wandered down the crowded sidewalks of Broad Street in a half-drunken stupor. I spent my days in a haze of alcohol, pain medication, and cigarettes, my nights with demons and insomnia. I wandered from pub to pub as each tossed me out to the next. It was as I turned a corner and discarded the remnants of an over smoked Turkish cigarette that, through the corner of my eye, I caught the flash of a blue uniform. Nervously, I spun around and headed in the direction from whence I came. Not wishing a confrontation, I hurried my pace only to be stopped by a second street officer.

"Morrow, constable," I exclaimed cheerfully. "What might I do for you this fine day?"

"Come with us, sir," he instructed as the first constable approached from behind.

I was lead to the Chief Inspector's office in New Scotland Yard. From across the room, I observed John MacKensie nervously thumb a stack of papers as he strained his brow with his other. It was the first I had seen of MacKensie in months. After Price died in disgrace, MacKensie seemed to be the logical choice for Chief Inspector. His new duties placed him not only in different work hours, but social circles as well. Suddenly, men such as Deos and I became a liability.

"What is the meaning of this, John!" I bellowed.

"Shut the door, Ian," he sighed irritably.

I kicked the door shut with my heel and continued to rant, "What the hell is so damned important that I had to be dragged by two uniforms?"

"I don't quite know how to say this…" MacKensie paused then looked up at me with forlorn eyes. "I'll just tell you the way it was told to me. It has been the request of certain parties that you not attend the funeral."

My mouth flew open as my blood boiled. How dare he tell me I can't attend the funeral. "The hell I won't!" I raved. "Are the powers that be so afraid of a little political embarrassment? Who doesn't want me there? Andrew, some damned Minister of something or another, God? Who, John? You can tell your aristocratic, high born, snub-nosed, two-faced, megalomaniac friends that the entire metropolitan police force couldn't keep me away!"

"If you go, I'll be forced to put you in irons," he threatened sternly.

I held my hands out in defiance and cast a colder stare than Deos or Clootie himself could ever muster. I wasn't about to be told by Benedict Arnold that I couldn't go to my best friend's funeral.

"That's the only way you'll stop me!" I hissed. With that, I spun on my heel and barged out the door. "You're no better than you're predecessor!" I accused as two constables blocked my path.

"William Price was a drug dealer and a murderer!" MacKensie fumed. "How dare you compare me with scum like that! I should throw you in the darkest, most rat infested hole I can find!"

I turned my head, which pulled at the cut on my neck and shoulder and cast a dark smile at MacKensie.

"Can I go now, mother," I mocked.

"Fine," John relented. "Let him go, lads."

The stern, blue gates parted, allowing me to pass. I knew MacKensie would cave. He may have turned his back on us, but he knew as well as anyone that I had more right to be there than the blue bloods that would inevitably flock out of a societal, old money obligation. I found myself sickened and slightly light headed as I stormed down the steps in a rage. As I approached the bottom, I rubbed my aching shoulder. I leaned with my back to the wall and banged my head repeatedly against the rough brick in disgust. I pulled the hand from my shoulder to reveal a thick, red brume across the palm.

"Son of a bitch!" I cried as I pulled a handkerchief from one of my many coat pockets. I rolled it along my leg and placed it under the collar of my shirt. As I began to apply pressure, I slid down the wall to the pavement in agony. Pain spread through the shoulder to the shoulder blade to continue down my left arm to my fingertips. Gingerly, I pulled my left thumb through my belt loop. After aggressively tossing the soiled handkerchief, I rolled onto my right arm and forced myself unsteadily to my feet. I fumbled through the plethora of pockets until I found a bottle of vitamin K and the painkillers. I tossed in five codeine tablets and three vitamin Ks, then washed them down with the remainder of my flask of scotch.

Afterwards, I did as I had for the past several days; I wandered from pub to pub in a drunken haze. I ran into Dan as he emerged from one of the most prestigious tailors along the Circus. Swung over his shoulder was a brand new, custom suit. It was far more conservative then I was used to seeing him in. Navy blue never entered his wardrobe. At first he tried to deny he had seen me in the many other faces along the walk, but I wasn't about to let him off that easy.

"Too good to speak to an old friend, O'Selle?" I taunted.

"Ian?" Dan exclaimed, shocked. "You look like Hell! Where have you been?"

"Everywhere, nowhere. I just came from the Yard, actually. Seems someone doesn't want me at the funeral."

I showed up at the funeral in full glory, after sleeping off some of my indulgence. I had a few razor nicks on my face and my tie was a bit crooked, but what can I say. It's not that easy to tie a tie with only one good arm. I cast a last smouldering cigarette to the wind as I climbed the stairs of the church, the tails of Deos' black trench ominously floating behind. Craned necks followed my every step as I approached the scarlet casket. Red! Only

Andrew would bury the Dark Knight in a red casket.

Long withheld feelings of anger and betrayal swelled within me as I gazed at his lifeless, unnatural form. Many said he looked natural, but nothing could have been farther from the truth. He looked like he belonged in Madame Trousseau's. He looked dead. I turned solemnly and glided to the back of the church and waited. I intended to have my say, regardless to what anyone else thought.

After Andrew's incessant whining and contrived tears of grief, I was reluctantly allowed to speak. Andrew's gaze followed me as I approached the pulpit. I stood before the duty bound audience with abhorrence. Throughout the church sat the same snobbish group I had encountered at Sir Charles' party and later at his funeral – a group whose only reason for being there was a feeling of class obligation. Their attendance was nothing more than an attempt to keep the last of the Kingstons (and their influence) on their side.

Then there were Deos' friends. A group made of clubbers, some music icons, artists, musicians, and even a few of the police force were forced to huddle in the shadows. I gazed over the motley array that were Deos' people and was sickened even deeper by the circus. Anger welled within me at the thought that those people, the ones who really knew Deos were the ones who were forced to huddle in the shadows and treated as though they weren't welcome.

"As many of you are aware," I announced as my anger threatened to rage like the Mississippi at spring thaw. "My name is Ian MacIntyre. A name many of you have no doubt heard and hold with a bit of contempt. I was taken to New Scotland Yard this morning because some of you would rather I not be here. But no one knew Deos the way I did. I had prepared a speech, but on the way here decided the words of Robert Burns would better tell of this heroic, benevolent man."

From the back of the church, Dan held a look of quandary. The more dignified of the group simply looked at me with a combination of dazed confusion and distain. For many, the parallel was a bit out of their range. Actually some of the group I thought would be lucky if they could count past five without the aid of their assistants. MacKensie wouldn't even look me in the eye as I proceeded with my tirade. I used the words of Burns' "The Epitaph (From On Captain Matthew Henderson)" to eulogize Deos, making sure to change a word or so when needed to fit.

# The Epitaph
### *(From On Captain Matthew Henderson)*

*Stop, passenger! My story's brief,*
*And truth I shall relate, man;*
*I tell nae common tale o' grief-*
*For (Deos) Matthew was a great man.*

*If though uncommon merit hast,*
*Yet spurned at Fortune's door, man,*
*A look of pity hither cast-*
*For (Deos) Matthew was a poor man.*

*If thou a noble sodger art,*
*That passest by this grave, man,*
*There moulders here a gallant heart-*
*For (Deos) Matthew was a brave man.*

*If thou on men, their works and ways*
*Canst throw uncommon light, man,*
*Here lies wha weel had won thy praise-*
*For (Deos) Matthew was a bright man.*

*If thou at friendship's sacred ca'*
*Wad life itself resign, man,*
*They sympathetic tear maun fa'-*
*For (Deos) Matthew was a kind man.*

*If thou art staunch without a stain,*
*Like the unchanging blue, man,*
*This was a kinsman o' thy ain-*
*For (Deos) Matthew was a true man...*

*If ony whiggin' sot*
*To blame poor (Deos) Matthew dare, man,*
*May dool and sorrow be his lot!*
*For (Deos) was a rare man.*

"I am proud to have been privileged enough to call Deos my friend," I continued. "I came to London a lonely outsider, but left a paladin. He accepted me when no one else wanted to be around me. I was a worthless, clumsy Yank. Deos saw the potential in me to be more. The potential to be something far greater – something like him. For that, I will be eternally indebted. My only regret is that we lost so many years while I was in Australia."

I finished my eulogy by playing *Dead Man's Party* and *Dust in the Wind*. By the time I was done, there wasn't a dry eye among Deos' friends, mine included. I could barely focus my eyes through the tears that set my face afire as I walked away. Filled with disgust, rage, and a heaviness in my heart I felt would remain for the rest of my days, I left the guitar Deos had given me propped next to his casket and swore then and there to never play again.

# Chapter Sixteen
## To Err is Human…

"The greater part of humanity is far too weary
And worn down by the struggle
With want to rouse itself for a new
And harder struggle with error."
{Johann Christoph Friedrich Schiller, 1795}

I stormed from the church. Dan followed me to the door and tried to lay a reassuring hand on my shoulder, but I abruptly brushed it away. I didn't even bother to wipe the tears from my eyes as I continued my walk. I refused to acknowledge him; I couldn't. I wanted to be alone, so I could drown myself at the bottom of a bottle. In a combination of frustration and disgust, he walked away.

I paused on the stone steps of the church and gazed across the busy thoroughfare to the pub across the way. After drunkenly dodging traffic, I entered the dimly lit pub to have everyone's eyes upon me. Arrogantly, I stole across the wooden floor. The sound of my boots followed my every step and voices fell silent at my approach. I stepped to the bar and glared around the room at the ogled crowd. I must have been quite the sight. Evil, grief, and hatred oozed from my body like the infection from my shoulder.

"I thought you were going to the funeral, guv," the bartender stated in a strong cockney accent.

"Where do you think I just came from?" I snapped, the tears mostly dried from my burning cheeks.

"Say no more," he replied as he set a large scotch before me.

I glanced over my shoulder as Mouse stepped into the bar, "I'll get his, too."

We took our drinks to an empty booth in a corner of the bar. Mouse nursed a pint as I overindulged further on bootleg Irish lightning and Scotch. Our conversation was simple – nothing much to speak of. We both tended to avoid the subject of Deos' funeral. I don't think either one of us were ready to deal with Deos' death. Mentally, emotionally, and physically, it was killing me. It was, after all the first time we had spoke since the day I left Public School. There was a little catching up on the old times. Mouse had stayed in London after school and worked freelance after college.

All through our conversation, one thought dominated my mind, Kat. The more I drank, the more I thought of her and the more I wanted to be with her. Deos' death had left a void I longed to fill. I saw Kat as the bridge that would span the chasm left by my best friend. I found I was just drunk and lonely enough to forget what she and Andrew had done.

"Why wasn't that girl with you today?" Mouse eventually asked of Katherine.

"Kat?" I stated, surprised that he had mentioned her. "We broke up."

We had differing ideas. She thought she should sleep with Andrew and tell him everything Deos and I did and I thought she shouldn't. It was as simple as that. Still, I felt badly about the way I'd acted at her apartment. It is said that absence makes the heart grow fonder. In reality, it only makes it more remorseful, and when doctored with alcohol's amber-coloured glasses, more longing. In that moment of weakness and alcohol, I saw Kat as a band-aid for my hemorrhaging life. My world had been disintegrated by the Atom Bomb of Deos' death and I was left my shadow permanently burnt into the pavement – evidence enough that I once existed, but lacking in substance. The longer I wallowed in pity, the more determined I became. I wholly intended to march up to her apartment and fully apologize. In short, I intended once again to ask her to marry me.

After one last douse of instant courage, I wobbled from the

table and made my way unsteadily for the door. As I began to cross the street, I was met by a voice calling, "Ian, stop!" I turned to find Ace running across the crowded street.

Her dark, lace jacket flowed behind the equally dark, nearly skin-tight dress. Her makeup formed dark streaks from the tears of mourning and despair we all shared. The sight of her was dynamic and uncharacteristic. Strength formed an aura around her and seemed to protect her like a shaman's charm. There was a look of determination in her eyes, she intended to save me from myself. There were times I suspected she was psychic. She knew me better than I knew myself. She was the sanity and common sense that I was desperately in need of.

"Where do you think you're going?" she demanded as she grabbed my arm.

"To do what I should have done the first time," I replied.

"She breaks your heart, uses you, and you want to propose! You don't think I miss him, too? She won't fill the void and she sure as hell won't replace him!" Her words stuck me in the back like a dagger. I knew she was right, but wasn't ready to accept it. Without another word, I entered the apartment building and raced up the stairs. Ace hurried behind calling, "Let it go, you're better off without her. She'll only hurt you again!"

As I approached Kat's apartment, I was overwhelmed by the cold, harsh air of foreboding. Before I could reach for the door, Ace's arm crossed my path. Even though her face was tensed with apprehension, she managed a faint smile. A tension wafted between us and thickened with each passing moment until it began to steal my breath.

"If this is what you want, fine," she stated. "I just don't want to see you get hurt again. You've been through so much already. Just think it over – sober, first. Ok."

Reluctantly, I turned and intended to leave, then changed my mind. My shaking hand reached out for the door. Upon the first knock, the door inched open with a loud creak. As Ace threw open the door, she forced my head to the wall with a stern push. Her eyes were wide in horror as she pulled the door swiftly shut. My nostrils were burnt by the pungent odour emitted in the slight breeze of the slamming door. At first, I knew not what it was, but came to quickly recognize it as the smell of week old hamburger.

It was the smell of old blood.

"What the hell!" I demanded, confused, as I reached for the door.

"Don't!" she cried as I turned the knob and opened the door.

I threw open the door to reveal the bloody, horrid scene within. Kat lay in the middle of the room surrounded by a lake of crimson and brown. Her golden hair was dark and matted with clots of drying blood. Her once lively skin was near translucent with patches of black. A suicide note was gripped in a cold hand, a knife driven deep into her prefect bosom. The roses I had tossed down the stairs were scattered around her like a fairy's ring. In a combination of rage and despair, I collapsed into Ace's waiting arms.

As she cradled my sobbing form, she whispered, "Jesus, Ian. I'm so sorry. This is horrible."

What seemed an eternity later, the building swarmed with a plague of police. As I sat sulking in a corner, Ace approached MacKensie. His suspicious gaze seemed to steal the very breath from my tightening chest. My mind and body were numb. The image of Kat's body haunted me like Deos' deathbed. It was an image that refused to be washed from my memory. With each condemnatory glance from MacKensie, I inhaled the harsh, sweet smoke from a Turk. All I could bring myself to look at was the matted, brown rug at my feet and hope the filthy, matted mess clouded the demons in my mind.

"Get off it, John!" Ace demanded as she gave the Inspector a stern shove.

MacKensie scanned her enraged form as two constables approached from behind. I admired her raw strength and courage. For someone to have lost so much and still retain the will to fight fired my envy and respect. I slowly grew to understand true heroism.

"Where were you?" MacKensie ordered of her.

"The same bloody place as you, you git!" she sharply retorted. "The funeral. That just happens to be where Ian was, too."

"Yes, but he did leave in a mad rush."

Ace turned in a circle and held her hands at her side. With

each moronic comment the Chief Inspector made, the harder it became for her to retain her composure. There was something to be said for redheads and their tempers. Ace was the positive litmus test. She glared at him with dark, wrathful eyes. I knew she had long past the point of tolerance and if the dear inspector didn't tread lightly he'd have more than me to worry about.

"Jesus, John," she cried. "That girl's been dead for days. If you were doing your job instead of badgering us, you'd have seen the note she left. Christ almighty! I could smell it the moment we opened the door. Get it through that thick skull of yours that we had nothing to do with it! We were just the sorry sots that found her."

"But your friend and the decedent were lovers," MacKensie informed.

"*Were* is the proverbial word there. He broke it off before Deos died. If you're suspecting lovers, ask Andrew. They were together long before Ian was with her. I'm sure he knows plenty! There doesn't seem to be much Andrew doesn't know these days!"

MacKensie continued to glare at me as he turned to enter the apartment. Not that there was much to see through the cameramen and police. I knew I should have been sickened by the display, yet strangely enough wasn't. I was numb. All I could do was wrap my arms around my knees and rock back and forth on that dirty, tattered rug.

Ace walked over to me and held out a strong hand to me. I took it and followed her from the building, leaving MacKensie speechless. As we entered onto the street, I became immediately aware that the media were already reapers across the street. Our names were shouted along with demands for information that went unanswered. With cold precision, I lowered my sunglasses and stared each and every one down in turn as we slid into Ace's car and sped off in a cloud of dust and rubber.

She took me to her place, a quiet, quaint flat off Hyde Park. I was nervous about being alone with her. She had always been a trusted friend, not to mention Deos' girl. The last thing I wanted to do was jeopardize that. The tension between us was a physical being, a smothering blanket of smoke that separated and choked us in its oppression.

"Do you want a drink?" she asked.

"Bring me two," I stated, my eyes fixed to the shining wooden floor below.

At first she looked at me with confusion, but brought three glasses of Scotch. The first I tipped back. Then, I took the second and poured it over the wound on my shoulder. The fire spread deep into my chest. Almost instinctively, she handed me her glass of Scotch. I tipped it back with force and slowly, the pain ceased. I leaned on my elbows and spoke to the floor.

"Aren't you afraid of what everyone will think?" I asked, unsure.

"Who cares what they think," she replied. "I trust you. Besides, you're a good friend who just happens to need a friend right now…Are you all right?" she drilled at my pain. "You look awfully pale. Maybe I should take you to the hospital. That shoulder should have healed by now."

I shook my head no to her. I had no intention of going to the hospital. The pain and weakness would pass, it always did.

The next morning, I paid a visit to the Hall. Andrew cautiously opened the door, and reluctantly let me pass. His face was drawn and haggard and his eyes held the tell-all dark lines of lack of sleep. The weariness in his step told me that he had been awake all night.

"We have nothing to discuss," he snapped. "If you came for your things I had them sent to her flat."

"I assume you heard about Kat," I countered.

His pale face flushed with anger as he gazed at me in sheer hate and horror. His tensed jaw quavered as he demanded, "What did you do to her?" as he forced me to the wall.

"I think I should be asking you the same question," I accused as I shoved him back.

Andrew forced his hands back into his pockets. Without so much as a syllable uttered, he began to retreat to his study. Before he could enter the door, I pulled him around and held him against the wall by the throat. His green eyes stared wide at me as I slowly raised his feet from the floor.

"It wasn't me…I know what you are," I hissed. "You may be able to fool everyone else with your grieving brother routine, but you haven't fooled me. I know all about your little plans and schemes…" I pulled the handkerchief from my pocket and unrolled the syringe from it. I spun it over my hand and thrust it into the wall next to Andrew's head. As I released him, I promised, "I'll see you hang if I have to do it myself!"

The sound of the bronze doors shocked me from my maddened rage. I looked over my shoulder towards the small, intelligent man that swung a black briefcase to and fro as he approached.

"Ah, good you're here," he chimed as he offered his hand. "My name is William Domino. I'm the solicitor in charge of the Kingston estate."

"Ian MacIntyre," I reluctantly introduced as I prepared to leave.

"Well, Dr. Kingston and I have much to discuss, if you don't mind."

Three days later, I received a message that my presence was requested at the reading of Deos' will. Truthfully, I was shocked that Andrew bothered to invite me at all. Then again, he only wanted me there so he could gloat, of that I was certain. He wished nothing less than my utter destruction. He knew having me there to see all of Deos' possessions passed to him would shatter me. I would have rather watched the Hall and everything in it of Deos' swallowed by the depths of hell than see Andrew get it.

All eyes were upon me as I walked into Deos' parlous study. Mr. Domino loomed behind Deos' antique oak desk and stared at me through horn-rimmed glasses. The hollow echo of boot heels reverberated through the room as I stole across the wooden floor. Andrew sat beside MacKensie and watched my every move with a mixture of vaunt and malice.

With more than a degree of arrogance, I sat upon the corner of the desk and reached for the etched box next to me. I slowly opened the lid and lifted a cigarette from within. As I lit the tip, I rose and the box fell to the floor. A thud reverberated through the room as it splintered and sent cigarettes and wood sailing across the floor. In the centre of the disarray laid a piece of tobacco dusted paper. Mr. Domino bent over and lifted the paper from the floor. His eyes widened as he scanned the hand written document. As if in disbelief, he compared it with the will then, with a sigh, placed both documents gently onto the desk.

"There appears to be a new will, dated three weeks before

Young Lord Kingston's death," he concluded as he rubbed his glasses between an embroidered handkerchief.

"What?" Andrew cried in disbelief.

He returned the glasses to the tip of his nose and continued, "It seems that in the event of the death of his Lordship, Harrison Ian Amadeus Kingston, that sum total of his estate is to be awarded to John Holliday Phoenix."

No one knew who this John Holliday Phoenix was and it didn't matter to me. All I knew was it was worth my while just to come. A sense of retribution filled my darkened soul.

In a fit of anger and defeat, Andrew rose from his chair and stormed from the room. Before he walked through the doorway, he bumped my shoulder and pushed me aside as I blocked his way. Involuntarily, I clenched my fist then smiled in satisfaction as he stormed across the marble floor and slammed the bronze doors behind him. I expected Andrew to gloat and bask in glory before me, but instead I watched him squirm, whine, and writhe in defeat. I wanted to find this John Phoenix and shake his hand!

The day called for a celebration and celebrate I did. By the early evening, I was two shots away from complete oblivion. That was when I passed the Jaguar. Andrew was parked against the wrong side of a curb, staring at Kat's building. He sat behind the wheel lighting a cigarette as I attempted to pass.

He looked through the open driver's window in determination as he placed an arm across my path. His eyes were reddened and full with an almost glassy hue. His sniffle and fine white residue across his nose told me all I needed to know of his recent activities. He had spent the afternoon in a blizzard of snow that doubtlessly left Deos spinning in his grave. Andrew was coked out of his mind.

"Get in," he growled almost incoherently.

Reluctantly, I walked around the car and slid into the passenger seat. Andrew's cold gaze fell upon me as I pulled the door shut. I had already begun to feel the effects of a bottle of bourbon, so by that point I could really have cared less what Andrew had planned. I resigned myself to fate at that point as I melted into the leather and let Bacchus lull me to sleep. We were only a few minutes down the road when I succumbed to the bourbon, codeine, lack of sleep, and blood loss.

I awoke in the same position I had passed out in, propped against the inside of the passenger seat door. I pulled the handle and fell immediately onto the sodden ground. I pulled myself up the side of the car and began to survey the scene. To my horror, I was surrounded by tombstones and the smell of freshly turned earth. Below me loomed the nefarious sight of a fresh grave.

I unsteadily made my way around the car to the driver's side, determined to leave any way I could. As I looked through the open window, my sight was caught by a reflecting light. I reached unsteadily through the window and pulled on the butt of a pearl handled revolver. With a shaking hand, I flipped the weapon to check the chambers. Three of the six were loaded. I was beginning to see a pattern to my life. If I'd been listening, I'd have known not to go off half-cocked.

The slosh of feet through water and sodden leaves caused me to whirl around with the weapon poised. Andrew's cold gaze followed the sleek barrel of an antique Colt. Together, we stood in infamy. Neither of us dared to speak, dared to breathe as we found ourselves in a twisted British form of a Mexican standoff.

"I know why you brought me here!" I called. "So just get on with your butchery!"

"You have no idea!" Andrew hissed.

"Of what its like to be a cold blooded killer? No, not that I'm not willing to learn."

I held the revolver fast and slowly began to squeeze the trigger. The tighter I grasped, the harder my hand shook. To my disgust, I discovered that regardless of how much I may have wanted him dead, I couldn't. I still regained some semblance of dignity and decency. Each time I stared upon the barren grave of Deos I became aware of how foolish I had been. I knew that to have pulled that trigger would have made me no better than Price, no better than Andrew. At that point, I simply opened my hand and let the weapon fall to the ground at my side and welcomed the release that Andrew's bullet would bring.

"Do what you will to me," I resolved. "I don't care anymore."

Andrew raised his weapon and took aim at my face. My gaze fell upon the remnants of my friend and I gently closed my eyes. A cockeyed smile passed my lips as I realized that the nightmare I had lived since the night Deos was taken to the hospital would soon be at an end. The sharp scream of discharge filled my ears and startled me to my senses with my heart in my throat. I looked at Andrew's contented grin as he pulled the weapon to his temple.

A monster clawed at my insides as I cried, "Andrew, wait! I'll make you a deal. You leave, you never return and no one has to know it was you."

"It wasn't me!" Andrew lamented. "Why do you keep torturing me like this? I had nothing to do with it!"

It was at that moment that he did the worst thing he could to me…

*******

I paused as I looked down the bar at the captivated group. I tried to forget the events of that day for a very long time. I had to just keep on living. Even at that moment, I could barely summon the will to continue my tale. My heart was in my throat and threatened to choke the words that I had to force into existence. I had never spoken of it before, but even though I may have wanted to stop and walk away, I knew I had to finish. I had kept it bottled for too long. The truth needed to be known.

*******

Andrew disengaged the safety once more, closed his eyes and pulled the trigger. Slowly, he fell to the ground in a pool of bone, brains, and blood. In a wave of guilt and disgust, I collapsed to the ground. Crippling pain engulfed me. The same pain I possessed the night of Deos' death. I reached for the revolver with renewed determination, the same determination that drove me to attempt to turn it on myself. I held the revolver to my temple and wanted to pull the trigger. I tried to pull the trigger. Intense pain involuntarily forced my hand to my chest as my heart raced sporadically in my chest, the last image before my eyes was that of a tombstone that read simply, *This is the grave of Mike O'Day who died maintaining his right of way. His right was clear his will was strong. But he's as dead as if he'd been wrong.*

I've always hated irony. . .

# Chapter Seventeen
## Death Isn't the Worst Thing

"Drunkenness is a temporary suicide:
The happiness that it brings is merely negative,
A momentary cessation of unhappiness."
{Bertrand Russell, 1930}

I awoke to the delayed ping of a heart monitor. I cautiously opened my eyes to reveal a haze of white. As my eyes adjusted to the surroundings, I became aware of where I was. I lay debilitated in the hospital surrounded by machines, IV's, and blank walls. I tried to rise only to hear the monitor go wild as I collapsed back onto the bed. My strength was completely gone. I had worn down my reserves to the point of no return. I was vulnerable, alone, and paranoid. All I wanted was to escape. As I attempted to rise a second time, an inrush of hospital personnel and a sea of hands reached out to restrain me met me.

"Lay down, Mr. MacIntyre," a nurse called. "You're a very sick man."

"Like hell I am!" I called as I ripped the pads by the wires from my chest and tore the IV tube from my arm. A squirt of blood caught one of the nurses between her breasts and I thought, "Good shot!"

All I wanted to do was leave and finish what I had started at the cemetery. I found myself despising the life that had been returned to me. I wished they had let me lie and rolled me into a hole next to Deos.

I forced my way to the side of the bed and sat with my hands in my hair. The muffled whispers of the crowd echoed in my pounding head. It felt as though my head was filled with air to the point of bursting. Pressure hammered at my forehead as I stared through floating stars at the floor. My palpitating shoulder echoed my pummelled heart and caused my left arm to go numb. The look in my eyes as I raised my spurnful head caused the group to whisper even more. Several left in disbelief and others in fear.

As I prepared to dress and leave, Dan entered the room. He feigned a smile as he approached the side of the bed. It was the first time I had seen him since the reading of the will, which for me seemed like only a few hours but in reality, was four days longer. The first two days at the hospital I had spent on life support.

"It's good to see you among the living again," Dan stated with a smug grin.

"What does that mean?" I snapped, purely unintentional.

What it meant was for the second time in my life I had managed to cheat death. The hospital personnel were shocked to see a man who had been brought to them days before no more than a corpse, awaken and want to leave. I had suffered a heart attack brought on by acute endocarditis; bacteria from the infected shoulder had attached itself to the valves and lining of my heart, as well as septic shock from infection. This combined with the stress, lack of sleep, blood loss, and a blood alcohol level that in itself should have bought me a six-foot permanent residence beside Deos.

Early on my fifth day of consciousness, two constables and John MacKensie entered my hospital room. In his hands, John carried a bundle of papers in one and a pair of irons in the other. With a tensed jaw and calculated coldness, John cuffed me, pulled me to my feet and forced me from the room.

"What is the meaning of this," I demanded.

"You are under arrest for the murders of Andrew Johann Kingston and Katherine Ann James," he replied steely.

So thus, I was dragged in the middle of a solemn procession to the interrogation room at New Scotland Yard. For hours I was continually questioned and subjected to lies and accusations of the vilest sort.

"I know you were seeing Miss James in the months prior to her death," MacKensie denounced. "I also know that she had been a long standing acquaintance of Andrew."

"I hate to tell you this, but..." I stated sheepishly before taking in a full breath to finish. "That doesn't prove a thing."

"You were the first on the scene at Miss James' death and Andrew's…"

I was becoming increasingly irritated by John's accusations.

"Half dead, I might add," I corrected. "Look I didn't kill Andrew or Kat. I went to her apartment to apologize for storming off days earlier. Ask Ace she was there! I couldn't have been there fifteen minutes before you lot arrived! And as for Andrew, he blew his own damned head off, for Christ's sake! If I would have killed anyone back there, it would have been me! I collapsed before I could get the shot off!"

I knew that in reality I had everything to do with both their deaths. I may not have thrust the knife or pulled the trigger, but I might as well have. I had driven them both to their damnable acts. My selfishness and drive for vengeance had clouded my judgment and had left me unrecognizable even to myself. MacKensie silently rose from his chair and left the room. I couldn't even look at myself in the two-way mirror. All I could do was to bury my hands in my hair and stare at my feet. As the anger and self-loathing welled within me, I rose, lifted the corner of the metal table and tossed it across the room, barely missing the mirror…

A few moments later, footsteps resounded through the corridors of New Scotland Yard. At the end lay the office of Chief Inspector MacKensie. Before the frosted glass, his young brunette secretary sat like a sentry behind a cold, steel desk. She stood and attempted to block the doorway to the office, as a figure approached.

"You can't go in there!" she ordered as Dan brushed her aside like a discarded toy.

"Watch me!" O'Selle seethed as he burst through the door.

Behind an over cluttered oak desk John MacKensie was perched with his legs propped on the edge and observed the ornate gold pocket watch in his hand. He gazed at Dan with a mixture of triumph and satisfaction as he swung his legs from the desktop and turned his chair to rise.

"You arrived sooner than I thought," he commented as he sauntered to the front of the desk. "News certainly travels quick."

With unwarranted ease, he sat down upon the desk and

gave an impassive grin as the intruder began to rave, "I demand to know why you're holding Ian! You received the coroner's report days ago! I should know, I handed it to you myself! Damn it, they were both suicides! You have no right to detain him!"

"I can do as I please!" MacKensie retorted. "I'll not be ordered around by a coroner's assistant!"

Dan's eyes glowed with restrained fury as he filled with distrust and abhorrence. Silence passed between the two men as they stood and bore down at one another. Finally, Dan uttered the ultimatum, "One hour, John! If Ian isn't released by then, I'll return…with my resignation and a call to the *Times*!"

With that, Dan turned on his heel and marched back through the glass door. He slammed it firmly shut behind him as he left. The sound of broken glass danced on the tile floor and echoed through the empty corridor as Dan trod tall and proud into the daylight.

Half an hour later, I was released, however reluctantly it may have been. MacKensie knew he couldn't prove that I murdered Kat and Andrew. Dan had called his bluff. As I emerged into the uncommon, blinding light of a cloudless London day, Dan stood at the foot of the stone steps with an outstretched arm.

"You all right?" he demanded as he heartily grasped my forearm.

"No worries," I lied.

I knew I should have been thrilled to be free, but it was actually quite the opposite. Instead of being overjoyed, I was indifferent, remorseful, and moderately paranoid. I found myself wondering what demons would lay in wait at the next alleyway or around the next corner. The thought of facing the world again sickened me to the core. I considered walking back into MacKensie's office, fabricating a confession to some wild tale of murder, and happily spending the remainder of my life behind bars just to avoid the pain and memories that awaited me on the bleak streets of London.

I'd have left for home, but I had no money to speak of, only a few pounds hidden in the soles of my boots. Now, with Andrew dead, I really had nowhere to go, other than Dan's or Ace's, and I really didn't want to bother them.

Dan and I met up with Ace as she stood next to a wire rubbish bin at the entrance to the Underground. Her eyes were masked by a pair of dark glasses. I watched my image grow and distort in the reflection as I approached. Gently, she took me by the arm, led me down the crowded stairwell, and into the welcome darkness of *Bottle Street Station*. As we paused to purchase our tickets, I wanted desperately to wrap my arms around her and never let go. Yet something held me back. The ghost of Deos still haunted me. To me, she would always be his.

# Chapter Eighteen
## 'Round the Twist

"Only the insane take themselves quite seriously."
{Sir Max Beerbohm (1872-1956)}

There were moments in the hours that passed since my release that I would sit alone in the dark of night and think. Perhaps that was my problem; I tended to think too much. I began to realize that if I hadn't been so busy fighting my own personal war, that Deos, Kat, and Andrew would all still be alive. I grew to blame myself for everything, even down to the most trifle of details. Perhaps, if I had never been sent to that damnable school so long ago, things would have turned out quite differently. The thought dominated every waking moment that I was cursed and everyone that crossed my maliced path was doomed to destruction.

Later, alone, I leaned on the rail of the now infamous Waterloo Bridge and stared into the cool depths of the Thames. My eyes became entranced by the minute waves and exonerate waters. I lit a Turk, tipped back the last of a bottle of bourbon, and slowly flipped Deos' lighter through my fingers. Through the corner of my eye, I caught the flash of a blue uniform approach through the mist. I cautiously slid the empty bottle into my left breast pocket and turned to face the constable.

"Evening, sir," he addressed.

"Evening, constable," I replied half-heartedly. "What might I do for you this fine night?"

"Just checking to see if everything is all right, sir."

"Fit as rain, right as a fiddle…or is it the other way around?"

I smiled a toothy grin at the constable who stood bewildered for a moment, shrugged, tipped his cap, and continued on his way. He shook his head joshingly as he Charlie Chaplined his way into the night's mist. When he had disappeared into the collecting fog at the end of the bridge, I pulled the bottle from my coat and tossed it into the Thames. I watched the glass shimmer in the artificial light of the bridge as it rolled end over end until it was swallowed with a splash by the lucid depths. I pulled Jean's chariot card from my pocket, stared at the image, distorted by the ribbon that was still tied around it, and wished I had listened to her warning. I raised the card to my forehead and closed my eyes, but all I could see was all I had done wrong.

It was then that I longed to disappear. Like the bottle, I wanted to be swallowed by time and eternity. I longed for my miserable existence to be over. I wanted everyone to forget that I had existed at all. I wanted to face Death and kick him where it counts, just so I would be guaranteed the most severe punishment possible for my transgressions.

So, I took it upon myself to be judge, jury, and executioner as I slid over the railing and allowed myself to fall from the edge. As I began to plummet, I caught a hold of a support beam and dangled high above my watery grave. A sudden flash of agonizing memories bombarded my brain, and spurred me to release my grip, and fall into an aqueous demise.

As I struck the water, I wasn't overwhelmed by terror, but rather hope, peace and the relief that comes from the realization that it was finally going to be over. I felt as though I had been wrapped in my grandmother's favourite hand sewn quilt. It was as I sank into my liquid bed that I spread my arms out wide and smiled. Yes, smiled. I had never been as content as when I thought I was finally, completely dead. Then a voice, strong, forceful, and demanding, like a Marine drill instructor, filled my shattered mind.

"Get up!" it demanded. "Do you hear me! Get up!"

In a panicked frenzy I rolled, swirled, and spun disoriented in the water. I lost all sense of direction as I struggled to reach the surface. I expelled the last of my breath into the dark depths with a silenced cry as the voice continued to pound at my brain. Then silence as the sound in my head slowed and quieted with the alarmed pounding of my heart. My arms and legs failed me as, unconscious, I floated to the surface.

*******

Gus and Al looked at me with a mixture of disbelief and concern. They both knew I had attempted suicide in London, but the details still surprised them. They hadn't really been prepared to hear the whole story in all its sordid details, regardless to what they may have said to the contrary. Slowly, reluctantly, I continued.

*******

I awoke to find myself in an all white room. The sheer sight of such brightness sickened my very nature. The creak of a door caught my attention as I lay in a bed and squinted at the ceiling. The towering door opened to reveal a stubby little bald man with beady black eyes. He sported a suit that was two sizes too small for his ample frame. The buttons over his opulent belly stressed the seams to their very limits. The clipboard in his short, plump fingers swayed as he shuffled across the dull, tiled floor. The closer he came to my bed, the more fake the jowls and pudgy fingers seemed. Though his cheeks were thick with years of tarts and crumpets, the wrists beneath his jacket sleeves were firm with the well-defined veins of a Greek god. I could see every vein rise above the youthful appearing skin as pudgy fingers gripped the clipboard.

When he smiled, it appeared as if his face would crack like a cheap plaster wall. He slowly presented his hand, which I brushed away dismissingly. I rose and approached the window to briefly look over a courtyard of white uniforms and pajamas. Then, I walked back to the bed and collapsed onto the mattress. A dull thud followed by the creaky din of springs filled the air as the mattress hit the floor then slowly rose.

"Mr. MacIntyre," the pudgy little man addressed, "my name is Dr. Pharisey. I will be helping you."

"Really," I hissed. "I seriously doubt that."

I rolled my head to face him as I glared the look upon him. His fingers forced a rattle of the clipboard, but his eyes never showed fear. I slowly reached out towards him ominously. With calculated ease, I slid the clipboard from his trembling hands and with a strong crack, broke in two and handed him the two halves with a smile.

"I don't deal with pudgy little charlatans like you!" I seethed. "If you value your miserable little existence, you'll not bother me again!"

With that repulsive sneer, the not-so-good doctor moved faster than I ever thought a walking beach ball capable. Perhaps I did overdo it a bit, but I didn't care. All I wanted was to be left alone. And so, filled with the satisfaction of a job well done, I slid down in the mattress and drifted into a dreamless sleep.

The beady little man made it look as though he knew what he was doing and tried repeatedly to incorporate me into their side show of crazies by having me participate not only in humiliating group therapy sessions, but also "arts and crafts." I was bounced from one activity to the next over the course of the following months.

First, I was placed in pottery. That is until I broke a pot over a manic-depressive's skull. In my defence, I was tormented by the bloke to the breaking point. Next came abstract painting. This I found moderately enjoyable. But I was quickly removed after trying to make an artistic statement. Actually, I shoved a paintbrush up some schitzo's nose and painted a rather life-like representation of the *Mona Lisa* with his head. He repeatedly stood too close and lingered so close to my left ear that his rancid, hot breath overwhelmed the little space between us.

Afterwards, came basket weaving (an institutional favourite!) in which I attempted to weave a noose to place over my overly energetic counsellor's neck. And I would have succeeded too if it hadn't been for those rotten kids...I watched one too many *Scooby Doo* reruns in there, but I'm feeling much better now.

It was a guard that had been placed at my side to keep me in line that intervened. Eventually, I was placed in finger painting where I was kept alone in an empty room with no easel or frame to hold the paper. I was resigned to sitting on a cold tile floor with the paper stretched between my legs, working with paint that was brought to me on sponges. A guard watched through a bulletproof window in the door as I faked contentment at my task.

Being a disruptive influence had become tiresome to me. Besides, I had begun to run out of ideas. I relied first on anger to see me through the incarceration, then humour. I realized if I was to have any freedom at all, the little charlatan and his minions had to believe that I was "making progress." In short, I was going to have to fake it if I ever wanted to see true daylight again.

A week or so later, I was awakened by the click of the lock on my door. I kept my eyes closed and listened to the rhythmic, precise steps that resounded through the room. They were too light to belong to the portly psychiatrist, yet, were a pattern I vaguely recognized, like the haze of reality in a dream. I lay perfectly still and listened as they paused at my bedside, then turned and left. The stranger issued three sharp raps at the door and waited for it to creak open leaving the echoed slam of steel and the click of the lock that left me once again alone.

The identity of this mysterious visitor would be revealed to me later that day when I heard the lock click once again. I kept my eyes closed, as I lay on the bed, and listened to the same rhythmic steps that had resounded earlier. As before, the stranger approached the bed and paused.

"I know you're awake, mate!" a familiar mix of New York and Sydney that always contrasted my mix of London boarding school and redneck, accused.

I opened my eyes to gaze upon a face I had almost forgotten. He shared my dark eyes, father's chin and mother's petite nose. Were it not for the dark hair with just a wisp of grey and the ever so slightly fuller jaw line free of any scar or blemish, I would have thought I was looking in a mirror. Only one face could so closely match my own.

"What do you think you're doing here?" I demanded of my older brother.

"Is that how you greet your big brother, runt?" Benton retorted.

"I take it you signed the committal papers! You always were in a hurry to get rid of me!"

"We have gotten hostile in our old age, haven't we?"

No one could infuriate me the way Benton could. Even as children we differed on most everything and I was a perpetual vent for Benton's over-inflated opinion of himself and crude cut-downs. At least he hadn't referred to me as "Urine" yet.

"If you've come to gloat, you can leave!" I snapped testily. "Unlike me, that option is open to you."

"Do you want me to go?" he asked, visibly hurt.

"As far as I'm concerned I was an only child! You were always an asshole, Benton!"

As Benton turned to leave, he looked over his shoulder one last time as he proceeded to the door. He paused halfway through and said, "For what it's worth, I wasn't the one that signed the papers. You have the Chief Inspector of Scotland Yard to thank for that."

It was to be the last time I would see my brother. Perhaps, I should have felt remorseful for what I had said, but at the time I didn't. To me, it was more a sense of apathy at that point. He hadn't so much as bothered to call since father found out about his appearance on Australia's most popular XXX game show. He had automatically assumed that I had told. I hadn't. Father had seen it for himself on an American special about foreign programming. A clip featuring Benton in the buff was aired to a worldwide audience. Then almost seven years later, out of the blue the invisible man appears at his mad brother's bedside and it is supposed to make up for years of his torture.

After Benton left, he sulked dejectedly down the all white hallway to Dr. Pharisey's office. Silently, he hesitated before the redwood door. He stared at his feet as he shuffled uneasily before the office before he slowly raised his hand and gently tapped the door once.

"Come in," the little man's voice squeaked from under the door.

Reluctantly, Benton turned the knob and slowly stepped through the doorway. He strode across the rug a man condemned. I was never to know the way I destroyed him that day.

"Mr. MacIntyre," the doctor greeted. "Please have a seat. I'm glad you've decided to talk with me. I know we both have your brother's best interest at heart here. To begin, I would like to first clarify a few points. If you don't mind, of course."

"That's why I'm here," Benton replied with false cheerfulness.

"Is everything all right?" the doctor commented. "I know this must be very difficult for you. Benton raised his brow in silent reply and the doctor continued, "Good…Now then, I have your brother's full name as Ian James MacIntyre. Is this correct?"

Benton nodded in agreement. The little man paused a

moment to overlook a tall stack of papers with his beady black eyes.

"Where were we?" he questioned absent-mindedly to thin air as he shuffled through the papers again. "Yes, here we are. He was born in Burlington, Vermont on October 31, 1960..."

"Actually," Benton corrected, "he was born in New York. Mother was working at the Met. Our family home was in Vermont."

After a stunned stare, a suspicious grin and a few hasty scribbles, the psychiatrist continued, "I have your parents listed as James Robert MacIntyre and Madeline Faye DeLacroix. They were married in London on April 10, 1952, and soon relocated to America. Your mother is Indian, I understand."

"She prefers Lakota," Benton sneered in disgust. "She unfortunately is American." Benton never really got along with our American relatives and took father's view of all things American. Be that as it may, they both married and later divorced American women, the hypocrites.

"Your parents divorced in 1975. Why?" Dr. Pharisey continued to prod.

"I'd rather not go into the sordid details, if you please," Benton replied as politely as he could. He knew to tell the truth meant accepting that father wasn't perfect. Something Benton was never capable of.

"I'm only trying to help your brother," the doctor explained.

"Why waste your time, mate? The bastard doesn't want to help himself! He wants nothing to do with me so why should I help him?" Benton raved.

Benton rose to leave when the doctor rushed around the desk towards him.

"Really, Mr. MacIntyre...Benton," he attempted to soothe.

"If you want any more information, call the Yard," Benton instructed. "Better yet, ask his good friend Mr. Kingston...Oh, I forgot! He's the reason he's here. Good day, doctor."

After leaving the hospital, Benton wandered from pub to pub. By closing time on that bitter winter night, he was too drunk, depressed, and tired to see the man that slowly stole in his wake as he strode along the banks of the Thames. As he approached the docks, his pursuer stalked silently from the shadows. In his inebriated state, Benton failed to notice until it was too late.

"Who..." he cried out just before a silenced small calibre handgun was raised to his forehead and fired with an echoed pop.

At around dawn the next morning, a jogger out for his morning run stopped along the banks at Kew Gardens. Through the corner of his eye, he saw a dark shadow in the early morning mist of the river. He cautiously approached to look at a waterlogged trench coat and air bubble warped pants afloat near the bank. The closer he approached, the more of the corpse became apparent. Dark hair swirled with the minute waves. Just as the jogger stepped along side of the bank, the corpse rolled to reveal the bloodless skin and hallowed eyes of death stare through the icy waters. An entry wound like a third eye sat in the middle of Benton's forehead. The jogger turned in disgust to expel the remnants of his breakfast over the frosted ground.

The media hounds arrived in full force, nearly beating the police to the scene. A crowd of curious "looky-lou's" had assembled themselves along a police barricade. Through the midst of the crowd, MacKensie made his appearance with Dan wandering solemnly behind.

"Who is it?" Dan asked timidly as the body was being pulled from the frigid water by two uniformed officers.

"Why don't you see for yourself," MacKensie toyed.

Dan slowly approached the rescue workers. Hesitantly, he gazed over the banks at the snow-white corpse. His heart sank in his chest as stark reality beat him senseless. He was sure the body was mine. MacKensie dug harshly through Benton's pockets. As he thumbed through a waterlogged wallet, he was surprised to find identification, traveller's cheques, two hundred sterling, and a faded photograph of a young boy and his look alike younger brother, nearly destroyed by the water.

"Sometimes, I think you're no better then a bloody grave robber!" Dan angrily accused.

"Relax, my boy," MacKensie soothed. "It was no robbery. I'll bet anything one of the gang Deos had a run in with had something to do with this. The bloke that pulled the trigger was probably too high to know who he capped. There's still a mint on him," MacKensie handed Dan a water soaked Australian driver's license. "Nice twist of events, wouldn't you say?"

"The resemblance is striking! They're identical except for Ian's scars," Dan exclaimed, partially in relief. Then his face darkened. "If they thought…What are we going to do about Ian?"

Mouse's camera was the last to arrive. The rumour mill was already in full force as journalists and observers whispered around him.

"Any idea who it is?" Mouse questioned.

"Its that Yank Indian friend of the Kingstons," an observer nearby related.

Mouse dropped his camera, forced his way through the crowd to corner Dan and MacKensie as he demanded, "Tell me what I just heard isn't true!"

Dan and MacKensie looked at each other then back at Mouse. Dan bent over and whispered into Mouse's ear, "We have to talk…off the record."

# Chapter Nineteen
## The Escape

"…Wild Spirit, which art moving everywhere;
Destroyer and preserver; hear, oh, hear!"
{Percy Bysshe Shelley, 1819}

Early that morning, I was awakened to the news that according to the system, I was officially sane. The word had arrived around dawn. I suddenly found myself turned loose with no explanation and nowhere to go. Relief mingled with fear as I forced myself not to think farther ahead than ten minutes at a time. I wasn't prepared to face the realization that I was homeless, friendless, and alone in London. The only connection I had to the outside world I had just alienated and was probably halfway back to Sydney, or so I thought.

I wandered the streets for a couple of hours before settling in Hyde Park. An empty feeling overwhelmed me as I lay in the grass and stared at the passing clouds. I was overwhelmed by the sense that I had lost something substantial, but didn't know what. I couldn't shake the primal longing that filled my core and left me distracted and jittery. The melancholy that engulfed me made me want to weep uncontrollably even though I had no idea why.

I was shocked to reality as I lay in the dying grass, letting the sun warm my face, by the high-pitched drone of a two-cycle engine. Before I fully realized what was happening, I was hit full in the face by clumps of dirt and grass as a black and red dirt bike slid sideways to a stop before me. I gazed up to see the stunning figure of Ace. Dark reflective lenses masked her eyes as she revved the engine with leather-gloved hands. She seemed radiant, in a brutal sort of way, as she straddled the seat in a leather cat suit and matching boots.

"Took long enough to find you. Hop on!" she ordered.

"What's going on?" I demanded.

"Just get on! Now isn't the time to explain. Hurry on, then!"

I shook the dirt from my hair as I rose from the ground and leapt onto the back of the bike. I wrapped my arms around Ace and briefly brushed my elbows along her firm breasts as the faint air of *Vanilla Fields* drifted from her hair and I hoped that nature wouldn't betray me. It had been so long since I had seen a "normal" woman that I doubted whether my body would obey my mind's demands for temperance.

With a cry of, "Hold on!" she lifted the front wheel and tore off through the courtyard. "MacKensie arranged for your release this morning," she explained over the high-pitched cry of the engine as we wove through the crowded streets and dodged our way through the dense noontime traffic.

"MacKensie?" I questioned. "Why?"

"You're dead if we don't," she replied.

"What do you mean, 'I'm dead if you don't'?"

With a sudden burst of power, I was tossed backwards, but held onto Ace's waist like a waif spider monkey to its mother as she began to weave dangerously through back alleys. The speed and danger of the drive forced any carnal reactions from my mind and body as I tried desperately to simply stay on the bike.

"I'll explain everything when we reach the Hall!" she yelled over the wind and the tormented wail of the engine.

We rode in relative silence, with the exception of the ringing in my ears from the pained cry of a full throttled motor, for the remainder of the ride. On the barren countryside we drove much too fast to sight see so I simply focused on the winding road ahead and was left with my thoughts. My mind wandered over the events of the past few months and I wanted to close my mind. I wanted to just forget everything that had happened. If I couldn't lock it away into an impenetrable vault in my mind, I wanted to be someone else so I could deny it had happened to me. I couldn't accept that it had all been real.

My heart sank as I gazed upon the state of Kingston Hall. In the few brief months since Andrew's suicide, the Hall had fallen into disuse and disrepair. The thought struck me that either this John Phoenix hadn't claimed his inheritance, or simply didn't care about the estate. The grounds had fallen prey to overgrowth and dust. Cobwebs had claimed the house. The golden glow of the afternoon sun filtered through the windows at the top of the stairs. The once shined marble floor was dull, dirty, and littered with dried leaves.

"Where is this mysterious John Phoenix?" I sneered as we entered the marble floored entry hall. Ace led me to a dust-laden mirror against the wall to Deos' study. I gazed at my hazy reflection as she whispered, "You're looking at him."

"Is this some kind of joke?" I demanded.

Footsteps echoed through the deserted Hall. Danny approached from Andrew's study with a distant, pained look in his eyes. His hands fumbled nervously in the pockets of his dark green dress slacks. His arms pulled back the tails of his grey overcoat to reveal the corner of a newspaper tucked into the breast pocket of his green double-breasted suit coat. Mouse wandered sheepishly behind, a look of disbelief darkening his usually jovial face.

"Will someone tell me what the hell is going on!" I declared.

"That depends on where you want to start," Dan voiced uncomfortably. "All this is yours now. That much is true. Since Andrew died before he could contest the will, all this reverts to the only party named in Deos'...John Phoenix."

"But how can that be? I'm not John Phoenix," I voiced, rather confused by it all.

Danny pulled a large manila envelope from the inside pocket of his overcoat and handed it to me. I opened the top and pulled from it a bundle of identification papers all in the name of John Holliday Phoenix, but the photo on the operator's license was mine.

"Why did you do all this?" I asked, stunned.

"We didn't," Ace confirmed. "Deos did. Just before he died... Just in case."

Dan and Ace passed a puzzled look to each other as if telepathically asking each other, "Should we tell him?"

"I demand to know what is going on!" I finally exploded

after losing my patience.

Dan directed me to a quickly handwritten letter in the back of the stack of papers that simply read:

*Ian,*

*If you're reading this it means two things have happened. The old kicker finally kicked me in the arse and I'm worm food. Two, you're in trouble. From what or who I can only speculate, but for one reason or another you need the security that only I can bring. So, old friend, congratulations. You are John Holliday Phoenix, the new Lord of Kingston Hall. I wish I were there to see the look on Andrew's face...*

My stomach churned at the thought of Andrew and I had to pause before continuing.

*Don't blame yourself for what happened to me. I know you're probably torturing yourself right now. Just remember this, you were my oldest, first, and best friend, my brother above all else. There is no one else worthy of my inheritance, respect or love. Take care of yourself and may you live a long and happy life, my friend, my brother – Lord John Holliday Phoenix.*

*I am with you always.*

*- Deos*

A lump formed in my throat and my hands began to tremble. My chest tightened as I fought back the long withheld tears of anguish. Dan laid his hand on my shoulder and I brushed it away as the note and papers fell from my hands.

"I didn't want to tell you like this..." Dan lamented as he reached for the newspaper in his pocket. I grabbed it and pulled it away before he could hand it to me. "Something like that," he tried to finish. "Deos did it in case of something like that."

My knees dropped to the floor as I read the headline, "*Local Musician Murdered.*" I found myself literally reading my own obituary and staring at a photo of my body being removed from the banks of the Thames in a black bag. Guilt swelled within me as I remembered how badly I had treated my only brother at the hospital. I wished I had said how I really felt, told him how I had always looked up to him. I wished I had finally told him that I loved him, that I had always loved him.

"Benton," I whispered with a shake in my voice. With a burst of anger I rose, grabbed Danny by the collar and forced him against the wall.

"Was it you!" I accused as Ace began to pull at my shoulders. "Answer me! Was it fucking you!"

"Ian!" Ace screamed forcefully in my left ear. "Get a grip!"

"I don't know who it was!" Danny replied as he pushed back at me. Slowly, I began to release my grip. "I'm telling the truth," he continued as he began to smooth out his suit. "I wish I did."

Mouse had entered the room, just stood at the fringe of the altercation, and looked on in apprehension. The day's events had left him numbed and speechless. He was emotionally spent and didn't know how to react anymore.

"Why tell me like this?" I demanded, genuinely hurt as I shook the paper in front of Dan's face.

"I didn't know how to tell you," Danny explained. "MacKensie and I were the first on the scene. MacKensie decided it was best if we let everyone think you were dead. There was nothing left at the scene. No murder weapon, no fingerprints, nothing. It was a class job. Benton's wallet was even intact."

"What did you tell my parents?" I demanded.

Danny nervously shifted his weight as he stared at his feet. Guilt and shame oozed from him as he struggled to formulate what to say. "We told them that both you lads were killed during a mugging and we were only able to recover Benton's body from the river."

I became overwhelmed with the drive to call home and explain everything. I knew mother would be devastated at the news that both her sons were dead. In a frenzied rush, I raced past Mouse to Andrew's study with Danny and Ace close behind. I lifted the receiver from the phone on the dust-laden desk. Danny placed a hand on the receiver and began to force my hand down.

"I have to talk to mother," I stated in a daze.

"The phone hasn't worked in months," he explained.

Anger filled me as I pushed him to the ground. I then turned my aggression to the phone. I ripped the cord from the wall and threw the whole unit across the room. I collapsed to my knees and cried. Ace wrapped her arms around me. I buried my head in her shoulder and just sat there. She never said anything. She just let me cry.

# Chapter Twenty
## Laird of the Manor

"Lords are Lordliest in thir wine."
{John Milton, 1671}

I adjusted my top hat and quickly ran my thumb and fingers over my well-trimmed beard and moustache. I resisted the urge to squirm uncontrollably or scratch my itching face. I know I had to stay in character. I knew I had to convince even myself. The solicitor's office held a foreboding that oozed from the pine panelling that reeked of *Liquid Gold*. Thoughts of *would he recognize me?* ran rampant throughout my mind and ebbed away at my nerve. Nearly half a year had passed since our last encounter, but given the circumstances of our meeting, how could he fail to remember?

I shifted my jacket as I stepped into a sparsely decored office. The solicitor looked much as I remembered him. His wisp of a frame sat perched behind a large oak desk with a glass top. A computer sat idle at his side. He shuffled a few papers then turned his chair around to file them as I entered the room. The silver tips of my shoes tapped on the hard wood floor and echoed as I crossed the cavernous room.

"Please have a seat, Mr. Phoenix," he stated as he turned his chair to face me.

"Thank you," I confirmed as I sat down before the glass-topped desk.

I reached inside my breast pocket and pulled out a gold cigarette case with a matching lighter. I flipped open the case to reveal ten aromatic Turks.

"Do you mind?" I asked as I gestured the case.

"Not at all," he replied as he slid an ashtray to me.

"Would you care for one?" I offered.

He shook his head and smiled. "No thank you," he declined. "I quit some time ago."

I placed a cigarette to my lips, closed the case and then lit the end. I took in a long, cleansing breath of sweet smoke to calm my nerves as I returned the case and lighter. I knew things were going well, but I still was cautious. I never did know who I could trust.

"I've taken care of all the arrangements," he assured.

"And the matter I discussed with you earlier?" I drilled.

"I was able to find Mr. Jones," he replied. "But I do have to say I could find you a much more able man…"

"No one is more capable of overseeing Kingston Hall than Jonesie! He's been with the Kingston's for three generations, I'm not about to trust just anyone."

With Jonesie back where he belonged, my worries were lessened. I knew I could trust him explicitly and he would follow every direction to the letter. Nothing irritated me more than people that would ruin a good idea by reading too much into it. Besides, I had grown to think of Jonesie as a grandfather.

Over the next half hour, I got the typical updates on costs, balances, and legal balderdash. I was completely bored. By the time we finished, shook hands, and parted ways, I was on the verge of a monotony-induced coma. The solicitor's voice hadn't changed from what I remembered. I could still imagine him saying, "Beueller, Bueller."

When I reached the loaner BMW, I threw my overcoat into the passenger seat along with my double-breasted coat, top hat, and walking stick. With a sigh of relief, I loosened my tie and melted into the seat. As I pulled away from the curb and into the flow of afternoon traffic, I began to laugh uncontrollably. A wave of relief and disbelief overwhelmed me. I had actually pulled it off. I had fulfilled Deos' last request.

I returned to the Hall in a near state of shock. Jonesie stood between the great stone lions and awaited my arrival. His eyes lit up as I stepped from the car and approached. Tears began to swell his ageing eyes as he walked down the steps towards me.

"Sir, can it really be you?" he trembled.

"Shhh," I coaxed with a childish grin as I threw my arm

around him. "Its good to see you again."

"I can't tell you how relieved I was to hear from Mr. O'Selle."

At first I thought nothing of the comment. Then once his words sank in, I paused.

"Who contacted you?" I asked.

"Mr. O'Selle."

"You mean the solicitor didn't call you to come back," I confirmed.

Jonesie looked at me bewildered, as if I were standing naked in Hyde Park playing a tambourine.

"No, sir," he replied. "The only time I heard from the solicitor was when he sent my advance."

At first I was irate at the thought that I had been lied to, but then I decided the solicitor must have been referring to finding Jonesie to pay him the advance check I ordered and set to the arrangement of more pertinent details. I stepped into the Great Hall to find a sparse crew of workers awaited me. Four construction workers, a gardener, and an interior decorator (who I quickly dismissed) stood in line as if for inspection. The maid and a secondary butler, Fairchild, appeared from the kitchen to join the others at the base of the stairs. Out of the corner of my eye, I glimpsed the door to Andrew's study. I crossed the floor without so much as a word, opened the door, and looked inside. Everything was much the same as I had left it. Even the shattered phone lay in pieces across the grey rug.

"Nothing has been touched, sir," Fairchild stated. "Just as you instructed."

I turned to face the group who eagerly awaited instructions.

"Jonesie will act as my voice. As will Mr. O'Selle and Miss Murdoch. You will treat them as you would treat me and attend to their instructions as you would mine."

"What would you have us do, Your Lordship?" the maid asked.

I stood dumb for a moment. Jonesie passed a cockeyed smile of recognition. I had never been called "Your Lordship" before. It was a term I'd heard heads of state, Sir Charles, and eventually Deos called. It was a term that recognized centuries of blue blood and breeding; not for a half-blood redneck like me.

"First I want everything of Sir Charles' donated to charity,"
I declared as confidently as I could, trying to live up to the title that
fate had placed upon my new-born head. "Anything of Andrew's
that can burn I want taken to the country house and left. I will deal
with it later. As for the Jaguar, crush it! I want nothing of
Andrew's to remain intact. Even if you have to melt things down,
just get rid of it!"

My unusual request, without a doubt, surprised the staff.
Everyone, with the exception of Jonesie, stared at me as if the
tambourine was accompanied by a pink and purple polka dotted
tutu. Jonesie was the only one who understood my feelings. If the
Hall were to be truly mine, I would have to do some serious
remodelling. The only things I kept, with the exception of the
contents of two of the guest rooms, were Deos' things. His
bedroom I had locked as a shrine of sorts and his study I also had
left intact. I felt if Deos had thought enough of me to be his sole
heir, I owed him at least that.

The Mercedes was another part of Deos I couldn't part
with. There were too many memories to deal with all at once. So,
in an attempt to distance myself and to help keep a low profile
while in town, I had Jonesie arrange to have the Mercedes shipped
to a long-term storage locker in New York, encased in a large
wooden crate marked *Foam Packing Peanuts.* I knew no one
would bother it then. I didn't know of any black market in foam
packing peanuts. With the largest of my pet projects safely on its
way to the states, I could concentrate on the restoration of the Hall.

I spent most of my time at the small country estate. It was
almost a week before the trucks arrived with Andrew's belongings.
As the movers carefully unloaded the items, I smirked and stated,
"All of this stuff goes around back, lads."

I got some questioning glares as the items were strew one
on top of another to form the largest bon fire I had ever seen. I had
the burn site set back in a clearing in the woods so it wouldn't
attract attention and I wouldn't have to worry about burning the
house down. After a couple of hours everything was in place and I
thanked the workers for a job well done, shook each one's hand,
and gave them all a hundred extra in appreciation.

Later that night, I lit the fire, watched with a bottle in hand,
and never moved. For the better part of a day, I watched the fire

burn down to just embers, ash, and burnt metal. Filled with satisfaction, I entered the house, cleaned up, and left for the Hall. The renovations were progressing nicely. Andrew's study was a shell of its former self and all that remained was the delivery of the new furniture. The staff kept busy and out of my way as I wandered through the house disposing of anything I found offensive. I was determined to rid myself of anything that had the even the slightest hint of a bad memory attached.

The only thing I did become attached to was Ace. I began seeing more and more of her when I got the chance. Their sideways glances and Dan's ever-present eye should have told me all I needed to know. But, when it comes to women, I have never been very observant of my surroundings. In fact, in the presence of women I became a Clydesdale, blinded and whipped.

"Ian," Ace called as she hurried across the marble floor, "we have some great news!"

I could never have been prepared for what was to come.

"I've asked Ace to marry me," Dan informed with a Cheshire cat grin upon his back stabbing face. "She accepted! Can you believe it?"

"No," I stated with unusual calm. "And I can honestly say that…so when is the big day?"

I felt my legs turn to jelly and knew how Nancy Kerrigan must have felt. A strange mix of betrayal, humiliation, and guilt overwhelmed me. *She had been Deos' girl. What business did any of us have with her?* Then, I began to feel foolish for not seeing what was blatantly blossoming before me. I really shouldn't have been that surprised. Even with his eccentricities, Dan was what any woman would be a fool to pass up.

"We've been considering Guy Faulk's Day," Ace replied. She gazed at the shining diamond on her finger and cried. "I can't believe this is happening. I never thought I'd ever want to marry, least of all love after Deos and look what's happened! This is unbelievable."

I'd second that. I left Jonesie in charge of the Hall and ran did what I had always done best, I ran away.

# Part III

"The having made a young girl miserable
May give you frequent bitter reflection;
None of which can attend
The making of an old woman happy."

-Benjamin Franklin-
(*On the Choice of a Mistress*)

# Chapter Twenty-One
## A Black Sheep in Wolf's Clothing

"Oh, well, I suppose it's right that the members
Of these old families should stick together
nowadays.
After all, their ancestors in those days
Were probably chained together."
{Billy Hughes, 1931}

I arrived along the river in mid-afternoon. As the rolling bluffs passed by, I relaxed into warm memories of my great uncle's farm. Nowhere had I ever felt more at ease than in the serene meadows and carved bluffs of the farm. I could spend hours exploring the caves that loomed high above the Mississippi. By the time I last saw Uncle Gus at the age of ten, I had become the local expert on Big Cave.

Gus, short for Fabius Maurice DeLacroix, had been the black sheep of the family. Most of my relatives thought him a crazy, drunk Indian, but I always admired his rogue spirit and imagination. As a child, Gus and I would spend endless summer hours playing Robin Hood in the forest behind his house, but some of my most treasured memories were of his aromatic pipe tobacco. I can't say what blend it was, but it always conjured up images of a Turkish palace and I would sit and imagine I was a sultan with my harem dancing around an emerald pool.

I pulled into the back pasture, hid the Mercedes inside the abandoned lean-too, covered it with an aging tarp, and concealed the front and sides with squares of rotting hay. A feeling of relief filled me as I emerged from the barn and made my way to the cliffs. As I passed through the woods, I was reminded of years long behind – a happier time when I didn't have a care in the world. How far away those days seemed now.

The boy that once wandered those woods free was gone and only a shell of a man remained. Even though the woods still held a mystic appeal to me, somehow they only seemed empty now. I passed the stream where Gus and I would recreate the staff fight from *Robin Hood* with Gus as Little John and me as Robin. I had to smile as the image of Gus wiggling feverishly to dislodge a crawfish from his backside as he cried, "You little sonnabitch! I'll make gumbo outta ya!" while lying in shallow water, floated to the forefront of my mind.

From there, I began my ascent up the cliff side to Big Cave. As I approached the humble looking entrance, memories of childhood adventure filled me. I nearly expected one of my old playmates to fall from a tree calling, "Halt! Who goes there?"

As I approached the cave, the hole in the cliff side appeared much smaller than I had remembered it to be. An entrance that as a boy I could walk straight through, I now had to crawl through on my hands and knees.

With an electric torch gripped firmly in my hand, I cautiously entered the mouth of the cave. The dim light shone on the rough stonewalls and bathed the cavern in an unearthly glow. I slid the heavily laden pack from my back and set a lantern on the shelf-like formation to my right. In my childhood, I had often imagined the first expanse to be my Banquet Hall with the shelf-like formations on each side as a line of chairs; the long, narrow formation in the middle as my table; and the rounded formation above as a chandelier. Yet, it seemed when I looked upon the room as an adult, I became aware of how dark, damp, cold, and lifeless the cave really was.

With spiritless interest, I set the table up as my bed and began to explore the rest of the cave. The cave itself consisted of three main rooms: the Banquet Hall; the Library; and the Conservatory, named for the unique formations found in each. The Conservatory held at its centre a formation that could only be described as the largest grand piano I had ever seen and the Library looked as though it held bookshelves from top to bottom. It was after backing my way out of the narrow Library that I proceeded to the Banquet Hall and squeezed back through the small opening to the sunlit expanses beyond.

For three days and two nights, I lived like a hermit in that dank cave. The only time I emerged was to walk to town for supplies. Supplies tended to consist of a bottle of imported Scotch and a six-pack of lager. By the end of the second day, the cave had begun to look like a fraternity house after homecoming and I had developed an excruciating cough from the cold, clammy conditions.

On the third day, not even laying in the warm summer sun would ease the dull ache entrenched in my chest. As I lay listening to the softly gurgling stream that flowed nearby, I drifted into a deep sleep. The first real sleep I'd had in weeks. I'm not entirely sure what awakened me, whether it was the snap of a dry twig, the murderous feasting of the mosquitoes upon my flesh, or the howl of a nearby wolf.

Night had fallen as I scanned the darkened horizon while warding off legions of bloodthirsty miniature vampires. From behind the trees emerged a dark figure carrying a twisted walking stick and a bottle of *Wild Turkey*. The pale red glow from a pipe illuminated the lines and bright eyes of the man, revealing his identity to me.

"You're looking pretty damned lively for a corpse!" Gus called in the Midwestern country drawl so typical of his generation.

"I thought you were dead!" I exclaimed only to begin one of my many coughing fits.

"I was told that you were, boy. Looks as though I'd better get you to the house. Sounds as though you've caught your death. That is if you weren't dead already…God, it's good to see you, boy!"

Gus threw his arms around me in a lengthy bear hug. Upon releasing his iron grip, he helped me down off the cliffs to the century farmhouse where I had misspent a considerable amount of my childhood. I sat down upon a dingy, floral patterned couch in the living room as Gus disappeared into the kitchen. He emerged a few moments later with a grey wool blanket and a cup of steaming, but spiked, tea.

"Guaranteed to cure or kill ya," he chimed as he handed the cup to me.

I pulled the blanket up around my shoulders with shaking hands and cradled the warm cup. Gus fell back into the same antique velvet chair he had since I was young. He looked at me in concern, and then turned his attention to his bottle. Together, we sat drinking in silence until Gus looked up at me.

"How's that tight-assed Brit father of yours these days? I haven't seen Lord Flaxseed since he and Maggie divorced," he commented.

Great Uncle Gus always referred to my father as "Lord Flaxseed" because he was "so goddamned tight you couldn't drive a flaxseed up his ass with a moll!" That and the fact that he refused to call Gus, "Gus" the way everyone did. He was always, "Your Uncle Fabius" or just plain, "Fabius". Gus hated his proper name. He thought it was, "too proper for a man of my stature, or rather lack of it."

Growing up, people looked at my mother strangely when she introduced her Uncle Gus. Only seven years separated them in age. My grandfather was almost sixteen when Gus was born. With Gus and mother so close chronologically, they were raised together like brother and sister, a relationship that never truly lost its closeness and a relationship that my father disapproved of wholly. He tried to separate us from mother's family, who he viewed as backwoods and socially inferior.

"Still a tight-assed Brit," I sarcastically commented. "Hell, I don't bloody know. Haven't talked to him since before I left Sydney. How's mother?"

"Better. She remarried six months ago," Gus explained. "Some retired Squid she met in Florida. Damned Navy men. You know she's just as impulsive as your grandmother was. I never could understand Agatha half the time either. The other half I spent wondering what my crazy ol' brother saw in her. And the rest of the family thought I was the loon!"

"You've got nothing on me in that department!"

As I sat with the mug still in my hands, I considered telling Gus everything. I knew he had heard some stories. After all, people were bound to talk. The only problem was how to tell him. The last thing I needed was to work everyone up again. After all, they had only just buried Benton and me.

"Look," I finally decided, knowing I could explicitly trust

Gus, "perhaps it is best if no one knew about me."

"On the lam are we?" Gus jested.

"Not exactly, but I think its best everyone thinks I'm dead. I've put everyone through enough already. Let mum have her happiness. Maybe now she can have a real life."

I thought it was easier to pretend I was someone else if I no longer existed. I thought I could save everyone the pain of what had happened. Let them grieve, soon they would forget about me, and go on with their lives. For in many ways, I was already dead.

"You forget, my boy," Gus stated with a gleam in his eye, "no one would believe a crazy old drunk Injin like me."

A cocky smile passed my lips as I realized, after all, he had a point. No one would believe him. My appearance would be explained away as easily as a pink elephant. People would say he had gotten drunk one night and imagined seeing his dead nephew. At times, I thought that perhaps my life was nothing more than a drunken nightmare and I would awaken next to the fish tank in my college dorm wearing a newspaper Napoleon hat and exposing my innards to *Whip It*. Now all I had to look forward to were headaches, chest aches, and self-pity. Some lord of the manor I'd make!

# Chapter Twenty-Two
## Meet the Boys

"A good old man, sir, he will be talking;
As they say, 'When the age is in the wit is out'."
{Shakespeare, *Much Ado About Nothing*}

After sleeping the remainder of the night, I awoke the next morning surprisingly refreshed. For the first time in over a year, I felt like shaving. As I begun to strip the whiskers away from my cicatrix cheek, I revealed the long, once bone white scar had began to fade to more of a pale pink. I knew it was still very noticeable, but I thought, *Who cares? If nothing else it will make me easier to spot in a line-up.* Still wiping my face with a hand towel, I walked from the bathroom into the living room where Gus sat in the same tattered recliner he had the night before.

"Now that looks more like you!" he exclaimed on my approach.

"Feels more like me, too," I agreed. "I thought about going to town and getting a trim. I could use a little off the top."

"Looks like the back could use it worse."

I was mildly offended, though I really don't know why. I felt like Samson before he met Delilah. My hair had become a part of my new persona and I wasn't about to let anyone near the back with a pair of trimmers. Besides, Gus' hair reached three quarters of the way down his back. Had anyone else made the comment, I would have told them where to go and how fast they could get there.

"On second thought," Gus began. "It suits you. You look better than some of the women I've dated. If you're a single guy around here the selection isn't worth a tinker's damn. Hell all the women my age are dead!"

"Hey," I taunted. "Watch it with the dead jokes; you happen to be talking to a corpse."

I had to laugh. Even at his age, Gus was still chasing the women. I guess you can't teach an old Gus new tricks. He always went for the younger women. To be frank, I never did see Gus with any women over thirty-five. Whatever it was he had, he knew how to use it.

As I emerged from the house, I was immediately struck by the vision of the Mercedes parked in the drive next to Gus' dilapidated '65 Ford pickup. The mirror finish on the hood reflected the passing clouds over the Stuart coat of arms. Even the tires had been polished to a spit shine. The impressive sight was certainly out of place in the dusty, worn driveway next to the corroding truck.

"I hope you don't mind," Gus stated. "But I've been watching you since you first arrived. You still can't fool your old uncle. Me and three of the 'boys' from town towed it here. None of us had seen a car with right hand drive, at least not since my last tour in Europe, that is. A couple of the boys even washed and waxed it for ya."

I was at a loss for words. I had hid the Mercedes for fear of drawing attention to myself. The last thing I wanted was to advertise my presence. Almost as if he could read my very thoughts, Gus reassured, "You don't have to worry 'round these parts. The most anyone has to know is you're just a friend visiting from England."

Gus thought of everything. While in seclusion, Gus took the liberty to begin a series of tales about the anticipated arrival of an overseas friend. I would definitely have to keep my wits about me on this one.

I quietly rolled to a stop in front of the small town, corner barbershop. The outside hadn't changed much. The candy cane barber pole had faded with the course of time, yet still spun with the same lazy momentum that gripped that part of town. Across the street was Riverside Park where, at the tender age of five, I hid from my father in a bush for the better part of four hours. Now the bush was gone, raised long ago to make room for a gazebo overlooking the river.

The building next to the barbershop had once been a five

and dime, but as was true of many things I would find, it too had changed. It was now a music store. The flamboyant posters in the front windows were a striking contrast to the anachronistic building next door. For in many ways, the barbershop looked as though it had been transported straight from the fifties. As I entered the building, I was overwhelmed by the scent of shave cream and tonic.

A kindly old man in overalls smiled at me from behind the morning paper and gave me a secretive wink to tell me that he was one of "The Boys". In the meanwhile, a tall elderly barber emerged from the back carrying a broom.

"What can I do ya fer?" he asked.

"A trim is fine," I commented.

"Have a seat."

I slid into the barber's chair and was nearly choked by a plastic wrap. As I looked at my image in the mirror, I could picture myself gazing into the same mirror as a seven year old with a far younger Gus standing against the wall in army greens with a buzz cut and cocky grin, saying, "Take a bit off the top…"

"…Say from the neck up," the older Gus finished, ending my momentary doldrums. Gus wandered into the room and stood against the wall with the same infamous grin. His dark Lakota eyes twinkled devilishly as he leaned against the doorway. His tanned, red tinted arms crossed over his tank-top covered chest. His lanky legs were crossed below his thin waist with the silver tips of his alligator skin boots shining in the mid morning sun.

"Very funny!" I stated.

"Who said I was joking," Gus snidely replied.

He walked over to the chair and laid a weathered arm over my shoulder.

"John," he stated to the barber, "this is that friend I was telling you about."

"Pleased ta meecha," the barber replied.

"Nice to meet you," I stated. "The name's John Phoenix."

The man with the newspaper in his hand shook a bloated bald head as he laughed, "Where you from, Arizona?"

"London, actually," I corrected.

The newspaper man continued to chuckle as a rough almost hacking sound emerged from his turkey-like neck. "I thought with a name like Phoenix that you'd be from Arizona."

"Frank, don't you have someone else to torment for a while?" Gus threatened.

The newspaperman just looked at Gus sulking and then returned his gaze to the print.

"What ya lookin' for?" the barber asked me. I was taken back for a moment. I had no idea what to say. "I mean your hair. What are you wanting done with it?"

A sigh of relief unintentionally passed my lips as I steadied my racing pulse. "A bit off the top, if you please."

"Looks like the back could use it worse, if you ask me," Frank continued to razz.

Gus' eyes darkened as his lips pursed in frustration with his neck turning a steadily increasing shade of crimson. "No one's asking you, Frank."

"If the boy wants a little off the top, then that's what the boy gets," John the barber finalized.

After a refreshing haircut, Gus and I proceeded down the streets of the small river town. I was led down a series of deserted streets to a small downtown café. The interior was decorated in an assortment of antique tools, pictures, and prints. Gus showed me to a vast, circular wooden table inhabited by a dozen older men drinking coffee. It reminded me of a cross between *On Golden Pond* and *Excalibur*. As we approached, each man watched every move intently, leaving me filled with nervousness. Feeling that I didn't exactly fit in with the geriatric convention, I reluctantly sat down.

"So you must be the mysterious friend everyone has been talking about," a bald, bearded man stated. "We heard there was a stranger in town. The name's Pete Johnson."

"John Phoenix," I introduced.

Each one of "The Boys" introduced themselves. There was John, the barber; Frank, the newspaper man; a Dick; two Toms; an Ed; Lyle; Clint; Bob; and finally, two Dales. Actually, I never really did get to know who was who, not that it really mattered much. In many ways, one was the same as the next. The men had spent so many years in this routine that they melded into one odd, hydra-like being.

"So," Frank commented as Gus shook his head as if

163

thinking *I'm going to fucking kill him.* "What's it like staying with horny old Gus?"

"Not much different than living in an asylum," I joked as Gus spit coffee out his nose. "Only I haven't shoved a paintbrush up his nose...YET."

The group erupted in laughter.  No one knew the full implications of the jest. Gus just looked at me sternly before returning to the cup of coffee in his hand. We sat and talked with the group for nearly an hour. I was surprised to find that for a band of old farmers, they could carry on some fairly lively conversations. Not that the usual shoptalk interested me much. Farm reports, commodities, hog prices, and fertilizer never really interested me. Well, maybe the fertilizer – After all, I did hold a BS in BS from Asshole U.

It was the stories of the area's history that I found most intriguing. Tales of river pirates, wars, a certain past resident named Mr. Clemens, paddlewheels, and the like littered the farm talk and kept the conversation just interesting enough to keep me out of a coma. The droll, monotonous tone would occasionally be interrupted by a piece of sharp country wit or a tale of personal misfortune (not to mention the frequent, "in my day...")

"When I was in high school," one of the Toms began, "the senior class decided to place Ol' Lady Dawson's wagon on top of the water tower. Only problem was getting' it up there, see? So, Bulldog Tambers and I climbed the tower and assembled the wagon piece by piece. Next thing ya know, we're assembling the last wheel and hears, 'What the Sam Hill do ya boys think yer doin'? We's look over the railin' to see the sheriff standin' at the bottom of the tower with Ol' Lady Dawson. The five other guys that was with us, see, had high-tailed it without so much as a howdoyado. You should have seen us tryin' to explain to our old men."

I didn't bother to ask how they eventually got the wagon down. I enjoyed thinking that the decaying wagon sat atop the water tower until the day they replaced it. I imagined the water tower toppling to the ground and the wagon exploding into thousands of pieces as it impacted at the bottom. There was something I found intriguing about that image. It embodied the essence of teenage farm-boy antics. The kind of relatively innocent prank that seemed to peak and wane with over-packed phone booths and VWs.

I spent the remainder of my time recuperating on the farm. I actually came to enjoy the tediousness and simplicity of rural life. Slowly, over time, I grew stronger. There seemed to be something about the lazy pace of the area that held unique recuperative properties to me. I felt as though I had found the Fountain of Youth. After a week, my pneumatic cough had dissipated along with the accompanying chest ache. It would be another week before my stuffy nose would clear.

The only part of the farm I didn't like was Gus' black and white tomcat, Dumb Ass. Every morning I would find Dumb Ass either sitting in the driver's seat of the Mercedes or crouched up under the driver's door laying in wait. As soon as I would open the door, he would pounce and attach his bloodthirsty claws to any available part of my body (which tended to be my face and neck) and held on like a morning commuter on the train to Calcutta.

Each time after the fierce attack, he would flee for the safety of the woodshed. Trying to catch him was futile because even for an ancient cat, he moved like a high-speed train across Japan. Gus would stand hanging out the torn screen door, chuckle his ass off, and yell at me, "That damned cat sure doesn't like you very much, boy!"

"I'm not too enchanted with it myself, you know!" I replied in disgust. "That hellion of a cat should have been shot a decade ago and you know it! I don't know why you keep that menace around!"

"I don't know why either. Must just be the fact that he reminds me of... me."

# Chapter Twenty-Three

## The Quarry

"Nature is full of freaks,
And now puts an old head on young shoulders,
And then a young heart under fourscore winters."
{Ralph Waldo Emerson, 1870}

By the time the Fourth of July came around, the town had sparked to life like Frankenstein. It seemed the entire population crawled from their hiding places for the Fourth of July festival. I was no exception.

I spent the morning wandering through town from garage sale to garage sale. As a child, I was forced to encounter hours of debate between my parents. My father would complain garage sales were, "Nothing but a silly Midwestern custom." Mother, on the other hand, took to garage sales the way pigmies take to headhunting. Except her hunt was for "hidden treasures" because, "People don't know what they're throwing away!" It wasn't that we couldn't afford new things, in fact we were always fairly well off, it was just the thrill of the hunt for her. And for as much as it pained me to do, I tended to side with my father on the issue.

I had wandered the crowded streets for the better part of two hours before I drifted into Riverside Park. I had begun to think I was back in London had it not been for the exception that festivalgoers were far more aggressive than any Rugby team I ever played. The park was filled to capacity with antique dealers, craft booths, assorted food vendors, a chili cookoff, and people, too many people. People packed into the streets like a 44DD into a 32B. The crowd seemed to ooze from every available outlet and began to squeeze the breath from my chest as the sweltering July sun added to the claustrophobia.

Lazily, I wandered by the fire department as the barrel race was ending and ducked into a cramped, enclosed trailer to escape the moving herds as they relocated to the next event. I passed by a sign stating *The Honey War: The War That Never Was* and was vaguely intrigued by the title of the strange little exhibit. An elderly man behind a well-worn card table rose and extended a hand as I approached. We shook hands as I ducked to avoid knocking myself out on the miniscule, narrow doorway.

"Welcome," he cheerily greeted. "Would you care to sign our guest book?" I didn't find it an unreasonable request as I hastily signed and then continued down the narrow trailer. "Mr...uh," he stammered as he examined my unique signature. "Oh, Phoenix." He scanned the address line where I simply wrote *London, UK*. "You're from London, are you?" he continued to small talk. "What brings you to the states?"

"Research, actually," I vaguely replied as I stared at the reproduction 1816 map of Iowa and Missouri. I don't know why I didn't say I was on holiday. It would have made the conversation so much easier. I gathered from the information and the segmented ramblings of the elderly curator, that war nearly broke out over the border of the two states, not far in fact from where we presently were. Beyond that, I didn't really care. All I wanted was to be free of the hotbox. The heat in the blast furnace seared my already white hot temper and singed the last remnants of patience and civility.

"Are you a scientist?" he continued to prod between ramblings about the exhibit.

"No, a writer," I replied with a hint of cynicism.

I had never been one for small talk and I was growing weary from the heat and the old man's ranting. From my first steps through the travelling museum, he followed at my heels like a lost terrier. I would have been perfectly content to read what was on the walls and be on my way. Instead, I was forced to endure the *War and Peace* version. After being cornered for a half hour in the sweltering heat of the tin can, I left a two hundred dollar donation after being guilted by the old man who explained the cost of the exhibit and inadequate federal funding.

*My God!* I lamented; *He has a lot of energy for an old man. I don't have that much energy now.*

I emerged from the baked potato and into the oven. Midmorning had been warm, but by middle afternoon, it was intolerable. I felt much as Jane Austen must have when she wrote, "What dreadful hot weather we have!  It keeps me in a continual state of inelegance!"

I had forgotten how hot the Midwest could be.  Then again, when you're a child you fail to notice (or at least remember) such trivial things.  My mind drifted over debates about climate change and global warming.  I pondered how my plains ancestors could have possibly functioned, least of all thrived in such sweltering heat.

A tinge of guilt and shame blew over me with a rogue, passing breeze at the realization that I had spent too long in England.  I had become soft to the heat.  I was acclimatized to milder weather.  Guilt emerged from the sense that I had somehow let my people down and I had become nothing more than another dark-skinned white man.  I felt less of an Indian and hated myself for the weakness.

I had spent the majority of the morning sweating moderately, but by the time I left the hot air balloon of a museum director, I was soaked to the bone.   I found that of late, I was finding it harder and harder to cope in intense heat, especially when compounded with Midwest summer humidity.  It seemed to steal my breath and drained the energy from my body.  I tried everything to cool off.  Finally, four lemon shake-ups and five beers later, I could bare the indignity no more.

I had a hatred of public pools since I was six years old.  My older brother had been forced to escort me to the local pool in Burlington, mainly just to get out of mother's hair for a while. Benton would reluctantly agree and I was led down the series of alleyways from our luxury apartment.

The first hour would go fine, until Benton would see Sheila.  Suddenly, being stuck with a snot-nosed little twit like me wasn't fun anymore.  Every time Sheila would swim by, Benton would push my head under water.  The first two or three times were fun, but by the tenth, when I was gasping for air and fearing for my life. It was getting old.

I would always be relieved, when the Grand Inquisitor was no longer bobbing me up and down like a buoy. Then again, that would just be because Benton would no longer be there. He would take Sheila and MY ice cream money and high tail it for the soda shop, leaving me to walk the twelve blocks home alone. And when you're six, twelve blocks seems like a marathon, even in suburban Vermont.

I knew the pool was out. Besides, it would be far too crowded for my liking anyway. After much thought, I came up with an alternative. I thought of a place out of the way where I could be alone with my thoughts.

I drove five miles outside of town to the abandoned gravel quarry. When I was younger, the quarry was where all the kids went before the pool was built. Since then, no one ever went there with the exception of the occasional skinny dippers. The only people that really ever went near the place were bass fishermen and hikers; even then they were few and far in-between due to the various *Danger* and *No Trespassing* signs.

I stripped down to only a pair of silk boxers and lay out on the barren bank for the better part of an hour, basking in the cool breeze that blew off the sonorous pit. The refreshing wind sighed over me as I lay in the shadow of an elm tree and watched the passing clouds. Not a single cloud brought to mind an image and in disgust, I rose and approached the high cliff's edge.

I gazed down the cliff face to the crystal clear depths below beckoning me with a shimmer that reflected the afternoon sun from fifteen feet below. For a matter of seconds, I hesitantly rustled the dirt with a bare foot before diving from the dry bank. As I glided through the icy depths, the temperature change nearly caused me to slip into shock. I felt as though my heart had stopped as I sank deeper into the near freezing water. After allowing myself to sink a bit farther, I forced myself to the surface.

With a gasp, I surfaced. Slowly, I swam to the low bank and warmer, shallow water. I braced myself against the bank with my left arm as I slicked back my hair with my right. I wavered there for a moment before pulling my shaking form to dry ground. The cool breeze hit me once more, leaving me to shiver worse than before. I collapsed on the shadowed ground and tried to regain my breath and steady my racing pulse. I hadn't remembered the quarry being that cold before.

As I stretched out on the hardened ground and tried to calm my nerves, I began to hazily remember the night I fell through the docks. I closed my eyes to ward off the increasing images only to have them strengthen. The sound of breaking boards filled my ears as impending darkness appeared below me. A feeling of disorientation that led to terror, gripped me in its cruel grip. As I tried to gasp for breath, I could feel distant arms grab my limp body and raise me. Even more distant were the desperate cries of young Kingston.

"Ian," I heard him cry out. "Ian, do ye hear me, lad! Damn it, don't you die on me! I won't let you die on me! You're all I've got!"

It was then that I realized what had happened that fateful night on the docks. As I began to put the pieces of my shattered memory together, I realized what Deos meant when he informed me of why I didn't recall anything, "Of course ye don't, lad. Ye were dead." He had saved me. He pulled my lifeless body from the Thames and brought me back.

His modesty kept him from telling me and I never got the chance to thank him. I realized, too late, all that he had done for me. He gave me back my life twice and I would never be able to express my gratitude or ever begin to repay him. He took the secret to his grave. He knew it would have forever altered the nature of our relationship and like me, he longed for normality – even if a lie was the only way to create the illusion.

I started to reality to find that I was no longer alone. Standing next to a neglected elm tree stood a young girl who couldn't have been a day over sixteen. I stared captivated by her large, dark eyes. Stray strands of ashen hair fell clumsily over her heart-shaped face from the tightly pulled ponytail on the top of her head. Strong farmer-tanned arms were crossed over the ample breasts she concealed under a loose tank top and long, muscular legs emerged from a pair of mid-length cut-off shorts. A mischievous grin passed her lips as she gazed over my damp, semi-naked body.

"The queen of hearts," she commented as I rose.

"What!" I expounded.

"Your boxers."

I was struck by the immediate realization that I was standing half naked in front of a strange girl. Suddenly, I once again became the odd, awkward, clumsy teenage outcast I had tried so hard to overcome. I stood in embarrassment as I feebly tried to cover what I could with my hands. Almost in answer to an unspoken prayer, she threw my clothes at me. As I pulled my trousers from my face, I turned to face the water.

"Do you mind?" I demanded.

"Jesus!" she cried. "You don't have anything I haven't seen before!"

I was rather distressed by the implications of that comment. She seemed awfully young to me, too young. I wasn't completely naive to the possibility that her purity had been sullied, but somehow I couldn't accept it.

"I have two brothers. Seeing a man in his boxers is nothing new to me," she finished much to my relief. A mild burden seemed to lift, as I was reassured that my first impression had been correct. The Midwestern girl next door did, indeed still exist. "But, if you're that self conscious, I'll turn around."

I struggled nervously with my trousers until I crashed to the ground with a dull thud. I heard a muffled laugh from the girl as I jumped to my feet and finished buttoning the waistline. She slowly turned around to reveal the smirk on her sun kissed face as I realized I was at least presentable. There was a palpable tension between us that left me feeling like nothing more than a dirty old man. I was repulsed by the attraction I felt towards her. It felt wrong and I couldn't forgive myself for recognizing it.

"What are you doing here?" I demanded. After all, I wasn't accustomed to strange women seeing me in my boxers – at least not uninvited ones anyway.

"I was out for a hike when I saw your clothes on the upper bank. I thought you might need them," she sheepishly explained.

"How long have you been standing there?"

"Long enough. What happened to your arm and face?"

The nerve! I didn't even know her and she was drilling me about my scars. Mainly out of embarrassment and spite, I decided to give her something to talk about.

"My last victim got a good shot in before I strangled her!" I sneered.

"There's no need to be hostile," she snapped.

"You're the one drilling me with questions!"

I bent over, picked my shirt off the ground and threw it over my shoulder. I brushed past the girl and started towards the Mercedes. As I began to climb the hill, I became aware that I was being followed. As I reached the top of the hill and the Mercedes, I jumped over the driver's door and slid into the seat.

"Nice car," she stated. "Where'd ya get it?"

"I stole it," I countered, "from an annoying little girl!"

I spun the tires and sped off leaving her engulfed in a cloud of brown dust. I drove for hours along the gravel back roads. Regardless of how cold hearted I may have become; I retained some of the sympathy that was my downfall so many times before. I felt terrible about the way I acted towards that poor girl. She never really said or did anything to deserve the way I treated her. Just because I was caught off guard was no reason to take my embarrassment out on her and the damnedest part, I knew it.

I returned to Gus' farm around midnight. I still didn't feel myself, but then again, I really didn't know who I was anymore. I was still guilt stricken over the way I treated that girl, but I convinced myself it was for the best. As I turned into the worn gravel drive, I was met by Gus' figure on the tailgate of his Ford. He raised a hand as I shone the headlights on him. A half empty bottle of whiskey sat next to him wavering between the ribs of the tailgate.

As I emerged from the Mercedes, I was met by Gus' question of, "Did you get some?"

"What do you mean by that?" I snapped.

"You'd been gone so long, I thought you might have gotten lucky."

Gus may have been what could be loosely termed a male slut, but I was trying to change my degenerate ways. Besides, I had a lot worse things on my mind than sex; in fact it was the last thing on it. Guilt was a terrible thing, even to a cold-hearted bastard like me. Gus followed me into the house where I collapsed onto the couch and threw my arm over my eyes. I wanted to sink into the cushions and never emerge. A portal to the darkest depths of hell could have opened below me and I wouldn't have batted an eye. I would have welcomed it openly.

"You look like your best friend just died," Gus stammered drunkenly.

"You forget, my dear Fabius," I explained, "he already did."

"What happened to you today?"

I didn't feel much like discussing the day's events, especially to my drunk great-uncle. I was guilt-ridden and hated what I had become. Part of me wanted to get drunk and howl at the moon while another part just wanted a cup of tea. I was perpetually in conflict internally, externally, and every way between. Physically, emotionally, and mentally I was coming apart like a worn out rag doll.

"Have a drink, my boy," he stated.

"I'm trying to cut down," I replied forlorn.

"Too good to drink with your old uncle?"

I slowly lowered my arm and stared into Gus' reddened face. "No," I bluntly stated, "but you wouldn't like me much if I drank right now. Besides, you drink that rotgut bourbon. That stuff'll kill ya. I know, I tried."

I ran into the girl from the quarry two days later as I wandering through town. At first, she didn't see me, but when she realized who I was, she raced to avoid me. I should have just pretended that I had never seen her, but something (that strangely resembled remorse) prompted me to act and I began to desperately chase her down. I had to have been a frightening sight to her. She was being chased by some rude, scarred-up Indian who had to be crazy because he sounded British and drove a British car. At times, I wasn't sure what to make of myself.

"I'll scream!" she called.

"Please," I stated as I grabbed her arm. "I only want to apologize for how I acted."

She looked at me puzzled then slowly relaxed.

"Will you let go of my arm!" she demanded as she summed up her courage.

"Of course," I replied as I released my grip. "Will you listen to me?"

"You have one minute, then I'll scream!"

I took in a deep, cleansing breath before I began, "I had no right to treat you like I did. It was stupid, arrogant, and inconsiderate. And it's been eating at me every waking moment since. I just hope you can find it in your heart to forgive me."

A blank stare would be my only answer and forlorn, I turned and walked away – my head low and my hands in the pockets of my jeans. I wouldn't see her again for several days until Gus' friend, Mick, came over to get the riding lawn mower.

She was sitting in the passenger side of a beaten up Chevy Silverado pickup. She was twirling her fingers through her bronze hair as she stared out the window at Dumb Ass. I kept my distance in the house and watched out a picture window in the living room. I wanted to go out and talk to her, but shame kept me in the shadows like some degenerate stalker.

Over the course of time, Gus and Mick would find things for Sarah and I to do together. Every weekend for close to two months found us locked in the cab of Gus' pickup on one errand or another until eventually, the ice melted and we became close friends.

# Chapter Twenty-Four
## When the Cat's Away…
## The Snake Will Play

"Let them hate provided they fear."
{Lucius Accius, 170-86 BC}

"I never thought this would happen to me," Sarah sobbed uncontrollably as I cradled her on Gus' couch.

It all started soon after Sarah began working for Paul's wife, Meg, as a waitress. Paul and Meg had been married forty years and their granddaughter, Mary, worked with Sarah on the weekends and Mary's mother, Barb, worked days for her elderly parents. At first, everything went well.

Sarah became quick friends with Meg and Barb. Business was slow in the afternoons following school, but that didn't bother her much. It gave her a little extra cash and something to do. Most of the time she wouldn't see Paul until after the restaurant closed and he stopped to pick up Meg on his way home from his job at the steel plant.

Sarah's troubles with Paul began innocent enough. There was the occasional pat on the backside or comment of, "I'm a dirty old man," and she thought nothing of it. Her two best friends were sophomore boys with twisted minds. Together, the three dubbed themselves *The Pervert Squad*.

As the voice of experience and having had considerable years on the three, I fell into a guru-style role. I related tales of goldfish eating contests, drunken nights in Sydney, and adolescent hijinks. I, did however, give full disclosure that I neither condoned nor participated in Benton's legendary debaucheries. Even so, the boys worshiped me like the Greek god of Nerdom.

Things didn't escalate until after Paul retired that April. Meg became seriously ill with cancer a few short weeks later and was hospitalized for several more. During the weeks following her colostomy and cancer treatments, Paul began spending more and more time at the restaurant, which was fine by Sarah. He was part owner after all. Many times it would only be Sarah and Paul in an empty diner just waiting for closing time.

Sarah in her child-like naiveté was oblivious to his lecherous intentions until the unthinkable happened. Barb was sitting at one end of the break booth and Paul sat in the corner across from her. Sarah was early for her shift and sat down next to Paul to catch up on the day's events – certainly nothing out of the ordinary.

Sarah had a bubbly personality and delighted in the conversation and company of everyone in the restaurant. Besides that, it was her unending sense of loyalty that kept her around. She enjoyed a good story and most of the customers had one ready at hand when they saw her.

After Barb left to finish up in the kitchen, Sarah kept her seat and stared through the large, plate glass window to the country highway and grain elevator beyond. The pre-storm darkened sky was an odd blue with the wind swirling up rogue dust on the empty highway. As if echoing the emptiness outside, not a soul had been in all afternoon leaving Paul to decide to call it quits early.

The prospect of any future customers looked grim and a storm entered from the west leaving Sarah pondering the rest of the night's endeavours. She thought Paul to be unusually quiet, but attributed it to Meg's worsening condition. Sarah flinched as Paul placed his hand on her thigh. She wiggled in her seat in a vain attempt to signal him to remove his hand.

He did just the opposite. He inched his hand up her thigh, rubbed it against her crotch and began to unzip her jeans. In silent terror, she jumped up and began to refill the napkins. She didn't want to be anywhere near him. Her skin crawled and her mind raced as she frantically tried to keep busy and for the first time prayed for the end of her shift.

I asked why she didn't just quit then and tell Meg and Barb. The only answer I got was that she didn't want to crush Meg and she didn't think anyone would believe her if she reported it anyway.

Meg had been the first person to give her a job. She figured that Meg and Barb would side with Paul when he denied the incident even happened. So, she resigned to keep quiet and act as though nothing had happened. She put up a front and convinced everyone, that everything was fine. Even the boys and I were oblivious to what had happened.

For weeks, things returned to a semblance of normal. Sarah was able to find ways to avoid being alone with Paul and no one was the wiser to what had happened. Not even me. We would get together after she left work and play darts. In the weeks following the incident she never spoke a word of it to anyone. To this day, she hasn't even told her grandfather. She feared what Mick would do had he known what Paul had done.

Eventually, Meg returned to work and things quickly returned to much as they had been before she left. It was at least a short reprieve for Sarah. But faced with the prospect that she was never going to get better, Meg resigned to sell the café to a former German beauty queen and her much younger Arab boyfriend from the next town.

Sarah couldn't stand to be in the same room as the new owner. Something about her presence made Sarah so nervous that she would fumble things. After an occurrence involving a tray of coffee cups, Sarah resolved that she wouldn't stay on after the German and Arab took over.

I drove Sarah to pick up her final paycheck from Paul. Paul was alone in the café when we pulled up in Sarah's rusted 1982 gold T-Bird. I watched her cautiously enter the back door. I waited on the wooden porch and began to smoke a cigarette. My concern was raised when I heard the click of the lock shortly after she entered the building. I became more nervous when she seemed to take longer than usual. As I paced in worry, I heard Sarah cry out, "No! Please!"

I didn't hesitate a moment longer. I tried the knob and then kicked in the painted steel door. Paul had Sarah pinned to the refrigerator. His lecherous hands and grizzled mouth were all over her. When I stormed in, he let her go and turned to face me. He had a large red mark on his jaw where she had punched him.

"Good girl!" I thought.

"You sick, bastard!" I cried as I grabbed him by the throat and pushed him against the nearby steam table.

I quickly gazed at Sarah to assess the damage. Her eyes were wide with shock and her hands were trembling. Her breathing was staggered with stifled sighs as she attempted to regain her composure and steady her racing pulse. Otherwise, she was physically unharmed.

"When a woman says no, she means NO!" I informed the terrified mass before me. I moved my hand down and grabbed the straps of his bib overalls, looked him dead in the eye and wanted to tell him exactly what I thought of him, but all I could only bring myself to utter these few words, "If I ever catch you doing this again, I'll kill you!"

With thus said, I let go, pulled two, hundred dollar bills from my pocket and stuffed them into the straps of his bibs. "For damages to the door," I stated as I took Sarah's shaking arm and started for the door. I looked back at the old man trembling in fear and told him, "You need help."

I tried to convince Sarah to press charges, but she wouldn't hear of it. She only wanted to try and put it all behind her. I could tell that emotionally, she was shattered and unable to cope with serious relationships. In the years following the attack, I watched her float from relationship to relationship, but none ever lasted for more than a few months.

But that night, all I could do was console her the best I could. As I caressed her in my arms and my shoulder became soaked in tears, I forced back the urge to find Paul and kill him for destroying the part of her I admired most, her child-like innocence.

# Chapter Twenty-Five
## The Date

"Up the well-known creek."
{Margery Allingham, 1965}

Several years had passed since our first encounter at the quarry. It took several weeks of gentle coaxing, but eventually, I convinced Sarah to go out on a date with me. By this time, she was a sophomore in college and had just turned twenty-one. We had often thought there was a conspiracy between Mick and Gus to get us together for quite some time. Mick would call me over to help with the most trivial of things – things I knew he was more than capable of handling on his own. And like clockwork, Sarah would either be sunning in her two-piece swimsuit or on her way to town. Mick would always come up with some lame excuse for the two of us to ride together and we would get a good laugh out of it.

I spent the majority of "Date Day" washing, waxing, re-waxing and waxing yet again, the Mercedes. I even went to the trouble to neetsfooting the leather and polishing every piece of chrome, down to the window cranks and radio knobs. I had to do something to ward off the growing nervous anticipation. At that point, I was still in a state of shock from her acceptance.

Our night began with a drive to Capital City for dinner at eight, followed by drinks and dancing at a nearby dance hall. Sarah was stunning in a long black halter-top dress slit to the thigh on either side and black knee high boots with four inch stiletto heels. She had her long hair pulled up into a bun with wispy curls falling around her heart-shaped face. I was astonished by the fact that she wore makeup. I had always found her attractive, even plain faced in cut offs and tank tops. That night, I lost my heart.

All eyes were upon us as we entered the dance hall and sat down at the bar. An uncomfortable feeling overwhelmed me as I realized the group was thinking me a dirty old man with a little girl. I was thirty-two and she was barely twenty-one, but looked more like fifteen. After a couple of drinks and some nervous silence, I summoned the courage to ask her to dance. I rose from my seat and extended my hand. She looked puzzled at first, then took a firm grip and followed me onto the dance floor.

At first we danced with disquieting distance between us. Then slowly, Sarah drew in closer until she rested her head on my chest. At that moment, everything else disappeared and we were the only two in the room. When the song ended, I brushed back a lock of her hair and gently caressed her cheek.

"I've been waiting for this for years," I stated as she peeped up at me.

As we returned to our seats through the mass of moving people, I heard muffled whispers emanate from a corner table behind us. I knew Sarah had heard it, too. I had tried so hard to make things perfect for her that night, but a few small-minded individuals were determined to ruin it.

"I didn't know it was prom night," one commented.

"I wonder where he found her, the school yard," another interjected.

"Looks more like the cradle to me," a third stated and the group immediately began to roar with laughter.

The last comment did it for me. If there was one thing I couldn't stand it was a bunch of obnoxious drunks insulting a woman. Obnoxious drunks in general I could handle, after all I was one, but I wasn't going to stand idly by and let them insult the woman I was with.

"Do you have a problem?" I enquired of the group as I helped Sarah to her seat.

"Please, don't, Ian," she pleaded.

The sound of those words flooded back memories of her attempted rape. Images of Paul holding her against the refrigerator and her cries of, "No! Please don't!" filled my ears and fuelled my already enraged temper.

"They're drunk," she finished.

"It's no excuse," I replied.

Fear and pain swelled in her tender eyes as I turned to face the aggressors. A short, heavy man stood up to face me.

"What's it to you? You blanket-back cradle robber?" he demanded.

"Ian, we should just go home," Sarah tried to soothe. "They're idiots! Just let it go!"

I just glared at the man, then turned to look at Sarah. She was fighting to hold back tears of hurt that were swelling her eyes and turning the lids puffy and red. Slowly, a single tear trickled down her cheek and I lost all control. I grabbed the man by the throat and forced his head to the bar.

"I think you owe the lady an apology," I demanded.

A second man knocked me in the back of the head with an empty beer bottle. A momentary weakness tried to buckle my knees, but I held fast. I knocked the man in the diaphragm with my elbow then immediately brought the back of my hand up against his face. After which, I grabbed him by the collar and forced him to the bar next to his friend. A third began to approach, but stood still when I scowled at him.

"Would you like to play, too?" I rasped evilly.

The man shook his head and sat down. The bartender came from around the bar, stood at the side and watched with arms folded. He looked at Sarah and then at me and smiled. He was enjoying the show. He'd grown tired of their mouths as well. That was the only reason I wasn't contending with the bouncer, as well.

"Now then, lads," I continued. "About that apology."

The pair trembled in fear as apologies began to spew from their mouths like a levy broken on the Mississippi. Their eyes stared at me wide in terror as they wondered what horrors awaited them next. I found a certain satisfaction in their fear-prompted grovelling. I have always been able to manage taunts and insults. I'd heard most of them at one time or another growing up. But, the one thing I couldn't tolerate was insulting a woman.

"That's all I wanted," I stated as I released my grip. "By the way, she does happen to be twenty-one."

I pulled a handkerchief from my breast pocket and wiped my hands. I then took Sarah's hand, raised it to my lips and said, "Shall we?"

We passed the bartender who shook his head in disbelief as

181

I reached into my pocket. I pulled a fifty out and concealed it in my hand.

"I apologize for the scene," I stated.

"They had it coming. You're one crazy son-of-a-bitch, man. Don't worry; they won't be back for quite a while. I threw them out a couple of nights ago and after you, I don't think they'll want to come back. I hope you two will be, though."

"Thanks, mate," I replied as I pulled my hand away and left the bartender holding the fifty. I then led Sarah from the building. As we reached the car, she gave me a stern shove and demanded, "What the hell did you think you were doing back there?"

"I couldn't let them insult you," I tried to explain. "They had no right to talk about you like that!"

"I don't care what people think," she continued. "People talk, so what! They're assholes! That doesn't give you the right to beat the hell out of them!"

Always my conscience. I reached up, gently caressed her cheek and then began to lean in. At first, she was startled by the gesture and shoved me away, but eventually relaxed. I pressed my lips to hers as she reached around the back of my head. I briefly winced with pain and Sarah pulled her hand away.

"Ian, you're bleeding!" she cried.

"I am?" I asked, surprised.

It was only then that I felt the blood run cold down my neck and drizzle to the middle of my back. I reached for a clean handkerchief and pressed it firmly to the glass riddled wound. With the other hand, I pulled the keys from my pocket and handed them to her.

"Looks as though you're driving, love," I stated matter-of-factly.

I backed up and let Sarah pass. I cocked my head to the side to watch her wiggle as she walked around the car to the driver's seat. There was a gentle shake of her breasts as she plopped into the driver's seat and placed the keys in the ignition. I sat in the passenger seat and slid down until my head was level with the dash.

"You should go to the hospital," she pleaded as she started the engine.

"Just take me home," I beseeched as my head began to

throb with pain.

"Are you sure?"

I snapped a little more than I should have when I replied, "Just take me home!" After a moment's contemplation and the sight of her flinch at the sound of my voice, I lamented, "I'm sorry. Could you just please, take me home."

"Home it is, then," she stated as we pulled from the parking space.

I closed my eyes, but never slept as silence gripped the car for the remainder of the two and a half hour drive home. With the handkerchief pressed tightly to my head, I wondered how things could have gone so terribly wrong that night. I thought that after all the time Sarah and I had spent as friends, my stubborn, arrogant pride would ruin everything.

When Sarah dropped me off at home, I stumbled to the house to find Gus waiting in his chair. A grin passed his lips as he shook his head at my arrival.

"Looks as through you had quite the time," he commented.

"Please don't start," I pleaded as I pulled the handkerchief from the head.

I collapsed onto the couch with a heavy sigh. I felt so drained and heart sick that I never even bothered to clean up, least of all change clothes. I only rose from the couch to get a six-pack from the fridge and a fifth of Islay Scotch from my private stock, then spent the remainder of the night with my head in a bottle and a cigarette hanging from my lips.

# Chapter Twenty-Six
## Remorse

"I would rather feel remorse than know how to
define it."
{Thomas a'Kempis, 1380-1471}

I was awakened by the smell of strong coffee. The back of
my head throbbed as I rose from the couch and staggered into the
bathroom. The small, chequered arm sleeve from the couch was
stuck to my hair by clumps of brown, dried blood. I held my hair
by a makeshift ponytail and braced myself as I peeled the sleeve
from my head and set it on the sink.

"Afternoon, boy!" Gus chimed as he passed by the
bathroom door.

"Afternoon!" I gasped. "What bloody time is it?" I peeked
out the door to a gold-framed clock at the end of the hall. It was a
quarter past two. "Why didn't you wake me?"

"Figured you could use the rest," Gus explained. "But I
was gettin' to wonder if you'd ever wake up."

With that, I finished cleaning up and emerged from the
bathroom wrapped in a terry cloth towel. Gus sat in the kitchen
with an Army surplus field radio that Sarah and Mick had picked
up at an estate auction the weekend before. The top was torn off as
Gus rummaged through the circuits and wires.

"Where the hell did you get that thing?" I asked.

Apparently, Gus wasn't listening. He just reached for a
pair of wire cutters and continued to tinker with the radio. I just
shook my head and proceeded to my room. I changed into a pair
of worn blue jeans and a torn tee shirt. As I passed by my
occupied great-uncle I stated, "I'm going to the back forty to chop
some fire wood."

"Have fun, boy," Gus mumbled.

I had the distinct sentiment that I was being ignored and just to prove my point I added, "While I was out I thought I'd bring back a couple hookers."

"Have a nice time…Bring me back a blond," he jested. "Didn't think I was listening, did you?"

"Asshole!" I stepped from the house and walked lazily to the large tool shed, grabbed the chainsaw in one hand, the splitting axe in the other, and wandered to the vast woods at the end of the property. Time passed quickly as I brought dead tree after dead tree crashing to the ground.

After I was satisfied that we would have enough wood to fuel the furnace through winter, I turned my attention to the chopping block. The block was nothing more than a well-worn stump scored with years of scars.

By then, the sun was beyond its peak in the sky and my shirt was soaked through. I peeled the sad soaked wretch of a shirt over my head, wiped my brow, gave it a toss, and began to chop. As I began to hack away, my mind began to wander over the previous night's events.

"What the hell was I thinking?" I expounded with the first chop. Flying splinters bounced from my bare chest, but brought little to no attention from me.

"The only good thing to happen to you in years and you throw it away!" I continued with a second blow.

"Stupid!" with a third.

"Arrogant!"

"Self-absorbed!"

As I raised the axe for a sixth swing, I heard a voice behind me ask, "Talk to yourself much?"

I was so shocked by the intrusion that I turned with axe still in hand, ready to swing. Then, much to my surprise, I saw Sarah standing in all her glory in a pair of shorts and a low cut tank top. I dropped the axe head to the ground and leaned, panting, on the handle.

"Do you have a death wish?" I asked. "You know better than to sneak up on me like that."

"Sorry," she relented. "So, this what English Lords do in their spare time?"

"Not very distinguished, is it? But fox hunts were never my style."

I picked my shirt off the ground and wiped my brow and neck. The back of my head began to sting from the sweat as I passed the soaked shirt across my neck.

"How's your head?" Sarah asked.

"I'll live," I replied matter-of-factly. "I'm surprised you're here."

"I brought your car back."

My heart fluttered as the thought that our relationship, along with our friendship, was irreversibly over, overwhelmed me. Whether it had been my brazen attitude, stubborn pride or explosive temper was meaningless at that point. I had destroyed what possibly was my last true chance at happiness.

A mischievous grin passed Sarah's lips as she pulled a six-pack of *Red Dog* bottles from behind her back.

"I thought you might be thirsty," she commented. "Consider this a peace offering."

"I'm the one who should be lighting the pipe after last night," I pointed out.

We spent the remainder of the afternoon into early evening lounging in the sun together drinking the beer. Elation filled me as the sun warmed our shoulders. Slowly, we melted into each other's arms as we lay in the lush grass. I leaned in to kiss her as my hands slowly wandered down the length of her back. She raised a hand to my chest and gently pushed me away.

"Not yet, Ian," she pleaded. "I made a promise that I wouldn't until I was married."

I was momentarily aghast by the statement. At first, I thought she was joking, but then I saw the sincerity in her eyes. I moved my hand and sat up. Looks AND integrity, certainly more than I had bargained for.

"You're mad, aren't you?" she began to cry.

I gently gripped her chin and turned her sorrowed head towards me. "No," I reassured. "Quite the opposite, actually. I respect it. I've never been with anyone that thought that much of themselves. I think it's admirable."

At that point, she was more shocked than I. She thought I would be like all the others and dump her like last week's garbage because she wouldn't "put out". I may have been an arrogant son-of-a-bitch, but even that wasn't my style.

"You're not just saying that, are you?" she questioned.

"Of course not," I continued. "There's a lot more to a relationship than sex. Tell you what, we'll go to the house and I'll shower. Afterwards, I'll take you to supper."

We walked arm in arm back to the house. I carried the chainsaw and Sarah carried the axe. After a stop at the tool shed, we entered the house. Gus was sitting in his chair with a glass of *Wild Turkey* and his pipe.

"Hey, Gus!" Sarah expounded as we entered the living room.

"Hi, Goofy!" Gus returned. "How's Mick?"

"Fine. He said he'd be by sometime next week with your riding mower."

Sarah's grandfather and Gus had been friends for years and exchanged so many things. Gus at any one time had at least fifteen of Mick's things, so what was one lousy lawn mower.

"Did you figure out what was wrong?" Gus enquired.

"Turns out the plug was fouled," she explained.

I wandered back to the kitchen as Sarah sat down across from Gus. As I opened the refrigerator, I called around the door, "Can I offer you something to drink?"

"No, thanks," she replied. "I think I've had enough."

Gus turned in his chair and addressed me, "Before I forget, someone called for you from London. He wanted you to call right away."

"London?" I asked, shocked. "They didn't happen to say what it was about?"

"No, but he left a number."

I grabbed a beer and wandered to the phone. Taped to the receiver was the number for Kingston Hall. Dread filled me as I nervously dialled the phone. After three rings, one of the staff answered. I was shocked that it wasn't Jonesie.

"Kingston Hall," the man's voice answered.

"This is Lord John," I stated.

"Your Lordship, I'm so glad you called. Although I am surprised that crude servant of yours remembered to give you the message. Really, sir, you must consider finding new help..."

My patience was beginning to wear thin with Fairchild.

"...I'll replace you if you don't tell me what is going on," I threatened. "Why didn't Jonesie answer?"

"That is what is wrong, sir. Mr. Jones has taken ill," Fairchild explained.

"What happened?"

"He has had a stroke, sir."

I couldn't believe what I was hearing. Even though I knew a day like that would eventually come, I was still never prepared for it.

"I'll take care of everything when I arrive," I decided. "Let Jonesie know that I'm on my way. I'll be on the first plane out."

With that, I hung up the phone and turned to Sarah. She looked concerned as I gently grabbed her shoulders.

"I'm afraid I'll have to give you a rain check on dinner, love," I stated.

"Unless you'd rather have breakfast in London," Sarah suggested. "I have some money set aside for college this fall."

"I'll not hear of it!" I snapped. "I can't have you spending your life savings to follow me halfway across the earth!"

She looked devastated as the words hovered over her in a dark cloud.

"I'll take care of everything," I guaranteed to her immediate joy. "Do you need a passport?"

# Chapter Twenty-Seven

## Bring Out Your Dead

"When we attend the funerals of our friends
We grieve for them,
But when we go to those of other people
It is chiefly our own deaths that we mourn for."
{Gerald Brenan, 1978}

We arrived in London late the following afternoon. Heathrow was unnaturally busy and we found ourselves fighting just to exit the terminal. I could tell that Sarah was tired from the long flight. Her eyes were heavy and she seemed to move slower than normal. Forcing our way through the crowd didn't seem to help her already tired disposition.

"Do you want to go straight to the Hall first?" I questioned.

"Can we stop somewhere to eat?" she propositioned. "I'm famished."

I took her to a nice restaurant in Trafalgar Square overlooking the statue. As always, the Square was a blanket of pigeons from the little old ladies and their sacks of bread. After a pleasant and relaxing meal, I hailed a taxi to escort us to Kingston Hall. As we approached the gates of the estate, Sarah's eyes widened as she gaped in awe.

"That bad?" I asked with a cheeky grin.

"You told me it was nice," she explained, "but I never expected Buckingham Palace!"

"Really! Buckingham Palace is much smaller."

I gave her a sarcastic grin as we stopped before the marble steps that led to the bronze doors. Fairchild stood between the lions to meet us. A stoic look was upon his face as he rushed to open the door of the taxi as it glided to a stop. I stepped from the taxi with Sarah close behind as the driver opened the boot for Fairchild to unload our bags.

"Welcome home, your Lordship," he stated. "I trust you and the miss had a pleasant flight."

"You don't want to know," Sarah whispered in my ear. She was visibly exhausted. Her usual youthful vigour was gone, replaced by a drained exasperation. Her face was drawn and haggard with dark circles encasing her gentle eyes.

"Fairchild, would you help Sarah to her room," I instructed. "If you would, place her in the room across the corridor from me."

"Very good, sir," Fairchild replied. "There is brandy and sweets awaiting you in the sitting room."

"Thank you, Fairchild," I replied. "That will be all for now."

Fairchild nodded a bow in acceptance and walked into the house. He didn't have quite the same impact on me that Jonesie did the first time I met him. Fairchild was far younger. Quite possible in his late thirties or early forties. His hair was jet black and slicked back with a shine. In fact, I had often thought if he wore dark glasses and spoke German, he could pass for Falco. Sarah looked a little reluctant to follow him, but I gave her a nudge and sent her on her way.

"Go on, I prodded. "I know you're exhausted. Fairchild's an all right chap, if he weren't, he wouldn't be working for me. Jonesie handpicked him. I'll see you in the sitting room later."

With that, I bent over and gave her a reassuring kiss on the forehead and another nudge. She reluctantly followed, looking a bit like a condemned man on his last walk. I watched until she disappeared up the stairwell then I retired to the sitting room for brandy and cakes.

It felt strange to be back within the confines of the Hall. The staff had done a magnificent job on the restoration. If it weren't for Deos' untouched study, I wouldn't have believed it was the same estate. I was uncomfortable with the luxury at first, but slowly began to adjust. Even years later, I had a hard time accepting the fact that it was all mine. I would return once a year to tend to affairs, but the Hall was never really home. There was an empty coldness that gripped me every time I entered and made me feel as if I were a guest in my own home.

One of the first things I did was to keep many of the paintings from the stairwell untouched. My only addition to the Kingston ancestral wall was a commissioned portrait of Deos. Of course, I had to have it three times larger than all the others and placed in prominence at the top of the first stairwell platform, just under the stained glass window, where the stairs turned to continue to the second floor. I wanted it to be the first thing anyone saw when they entered Kingston Hall. Jonesie at first mildly protested, but when the work was finished and the painting was seen in all its glory, he was as pleased as I.

After resting comfortably in a plush lavender chair before the fire, I decided to pay Jonesie a visit. After all, he was the reason I was here. I thought it best to find Sarah and let her know where I was going. As I paused before her open door, I resisted knocking for fear of waking her. From somewhere inside, I heard the hollow rustle of drawers.

With a cockeyed smile, I knocked to hear the cheerful chime of, "Come in!" I entered to find Sarah's suitcase open upon the bed and she was leaned over one of the drawers unpacking. I paused for a moment and watched her backside as it gently waved back and forth, then approached and grabbed her by the waist, pulling her close.

"I have to leave for a bit," I apologized. "I'll be back as soon as I can."

"Where are you going?" she asked timidly as I held her tightly before the large, antique mirror.

"I'm going to the hospital to see Jonesie. You can go along if you want, or I can drop you somewhere if you want to sight see."

She looked peculiarly at me through the mirror before she said, "I think I'll come with you. I don't want to sit around here by myself."

I pulled the Bentley from the garage and drove into town with Sarah in the passenger seat. As we pulled into the hospital parking lot, I was struck with the memory of the night of Deos' death. Phantoms of the past gripped my fluttering heart in a cold grip and caused me to hesitate entering the building as it momentarily stole my breath and lightened my head.

"What's wrong?" Sarah asked.

"Nothing," I lied.

With a heavy sigh, I entered the sliding glass doors that led to the main floor lobby and made my way to the information desk. The girl behind the counter smiled a faint smile as I approached.

"Can I help you?" she asked.

"Yes, actually," I replied. "I'm here to see Mr. Trevor Jones."

"He's in room 515."

I was taken back. It was Deos' death room. I would have to see to Jonesie's immediate move. I thanked the girl and we proceeded to the elevators. We passed a father and his young dark haired son as we entered the quickly closing doors. When we reached Jonesie's room, he had his bed propped up and was reading a collection of poetry by D.H. Lawrence.

"You still read that crap!" I exclaimed as Sarah and I stepped into the room.

Sarah strode behind as I approached Jonesie's bed. The effects of the stroke were evident on his aged face. His eyes were still bright with the same youthfulness they had always possessed and half his mouth curled into a childlike grin as he laid the book aside. He held out a long, leathered arm as I approached. My mind painfully flashed between past and present as images of Deos in that same bed mingled with Jonesie like the pages of a flipbook.

"Master Ian!" he stated, pleased. "I can't believe you're here. I expressly told Fairchild not to bother you with this unfortunate mess."

"How could he not?" I replied as I sat upon the edge of his hospital bed.

Sarah tugged at my arm and I turned my head to find her standing uncomfortably at my side.

"I should leave you two to talk," she commented. "I'll be in the cafeteria."

I pulled out some money and handed it to her. "Take this," I explained. "I'll catch up with you later."

"It was nice to meet you," she addressed Jonesie. "I've

heard so much about you from Ian."

And with that, she was gone.

Jonesie winked at me and asked, "And who might that have been?"

"Sarah Donahue," I replied.

"Reminds me of my Sadie. I never told you about her, did I?" I shook my head as he continued, "We were married a long time, twenty years to be exact. She passed a long time ago. If it hadn't been for the Kingstons, I don't know what I would have done. That boy was a godsend."

I knew he was speaking of Deos. I had often thought the same thing. He was never meant for this world. Men like him come along once in a generation, only to burn out and fade far too soon. As I watched Jonesie pour his soul out to me on that narrow bed, I felt closer to him than ever before.

He slowly leaned over to whisper in my ear, "Keep a hold of this one, my boy. Don't ever look back. You'll be glad you did."

He then laid his head back onto his pillow and drifted into a sedative induced sleep. I stood up and proceeded from the room. I knew then that it would be the last time I would see Jonesie alive.

As I walked to the cafeteria, I tried to block the thought from my mind, but Jonesie's words kept echoing in my ears, "Don't ever look back." I found Sarah overlooking the city with a soda in her hand. As I approached, she turned around and leaned her back against the window.

"How is he?" she asked.

"Surprisingly good, I think," I replied more to convince myself than her.

She threw her arms over my shoulders as I pulled her close for comfort. I buried my nose in her strawberry-scented hair and closed my eyes. I never wanted to leave. I could have lived out my days trapped in that moment, surrounded by warmth and the gentle scent of strawberries. Slowly, Sarah pulled away, ending my serenity and returning a knot to my chest. Together, we left arm in arm.

*******

I paused to order another pitcher of beer for Gus and the Admiral, and a glass for me. I knew I'd had too much Scotch.

Gus looked at me in credence before rising from the barstool, relieved for a break. A flash of lightning lit the room followed by the sharp crack of thunder; my shaking hands gripping the glass as I tried to quell the growing uneasiness I felt. The thunder was drawing closer and it brought a sense of doom with it. When Gus returned, I continued my tale.

*******

Jonesie died the next morning. I received the call in the middle of breakfast. I had let Sarah sleep in. I knew she was still exhausted from the day before. When she finally came downstairs at ten, she could tell by the look in my dark eyes that something was wrong.

"What's wrong?" she asked still sleepy eyed.

"The hospital called early this morning," I stated. "Jonesie died."

"My god! Why didn't you wake me?"

I did my best over the following days to organize the funeral. I let the staff handle the obituary and other arrangements. Even though I tried hard to forget, our last conversation haunted me. Every time I would gaze at Sarah, I could see Jonesie's face and hear his voice echo in my head. By the day of the funeral, I was a certifiable wreck. Sarah was more than supportive through it all, I have to admit. Her patience and understanding seemed endless. No matter how apparently short-tempered or unstable I became, she would shrug it off, give me my space and return with the support I needed.

The service was brief with little ado, just as Jonesie would have wanted. There was mostly the staff in attendance and a few elderly men from town. Sarah stood at my side, gripping my arm tightly as I laid a lone rose on the casket and whispered, "Good night, sweet prince." Jonesie had always been a sucker for Shakespeare. I choked back the growing tear-laden mass in my throat that threatened to erupt a decade of pain as I was overwhelmed by the cold chill that ran down my back and tried to weaken my knees.

That night at dinner, with the words of Jonesie still reverberating in my head, I got down on one knee, my heart pounding feverishly in my chest as sweat rolled from my brow, pulled a large diamond engagement ring from my coat pocket and proposed to Sarah. Her reaction was admittedly, initially one of shock. Once the question set in and I placed the ring on her shaking finger all that changed.

"Of course!" she stated finally.

She leaned over and kissed me. It executed like some cheap romance novel. I had felt foolish doing it, but also felt it was just grandiose enough that I wouldn't be rejected. I rose to a rain of applause from the restaurant and my face blushed slightly from embarrassment. I momentarily questioned whether my answer was bore from sincerity, obligation, or pity. I brushed doubt from my mind as I took my seat and gazed at Sarah who was entranced by the glitter of the diamond.

I realized how I had thought that I had been smote in love once too often and had resigned myself to being alone. Jonesie taught me not to let the rest of my life pass by and to grab happiness when you find it. I gambled my heart that day expecting to throw snake eyes, yet again, but instead found a wife.

# Chapter Twenty-Eight

## The Appaloosa

"One is never nearer by not keeping still."
{Thom Gunn, 1957}

The plane ride from London was unusually quiet. Sarah sat in silence as she just stared out the window and rolled the engagement ring through layovers, turbulence and refuelling for close to eighteen hours. Glazed eyes and a blank expression carpeted her usually bright face with a grey haze. I feared that she had changed her mind. How could I have been so stupidly impulsive? For the second time, I had risked throwing away the one good thing to happen to me. I never seemed to learn the first time. Even as a child, I was thick. Most kids would learn after touching a hot stove the first time. It took me four.

*She's feeling pressured*, I frantically concluded as forced-back doubts and fears emerged. *I'm rushing things. I never should have opened my big mouth! She's leaving me as soon as we touch down...I'm such an asshole!* Fear crippled my reason until I could no longer deal with it and out of frustration I did what I had always done best – I ran away.

I climbed onto Sarah's primer grey and red oxide appaloosa spotted Suzuki 350, kissed Sarah's cheek goodbye and left without a word spoken. The vacant stare of Sarah as I peeled from the driveway haunted me. Her face lingered in my vision as I howled down the empty country highway. I rode for hours with only the wind, sun, and my rampant thoughts as my companions. All the scenery looked the same; dark and desolate, until eventually I arrived across the state line.

From the highway I eyed a small bar on the outskirts of a town not quite large enough to be termed "one horse." Strewn out behind the building was a long line of Harley Davidsons, cars, and beat up farmer trucks. After circling the building, I squealed to a jerky stop before the front door.

I released the kickstand, set the bike effortlessly down, and walked stiffly inside. My hands were numb from the vibration of the motor and the tires on the road - my legs stiff, numb and achy from hours of disuse. I paused in the doorway to remove my riding goggles and scanned the bar. I found an empty stool just inside the door and squeezed in amongst the plethora of farmers, hillbillies, bikers, thugs, and biker chicks. I fit in perfectly with my wind tussled long hair, ragged blue jeans, bush boots, torn sleeveless shirt, and road dust laden face.

I wiped black sweat from my brow as I sat down at the bar. A bushy bearded, aging, potbellied bartender in a stained sleeveless tee shirt three sizes too small waddled over to where I sat, passed a suspicious glance, and growled, "What do you want?"

"Double shot of Scotch with a chase of whatever you have on tap," I replied.

The bartender shrugged, got the drinks, and plopped them down before me with a grunt of, "Five fifty."

I gave him a ten and motioned to keep the change. I had my drinks along with several others as I stared off into nothingness. Emptiness gripped me as my mind flashed over the events of the past few days. All I could see were images of Jonesie laying in the hospital bed, then later in a casket, the haunting images of Deos' grave, and finally Sarah's blank stare as I rudely peeled away. Guilt, shame, and fear overwhelmed me. The alcohol only seemed to dull the thoughts that prodded at me.

I wanted to keep driving until I reached the Pacific, then drive on in. I couldn't go back. I was too afraid of what I would encounter. I was afraid that I had disappointed her. I knew I could never live up to what she deserved and it was better if I broke her heart by leaving now then putting her through a lifetime of hell later.

I was shocked back to reality by riotous laughter and a drunken cry of, "What the hell is that supposed to be?" by a group of bikers in a corner by the door.

I looked over my left shoulder to see the group gawking, pointing, and laughing at Sarah's bike. Shock and anger gripped me with rage as another member of the group cackled, "If it was a horse, I'd have it shot!"

By now I was fuming. Half drunk, I walked over to the table, stood there, and waited as one of the group voiced, "Goddamn rice burners! It probably runs on that there sack-ee!"

"It's pronounced sake, get it right!" I corrected.

"Got a problem, Chief?" another sneered.

"No, but you do. That happens to be my fiancé's bike you're insulting."

The group exploded into laughter yet again. Even the women hanging over the men's shoulders couldn't contain their amusement. I involuntarily took in a long, slow breath as I glared coldly at the group. Rage began to swell within me. Once again I was operating outside my senses and was becoming an observer in my own body.

"Yeah, and what are you going to do about it?" the instigator questioned.

At that I simply raised my eyebrow and invited, "Would you care to step outside and find out?" A giant of a man rose from the chair. My chin met his broad, hairy chest. A strong whiff of whiskey, motor oil, and body odour stung my nostrils. "I'd say after you, but I wouldn't want to be downwind."

As we exited the back door, the oaf of a man aired venomously, "You smart mouthed son-of-a-bitch! I'm gonna pound you in the dirt, little man!"

The man then punched me in the jaw with the force of a rampaging bull. I fell back onto the concrete of the parking lot. After shaking my head to clear it, I rose and charged. I forced my shoulder into the man's stomach and threw him into the bumper, then onto the hood, of a nearby car, eventually bouncing his head off the windshield. Slightly dazed, the man rose and knocked me in the chest. The blow silently stole my strength and I fell to my knees as I watched in slow motion as my opponent tried to charge once more before three other bikers pulled him back.

"The Chief's done for," one tried to soothe.

"What the hell do you think you're doing, Stumpy?" one

drilled my assailant.

"I'm gonna kill that pansy ass, blanket-back, son-of-a-bitching bastard!" my assailant cried wildly.

"Get him out of here!" a large, bearded man in a black leather jacket, tee shirt and jeans ordered.

The stranger then approached me as I tried to catch the breath that was quickly becoming shorter in my chest. He reached an arm out to help me to my feet as I stumbled unsteadily as an odd feeling like a frog jumping gripped my chest and pressure built before my shortening sight.

"You okay, dude?" he asked with genuine concern.

"Fit as rain, right as a fiddle," I confused intentionally.

The man grinned a toothy smile and stated, "Where you from, man?"

"London," I replied.

Astonished, he shook his head then stated, "How the Sam Hell did you end up clear out here?"

"Long story," I gasped.

We walked as we continued our conversation, until we arrived on the other side of the building at Sarah's bike. I swung my right leg over the seat and sat down. Tightness entrenched itself in my chest causing me to take a deep, steadying breath. My hands were still shaking when I kick started the motor, raised the kickstand, and shook the man's hand.

"You gonna be able to ride, man?" he asked noticing the tremble in my hand.

"I'll be fine, mate," I replied confidently.

"Call me 'Tiny'."

Tiny? In a way it suited him. He had the heart of a preacher in the body of a rough and tumble biker. I always had a soft spot for walking contradictions. After all, we had to stick together.

"John Phoenix," I introduced as I pulled the goggles over my eyes and prepared to leave. "Thanks again, mate."

I pulled away to the faint call of, "Cool name, man! Take it easy, dude! You got real balls!" echoing behind me.

I rode for half an hour in the dusk before arriving at the nearest hotel along the highway. I parked the bike towards the back of an empty lot and walked into the lobby. After getting a room for the night, I settled in and passed out.

The next morning, I awoke to find I had left the air conditioner on high. Goosebumps covered my body and breath clouds circled my face. I ran to the window and turned on the heater before dashing to a hot shower. The steam and heat combined to stagnant the air that cried, "Bring out your dead!" as it avoided my lungs.

Upon finishing, I emerged slightly dizzy. I wrapped my waist in a towel and lay on the bed to watch television. The chill was gone from the air and it felt good to just lay back and relax, if only briefly as I struggled to catch my breath. The ability to move seemed to elude my lethargic form. I could think of moving, but was incapable of fulfilling the action. After a half-hour of vegging on the bed, I was able to dress and prepared to leave.

Upon emerging from the building, I got the first glimpse of Sarah's spotted appaloosa. Both tires were slashed. From the shattered engine bled motor oil and gasoline. A tire iron was carelessly tossed aside in the empty parking stall beside what was left of the destroyed handlebars, gas tank, and splashguards.

Anger swelled within me as I gazed at the battered remnants of Sarah's joy. I was more concerned about how I'd explain to Sarah what happened when I eventually did go home. She had spent the sum total of her summer's savings on that bike. It was all she had talked about for weeks, even years, before she bought it. It may not have looked like much, but it was hers, lock, stock, and tailpipe. The thought of how I'd get home was the last thought on my mind at that point. I was a dead man!

Out of frustration, I kicked what was left of the bike. I had to think of what to do. All I could see was Sarah's shattered spirit scattered amongst the carnage. I knew I had disappointed her, but could not bring myself to injure her more. I convinced myself that it would be easier for her if I just disappeared. Slowly, my conscience and better judgment began to take control. After swallowing my pride, I returned to the hotel and phoned Gus. My heart sank as I listened to the seemingly endless ringing of the phone.

"You're dime, I'm wasted, speak to me," Gus groggily answered.

I hesitated before stating, "Gus, just shut up and listen. I need you to bring the truck. I'm across the state line in Everson. I'll be in the bar across the street from the *Holiday Inn* on the interstate. No questions, I'll explain when you get here."

I spent the remainder of the four-hour wait drinking myself into oblivion and trying to think of how I could ever make this up to Sarah. The fact was, no possible way existed and I knew it. I wouldn't blame her if she slapped me in the face, told me she never wanted to see me again, unless it was my funeral and then only to piss on my grave. I had a cigarette in one hand and the last of a once full bottle of scotch in the other when Gus wandered in the front door of the bar. He rushed over to me, placed his hand on my shoulder, and asked, "What happened, boy?"

"Don't ask," I surly replied. "Follow me."

I finished the Scotch and took Gus to the hotel parking lot. As we stood before the mess of twisted metal, broken plastic, and mixing fluid, Gus stared in disbelief. A muted Sutherland "Hawkeye" whistle emerged from his lips. He gazed momentarily at me, then back to the bike and shook his head in astonishment.

Without a word passed between us, we loaded the remnants of the bike into the topper-covered bed of Gus' truck. After finishing, I paused, almost shaking, before entering the passenger door. I didn't want to return to Sarah. It had nothing to do with not loving her; in fact I don't think I ever loved her more than at that moment. I couldn't stand to break her heart like this. I was an arrogant, selfish fool and it had come to not just bite me in the ass, but take a Great White's mouthful of my pride. That drive was the longest four hours of my life…

Sarah was waiting when Gus and I arrived early the following morning. I could tell by the look on her face that she had not slept and had done a considerable amount of crying. Guilt devoured me and I couldn't look her in the eye. I stepped from the truck, dropped the tailgate and raised the topper door, exposing the battered mess. Tears welled in her child like eyes as she gazed at her bike then at me before sobbing to the house.

I stood paralyzed with grief with my hand still on the topper. Pain began to swell through my left shoulder as the frog returned and my knees buckled beneath me. As I tried to catch myself on the way down, I smashed against the tailgate with my elbows. Gus heard the crash, came running to where I laid on the driveway and helped me unsteadily to my feet.

"What happened?" he asked.

"I tripped," I lied. "I'm fine."

"You go in the house. I'll finish here."

I did as Gus instructed and went inside. Sarah was sitting in Gus' chair with tears still in her eyes. She said nothing as I walked past and grabbed an ice pack from the freezer. I wrapped it in a hand towel as I made my way back to the living room. I pulled the pack of cigarettes from my pocket, laid an ashtray on the floor beside the couch and myself down with the ice pack on my aching shoulder. Just as I pulled a cigarette from the nearly empty pack and placed it to my lips, Gus entered.

"What's wrong with your shoulder?" he asked as I lit up, the colour draining from my face.

"Must have pulled my shoulder loading the bike," I replied. "Hurts like a son-of-a-bitch!"

Sarah looked up at Gus and asked, "Would you drive me home, please."

"Sure thing," Gus replied as he continued to study me with a sour look on his dark face. "Be out in a minute."

As soon as Sarah was out of the house, Gus slapped me up side of the head and demanded, "What the hell were you thinking?"

Involuntarily, I raised my fist only to be met with a sharp, "Do it, you stupid son-of-a-bitch!...You're just going to let her walk out of here without a word, aren't you?"

I lowered my head and tried to calm the frog that was attempting to emerge from my chest. "I'll talk to her in the morning."

"Ifin' you don't talk to her now, there ain't gonna be a in the morning."

I just shrugged, rolled my eyes, and turned the other way. Out of disgust, Gus left without another word spoken. I wallowed in self-pity, Turks, and Scotch until Gus' hasty return with the frog intermittently reminding me of its presence as the pain in my shoulder intensified.

# Chapter Twenty-Nine
## The Homecoming

"The rich man has his motor car,
His country and his town estate.
He smokes a fifty-cent cigar
And jeers at Fate…"
{Franklin P. Adams, 1881-1960}

Gus seemed to return in a rush. He came in the door, gazed at me in a mixture of concern and disgust, then flopped into his chair. I tried to disguise the fact that I had Two-ton Tammy sitting on my chest and a jackhammer pounding its way through, but the look on my face inevitably gave me away. The colour had drained completely away and my face was drenched in sweat.

"You ain't talking me out of this one, boy," he stated as he picked up the phone. "I'm calling Doc Gardner."

Within twenty minutes, Gus had dropped me off at the entrance to the clinic on the far side of the hospital. Upon entering, I was immediately rushed back to an examining room where an attractive young nurse took my vitals. As I sat at the edge of the narrow examining table, I glanced her over and began to feel a strange sense of arousal when she brushed against me as she reached for the blood pressure cup. Guilt swelled within me as I began to think that I had spent too much time with Gus. The old dog had begun to rub off and I wasn't at all sure that I liked it.

It seemed as though the nurse had no more than left when the doctor entered, a little more rushed than I felt warranted. Doc Gardner was a young man, about my age with dark, Mediterranean features. He had a manner I found uncommon amongst his profession – a way of making a person feel as though they were old friends.

"So what's going on today, Buddy?" he asked very conversationally. "Gus said you're having chest pain."

"Gus is a mother hen," I dismissed. "He's overreacting."

Doc then placed his stethoscope to my back then switched to my chest where he seemed to hover as he continued to speak, "Been under any strain lately?"

"Pulled my shoulder this morning moving a wrecked motorcycle," I shrugged.

He looked at the fist-sized bruise in the centre of my chest and the one on my chin, raised his brow and questioned, "Anything else I should know."

"Got in a fight with a biker across the state line. Nothing I couldn't handle. Bloke got in a cheap shot's all."

This seemed to concern the doctor. He checked my chart, what there was of it, then listened to my heart again.

"Has anyone told you, you have a heart murmur?" he asked.

"Yes, in London," I replied shocked and a bit nervous about where this was going. "Why?"

"How long have you had it?"

Now I was really beginning to get concerned. I didn't like where this was going. Fleeting images from the past cascaded me. I was once again standing in the cemetery, then awakening in the hospital. I squeezed my eyes to shut out the images, but found myself haunted by Deos in his hospital bed.

"Since '85. It showed up after I had an infected shoulder wound. I was told it was innocent. Would never cause me problems."

The doctor looked at me in concern as he stated, "John, I'd like to admit you over night for observation."

"I don't have time for this," I protested as I rose from the table.

Doc placed an arm in front of me as I attempted to leave, looked me sternly in the eye and stated, "Humour me."

There was forcefulness and determination the man exuded that made me pause. The sternness in his eyes paralyzed me and reluctantly, I relented. As I lay in the hospital bed with wires stuck across my chest, I wondered how I would break the news to Gus.

I'd have to tell him, but I didn't want Sarah to know. I'd done so much to her already. Besides, she probably wouldn't care after how I'd treated her and I really couldn't blame her.

With a nervous hand and my heart in my throat, I picked up the receiver and dialled the bar. I paused as Gus was handed the phone and nearly hung up. Relieved, I joked, "The funniest thing just happened and you'll never guess where I'm calling from…"

"They admitted you, didn't they?" he snapped with on overwhelming sense of disgust.

"It's only for observation. It's nothing big, really," I babbled. "Don't tell Sarah. I've done enough to her already."

I heard Gus exhale irritably before he barked, "Damned right you have! That poor girl's been crying her eyes out since last night because of you! Maybe while you're in there they can surgically remove your brain from your ass or else they'll be extracting my boot!"

With that, he slammed the phone. I held the receiver loosely in my hand for a moment before hanging up. I then banged my head against the headboard in frustration. All in all, it went better than I anticipated. A nurse entered the room as I finished punishing myself. She looked at me curiously as she took my vitals.

"You're blood pressure is sky high," she gasped. "Everything all right?"

"Just another day in paradise," I replied. I looked up at her as she pulled the sleeve up on my speckled hospital gown. "I've been better," I stated as I noticed her eye the scar on my neck and cheek. "Been worse, too."

"Pretty nasty scar," she commented as she inserted an IV line. "Doctor wants to start a line of nitro. If you need anything just press the call button. I'll warn you, it could give you a headache."

"Pressing the call button?" I joked.

She playfully slapped my arm, as she laughed, "No, silly, the nitro."

I thanked her as she left the room. Over the course of the remaining day and well into the next, one nurse after another came and went as I was shuttled around for this test or another. They took blood, vitals, checked leads, took X-Rays, and even ran an ultrasound of my heart. I was beginning to feel like my room should have a revolving door.

A vague fear plagued me as I was haunted by long withheld images of Deos. I wanted to believe that everyone was overreacting, but lingering doubts remained. Other than a little weak and out of breath, I felt fine. Surely it couldn't be that major; I was only thirty-two. I was in excellent shape and clean; my only vices were cigarettes and alcohol. Then, I would think of Deos. He was far younger and shared my two vices. I couldn't help but think of what happened to him and speculate if I was doomed to inherit not only his estate, but fate as well.

On one level, I didn't care much what happened to me. Then I would begin to think of Gus and Sarah and wonder how they would react. How would Gus explain to my mother that not only had I been alive all this time and had never contacted her, but now was dead – again. Losing a child once had to be hell, but I was doubling the injury.

Finally, I could take no more. When the next nurse entered, I stated, "I need a cigarette before I go bloody crackers, lass!"

She smiled sympathetically as she said, "You can't smoke in here." She lowered her voice to a near whisper as she continued, "But I just received orders to remove the nitro and there is a smoking area on the backside of the hospital on the first floor. Tell you what, if you can wait another ten minutes, I'll walk down with you on my break. I could use a smoke myself."

"I've waited this long..." I resigned, "and I have imported Turkish studs, if you're interested. Miss, you've got yourself a deal!"

Like clockwork, ten minutes later, we were on our way to the smoking area. The portable monitor box banged against my chest as it flipped on its chain as I walked. I felt like everyone's eyes were on me as I wandered through the hospital. The draftee, ill-fitted gown did little to conceal the wires that ran from my chest to the dancing box that slapped against me. Shame welled in me as I thought not only of what everyone must have been thinking, but also how I much I felt I didn't belong there. I wished it had all been some twisted nightmare and I would awaken to find a half empty bottle of Scotch in one hand and the star-filled sky above me.

Eventually, we arrived at a primitive looking shack overlooking the back parking lot. I hurried inside and lit up as the nurse entered behind me and lit a cigarette as well. She sat surprisingly close in the chilly smoke-filled shack. The wind whistled through the poorly fit Plexiglas structure from the over-cast skies and fog that threatened ominously to the approach of a severe thunderstorm.

"We don't get many like you in the cardiac unit," she stated.

"What do you mean?" I asked, confused. "I'm just here for observation and a couple of tests, it's a waste really."

"Actually, I meant young, in good shape…good looking."

I choked on my cigarette as I inhaled. Her face turned red from embarrassment and was still blushing when she asked, "So, what happened to your shoulder and face?"

"I was in the wrang place at the wrang time, lass," I replied sounding a bit more like Deos than intended.

"What?" she asked.

"Nothing. I really don't like to talk about it. My fiancé doesn't really even know."

"You're engaged?" the nurse asked shocked and a bit disappointed.

"I was. Not so sure now. I was a real asshole this weekend."

She looked at her watch and yelled, "Shit!"

"Something wrong?"

"I'm late! Sorry, have to run."

I had one more cigarette in the draftee shack before returning to my room. When I entered the room I didn't see anyone at first. Then out of the corner of my eye, I saw a dark figure huddled in a chair in the corner. I turned to find Sarah's sombre form sitting in the shadows behind the door.

"Gus told me you were here," she commented.

"I told the stubborn old son-of-a-bitch not to say anything," I ranted.

"Is it true you had a heart attack?"

I curled my lip and poshed at her. "Hell, no!" I snapped. "Gus is just overreacting."

"As a matter of fact, he isn't," a voice stated behind me.

I turned to find Doc Gardner standing behind me with my chart in his hands. A disconcerting look adorned his usually jovial face as he drummed his fingers on the manila folder.

"Give me a break," I retorted. "I'm thirty-two."

"You may want to have a seat, John," he continued. "The tests show that you've had a mild heart attack and it's not the first. There's evidence of damage from a prior attack some time ago."

"Shit, that was a decade ago!" I continued to rave. "This is bullshit!"

With a slight air of command, the doctor informed, "Any first year med student could tell from your EKG alone that you've had a heart attack. If you don't start slowing down and keeping calm, there's no guarantee that the next one won't kill you."

"Oh, my God!" Sarah began to sob uncontrollably.

I placed a hand on the bed and began to sit. "I think I'd better sit for this," I agreed, suffering an overwhelming sense of shock and irony. I wondered if this was how Deos had felt all those years ago. I could barely handle the news at thirty-two, I couldn't conceive how a fourteen-year-old had coped.

Doc Gardner continued, "It seems you've developed a restrictive myopathy. The good news, however, is we're catching it early and there isn't any enlargement of the heart."

Sarah's eyes were wide in disbelief and I found it impossible to look at her. Once again, I'd caused her pain. I was beginning to hate myself for this seemingly endless stream of injury. I was torn apart by the tears in her eyes and the pain in her face. I knew I was no good for her. She deserved better than I was putting her through.

"What's caused it?" I asked, still unable to fathom what I was hearing.

"It appears that after you're infection healed, the damaged areas of your heart began to develop scar tissue. It's taken years to advance. I suspect that little brawl you got yourself into, exasperated matters and caused an arrhythmia. It was this arrhythmia that caused your collapse yesterday."

I found myself involuntarily breathing heavier. All I could do was stare at the floor in disbelief and let the news slowly sink in. I felt as though my life was over, that all I had fought for, all I had been through, was all for nothing. I had my last chance at happiness within grasp and it was slipping through my fingers. I couldn't do this to her. How could I ask her to stay and watch me die? Almost as if in answer to the rampant doubts and fears compounding my mind, Doc Gardner reassured, "I don't see any need to transfer you to another facility."

"Are you saying that I won't need surgery?" I asked.

"Lord, no!" he laughed. "Like I'd said, we've caught it early. Yes, you're prone to ventricular tachycardia, an arrhythmia, dangerous especially given the restriction, but it's nothing that can't be controlled by medication. I'm putting you on four medications and I'm also writing a script for nitroglycerin tablets. These you'll take as needed for chest pain, since you've developed angina as well."

Doc Garner walked over to my bed, placed a hand on my shoulder and stated, "Don't worry, John. I'm confident that this will get things under control. It might take a couple of weeks for the medications to take full effect, so in the meanwhile, if you have any symptoms at all, day or night, call me right away."

I nodded as Doc Gardner patted my back, handed me the prescriptions, and started for the door, "By the way, I want to see you in my office in two days to see how you're doing." Then, left the room.

Sarah's eyes were glistened with tears. It was tearing me apart inside to see her so upset. I choked as I said, "Please, Sarah, don't cry. You heard Doc Gardner, I'm fine. It's just a little glitch. Look, I'll understand if you don't want to marry me anymore."

She looked up at me and said, "What would make you think that?"

"Well, I'd understand if this scares you off. I don't want you spending every moment fearing the worst. So, if you think it better we call things off, I understand."

"Is that what you want?"

I wasn't sure what I wanted. All I did know was I didn't want this to overwhelm my life. I didn't want to become just a condition. I was beginning to understand where Deos had come from and why he hid that part of his life from me. I also knew that if Sarah and I were to be married, I wanted her marrying me, not my condition. I took a deep breath then confessed, "Look, I want you married to me, not this," as I pointed to my breastbone.

"That's not what makes you, you," she sobbed as she walked over to me. "I loved you before this and I'll love you after."

"And what if Doc Gardner is wrong? What if this develops into something more?"

"Then we'll cross that bridge when we get to it."

Inside, I was shaking, "I don't want you to be a young widow. Not if I can help it."

She turned my cheek to face her as doe eyes smiled at me, "Don't you think that should be my decision. I'm willing to take the chance. Are you?"

# Chapter Thirty
## The Houseguests

"The English are polite by telling lies.
The Americans are polite by telling the truth."
{Malcolm Bradbury, 1965}

Forlorn, I wandered through the grounds of Kingston Hall. I paused before Pallas Athena and stared at the crystal waters of the lake. My mind wandered aimlessly and my shoulders were heavy with nervous anticipation from the rampant thoughts and fears that dominated my mind. Lingering fears and doubts slowly consumed me. I was once again in London and feeling like not only a ghost in my own home, but in my own skin as well. I had a hard time adjusting to medicine regiments and the physical effects that intermittently still plagued me. I hated myself for the drained energy that seemed to hit out of nowhere. I felt like a weak fool for not being able to bully myself back to health as quickly as I wanted.

I met Sarah in the circle drive. She was stunning in a pastel flowered sundress and straw hat. Fairchild held the driver's door of the Bentley in wait. "I'm going to Heathrow to meet Gus, grandpa, and my brothers," she informed. "The rest of the family will be arriving in the morning."

"That time already," I pondered, scarcely able to believe it was less than a week until D-Day. It still seemed like a distant dream, intangible, and never to be. "Well, then I'll see you when you get back."

Sarah's three cousins giggled from the backseat as I leaned in and gave her a reassuring kiss before I walked to the garage. I lightly patted my coat pockets to make sure that I had everything before I ventured out.

As I found my way to the Mercedes, I scanned the spotless expanse of the building. Fairchild had done a fantastic job, but even I was a bit astounded that the staff was worried about a dirty garage. I could have cared less myself. It was just a bloody garage.

As I slid into the driver's seat of the Mercedes for the first time since having it shipped back, I let out a heavy sigh. The garage door opened to reveal the blinding sun beyond as I slid my dark lenses over my eyes. With a mighty roar, the engine fired to life, and I pulled away from the estate.

I drove for what seemed hours until I arrived at the gates of the cemetery. I hesitated at the ornate gate, wondering what had drawn me there. The frog jumped in my chest as I began to shift into reverse and back away. Expecting the worst, I started for my pockets and then decided to wait it out. As I tried to leave the drive, the engine inexplicably stalled. My heart skipped several beats from shock when I cranked the engine to no avail as a strange anxious anticipation gripped me further.

"All right! All right!" I called to the heavens in frustration. "I get the bloody point, mate!"

I steeled my nerve as I stepped from the car. Fear gripped me as I wandered the tombstone-laden expanses. It had been nearly a decade since I last set foot here. I vaguely wondered if I'd still know my way around. As if in answer to my primal fears, my feet guided themselves until I found myself within sight of a massive black marble monument of a knight upon a midnight steed. A smile passed my lips from satisfaction.

I had ordered the monument at the same time I commissioned the painting for Kingston Hall, but had never been able to bring myself to view it. The striking resemblance on the face of the knight brought a lump to my throat. Everyone thought that I had gone overboard, but it was certainly a fitting tribute. I swallowed hard as I neared the impressive sight. The wind rustled my hair and flipped the tails of my coat. Even though it was a warm summer's day, the air was chilled, stale and tried to steal my breath.

"Well, you've finally done it," I stated as I knelt before Deos' grave. "You made me into you, mate." With a heavy sigh, I continued, "How did you live knowing?"

"Live knowing what?" an Irish voice behind echoed. I turned to find Dan leaning on a tree, picking at the twig in his hand. "I went by the Hall, but you weren't there…I thought I might find you here."

"It's been a while," I greeted. "How's Ace?"

"Fine, I guess. She ran off with a roadie for *Oingo Boingo* years ago. I guess I was the 'transition guy'." I wondered how long that lasted. Every time she heard *Dead Man's Party*, she would cry.

"How did he do it, Dan?" I pleaded.

"Do what?" Dan questioned curiously.

"Live knowing what was wrong. How did he handle it?"

Dan looked at me in disbelief before asking, "Why, what's happened?"

I reached into my pocket and tossed a bottle of pills towards him and sighed, "I'm too young for this shit!" Dan examined the label as he continued, "He just had to give me his curse, too."

"Now don't go blaming that on Deos." Dan tapped me on the shoulder with the twig before flipping the pill bottle in the air. "You brought this on yerself. It was endocarditis that caused your first heart attack, remember."

"Oh, stop preaching, reverend!"

"So, how bad is it?" I stuck my hands in pockets and rocked on my heels, stalling for time. I didn't like to admit it. To have said it aloud, would have admitted that I was mortal. It would have also meant admitting that I was weak, too weak to control even my body.

"Had a minor heart attack a while back," I reluctantly admitted. "Was told it wasn't the first."

Dan raised his eyebrows and tapped me on the shoulder again, "Remember."

"I've tried hard to forget, Dan. Then I had nothing to live for, but now…Sarah's been hen-peckin' the hell out of me ever since I got out of the hospital. You know the damndest thing, I'm to be married in less than a week and my best friend is six feet under."

"So why is that a problem?"

Dan returned with me to the Hall. The Bentley was in the drive and Gus stood outside smoking his pipe with a glass of whiskey in his hand as we approached in the Mercedes.

"Damn, boy!" he cried as we stepped from the car. "You had all this and you chose to live in a dump like mine! You sure you don't have a fever?"

"Piss off, Gus!" I expounded as he gave me a lengthy bear hug. "I'd like you to meet my old friend, Dan O' Selle. Danny-boy, this is my asshole uncle Gus."

"Pleasure to meet you," Dan announced as he and Gus shook hands.

"You actually claim to be friends with THIS guy?" Gus asked.

"Sometimes, I wonder why…must be for the money!"

Laughing, the three of us entered the Hall. Sarah met me with a snide smile on her face.

"Um," she stammered. "You have visitors in the study."

"I wasn't expecting anyone," I informed in surprise.

Gus elbowed Dan in the ribs and grinned like the Cheshire cat as they followed. As I entered the study, my eyes opened wide with shock at the sight of my mother, seated on the scarlet couch next to her husband, the Admiral.

Admiral Albert Cavelli was a forceful, weathered man; hardened by years of service and three tours as a Navy pilot in Viet Nam. Even before the service, he was a rough New York Italian, raised in a Brooklyn orphanage, and on the streets. He had the personality and presence of a man twice his size and height. His thin, short frame was masked by an overwhelming realization that while he could be your best friend, he could still kick your ass. I found myself pitying any ensign that crossed that Admiral.

Mother rose shaking, the Admiral gently grasping her arm for support. We both feared she would faint when her eyes welled with tears as she approached and gently caressed my left cheek. She ran her fingers over the lengthy scar and immediately began to sob, "I didn't believe it when they told me…I knew you weren't dead…Grandfather wouldn't take both my boys from me…My God, what have they done to my little boy…"

She buried her head in my chest as I held her close. Sarah cried in the corner with Gus smiling contently at her side.

"Mother," my voice quavered as a tear ran down my cheek. "I'm so sorry."

"I couldn't let you get married without your mother," Gus explained, the Cheshire cat grin still on his face.

I turned, pointed at Gus and said with a wink, "I'll deal with you later."

That evening after dinner, we sat having drinks in the dining hall around the large, antique oak table. To my right was Dan, mother, and the Admiral. To my left sat Gus, Mick, and Sarah's two brothers: Sam and Mike. Sarah sat across from me at the far end, looking more dissatisfied the more I drank.

"You know," I stated. "There hasn't been much life in this draftee auld place in a decade. You know what we're missing? Music." Mother looked shocked and slightly embarrassed by the comment. "C'mon, boys! Everybody ante up!" I placed a five-pound note under my empty Scotch glass. Everyone looked at me confused, with the exception of Gus who reluctantly followed suit as he shook his head and whispered, "She's going to kill you, kid."

"Fairchild, bring me some of my finest Australian crystal." Fairchild returned a few moments later with a large crystal goblet.

"Ian, I don't think," mother begged.

"When Benton and I were little," I continued. "Mother would take bets at parties that she couldn't," I tapped the crystal with my finger, "shatter a goblet."

The Admiral looked shocked at mother, then smiled as he said, "This I have to see."

"Oh, damn," Gus expounded. "Here we go."

Gus removed his glasses and rolled them in his shirt, then addressed the Admiral, "Squid, I suggest you do the same."

After a little more drunken coaxing on my part, mother relented. Sam and Mike looked stunned and confused as mother rose, cleared her throat and took a sip of water. Her voice quavered at first, then grew stronger as she regained her courage. Fairchild leaned over my shoulder, "Lovely voice, sir."

"Shh," I prodded. "Just wait," I reached up and grabbed his monocle. "You may want to wrap this in cloth."

Just as Fairchild had finished wrapping the monocle,

mother hit the high note. With a loud crack, the goblet split down the side. Gus began laughing, whistling, and clapping; Sam and Mike gasped, "Goddamn!" and the Admiral grabbed mother's hand dotingly and kissed it as he breathed, "Really, Maggie, I had no idea."

Mother raised the glass to examine the crack and shook her head in disappointment. "Not as good as I used to be," she dismissed. "Fifteen years ago, this would have been dust." Then she scooped up the money, "Thank you all," stuffed it in her bra, "Tomorrow night, drinks are on me," then turned to step from the room.

"Shall we adjourn to the study?" I asked as a piece of crystal from the chandelier above hit the table before me. "Not as good as you used to be, huh?"

Mother shrugged her shoulders and gave me a wink as she started for the door. As we entered the study, Sam and Mike were in awe of the display of weaponry. Mike paused before the case inside the doorway and asked, "Are those Peacemakers?"

I placed a hand on his shoulder and stated, "God created man, Colonel Sam Colt made them equal...Would you care to fire one?"

"Would I!" Sam cried.

"I'll take you to the country house tomorrow for a little target practice."

"Sis!" Mike called. "If you don't marry him, I will!"

The next morning, mother and Sarah left with the cousins to meet Sarah's parents at the airport and I took Gus, Mike, Sam, Mick, and the Admiral to the country house. The vast country estate hadn't changed much since the last time I was there. The burn pile had long since become a forgotten memory and the grounds were as green and lush as ever they were.

"I still can't believe all of this is yours," Mike stated in awe. "I just thought you were another broke guy with a really cool car and all that English Lord stuff was bullshit."

"Honestly," I replied. "I still have a hard time believing myself."

"Did I hear right," the Admiral addressed, "that you inherited all of this?"

I paused a moment before replying, "In a manner of

speaking. It's a very long, complicated and painful story. But to answer your question the best I can, it was left to me by my best friend and name sake, sort-of-speak."

Stopping at the rifle range, we set out the coolers, weapons, and ammo. Gus hurried down the hillside from the house to catch up to the group. He had paused for a short pit stop and lagged seriously behind the beer. I grabbed a beer from the cooler and tossed it to the Admiral before tossing one to each of the group before opening one myself. The Admiral lit a fat cigar as we sat down in the shade of an ancient oak. The smoke from the cigar mixed with the aroma of my Turk as we continued our conversation.

"He must have been one hell of a man for you to think so highly of him," the Admiral explained.

"He was," I admitted.

Gus wandered down the hill, a walking stick in one hand, his pipe in the other. "What's a brave got to do to get a cold one around here?" he complained as he shoved Sam off the cooler.

"You know this is really smart," Mike quipped. "Grown men liquored up with loaded guns."

"Kick in the butt, ain't it?" the Admiral voiced as he rose to his feet.

As promised, I let the boys fire the Colts. The disbelief in their eyes, as they each held one, took aim, and fired, was paled only by their awe.

"I feel just like Wyatt Earp," Sam commented.

I reached across my chest, pulled one of the Remington's I had positioned backwards, high on the hip, and stated, "Really, boys…Wyatt was overrated," as I stood sideways, raised the barrel, quickly took aim, fired, twirled the pistol, placed it back in the holster, and finished, "Doc was the man…and I'm not just saying that because I'm named after him."

"Damn, boy!" the Admiral cried. "Where the hell did you learn to shoot like that?"

"Waterloo Bridge," I enigmatically replied as I walked away towards the house.

The Admiral tried to follow, but Gus grabbed his arm and whispered, "Let him be. Waterloo Bridge was how he got those scars."

I wandered up the steep hill to the house and straight to the liquor cabinet. The Admiral walked in as I was finishing my third Scotch. Outside, I could hear the discharge of weaponry and the occasional drunken, "Hot damn!", "Take this Custer!", or "This is livin' boys!" uttered by Gus. The Admiral walked over to the liquor cabinet and asked, "Do you mind?"

"Of course not. Help yourself," I offered.

He poured a drink and took a seat across from me.

"You probably didn't know I was a POW, did you?" he asked. I shook my head in reply. "Took me years to get over...Shit, what am I saying, you never get over it. You just get through."

I demanded, "How do you get over watching your best friend's brother blow his head off in front of you? How do you get over knowing that you're the one that drove him to it?"

"You can't. And I'm not going to blow smoke up your ass and tell you that you can or feed you some cock and bull story about putting it in God's hands because I heard enough of that crap over the years to tell you it don't work. I gave up believing when I was sixteen and my sister was raped in the orphanage by one of the staff...Killed herself over it... That, and I've seen too much action to believe that there is any almighty force for good somewhere out there. I even went to space looking for answers, you know what I found," I shook my head, "darkness and cold." I was really beginning to like this guy. "All I'm saying is you try your damndest to forget and move on with your life. It took me three ex-wives and a string of girlfriends to discover that one. You got a good girl; don't let your past destroy you."

With that, he rose and left the house, leaving me once again, alone with my thoughts. For a career military man and former NASA commander, I was shocked by how personable he was. I had always envisioned career military to all be the same – loud, domineering, and stern. Al's humanity, humour, and unflinching loyalty to family endeared him to me from the first moment I met him.

# Chapter Thirty-One
## The Dark Side

"Not on sad Stygian shore, nor in clear sheen
Of far Elysian plain shall we meet those
Among the dead whose pupils we have seen
Not those great shades whom we have held as
foes…"
{Samuel Butler, 1898}

The air was refreshingly brisk the following morning. I had ushered in the dawn with a cup of coffee in one hand and a cigarette in the other as I stood on the balcony gazing over the wide country expanses. The smell of gunpowder still lingered in the misty air and summoned up ancient images of the morning after Gettysburg. In contrast, the call of birds through the still air was a soothing symphony that entranced my soul.

"Use some company?" the Admiral asked from behind. "You an early bird, too?"

"Nah," I replied. "Haven't slept yet. I've had a lot on my mind."

"Cold feet?"

I shook my head, "No, old demons."

After an uneventful drive to the Hall, I greeted my soon-to-be in-laws before sitting down with Sarah to discuss the last minute arrangements.

"The landscaper and the caterer will be here in the morning to go over the final details," she began as my mind drifted. "Did you hear me?"

I raised my eyebrows and stated, "No rest for the wicked, I

take it."

"Ian, could you be serious!  Sometimes I don't even think you listen to me anymore!"

I let out a sigh as I ran a hand thorough my hair.  Then rose and approached the liquor cabinet.  This only seemed to enrage her further.  She scowled at me as she fumed, "Do you really have to drink right now?"

"Something wrong?" I seethed.

"It seems all you do anymore is drink and ignore me…and its only gotten worse since the guest started arriving!"

I threw my head back and stared at the ceiling.  "You're the one that invited them!  I wanted something small and private.  You're the one who had to have this circus!"

Sarah rose incensed from her chair and stormed from the room.  Tension had been high for weeks.  We'd fought countless times over the most trivial of things.  I wanted her to be happy, to have the wedding of her dreams, but I sometimes wondered if I was going to survive it.

A knock echoed through the Great Hall.  I really don't know why I noticed; people had been coming and going so routinely of late that I considered installing a revolving door.

As a forceful voice thundered through the entry, a knot embedded itself in my stomach and I thought I was going to be ill.  The voice addressed, "Madeline," passing my mother as she descended the staircase.  It wasn't until I heard the visitor state, "Fabius" as he met Gus that I knew who it was.  My father had arrived, Sarah's handiwork, no doubt.  Even the devil wouldn't have dared.

"Lord Flaxseed!" Gus insulted.  "What's it been?  Twenty, twenty-five years?  Not long enough."

As Fairchild entered the study to announce the new arrival, even his voice held an air of caution.  "Your Lordship," he acknowledged.  "Mr. James MacIntyre."

"Thank you, Fairchild," I dismissed as I sat facing the fire with the back of Deos' chair to the door to conceal me.  I heard my father's footsteps enter and stop just inside the doorway.  The stereo played softly in the background as I sat with a half empty glass of Scotch.

"Its an unexpected pleasure, m'Lord," father cordially

began. "I have to admit, I was surprised, in the least, when I received the plane ticket with my invitation."

"My fiance's doing, I assure you," I replied venomously as I rose to turn and face my father for the first time in fifteen years.

His face flushed as he struggled with the shock. I was surprised that he didn't have some new tart on his arm. I felt nothing as I looked at him. I'd never wanted him there, I certainly never needed him. Even as I looked at his rapidly aging face, I felt nothing but contempt. When I looked at Al, I felt a sense of understanding, but with James there would always be disgust.

"Ian?" he stammered. "Can it really be you, son?"

"Don't call me son," I seethed.

"I thought the Lord of Kingston Hall was John Phoenix."

I raised an eyebrow, widening a dark eye, took in a deep breath to steel my nerve. I finished my glass of scotch before answering, "I am John Phoenix. Ian MacIntyre died a long time ago." I raised a Turk to my lips and lit up as I continued, "Why did you come if you didn't know whose wedding it was?"

"What do you want from me?" he pleaded.

"Nothing!" I coldly admitted. "You shipped me out of your life when I was fourteen. I've only seen you four times since, but you fly halfway around the world for a stranger's wedding, just because of some damned title! All this from the man who couldn't bother to attend his son's funeral…" Father looked shocked by the revelation. "Yes, I heard. Gus drove to Vermont from the farm, but you couldn't be bothered to drive from Boston and Benton was the one you liked!"

"If you didn't want me here, why send for me?"

I turned back to the fire as I seethed, "I didn't, I can assure you. But since you're here, you're welcome to stay for the wedding if you wish. If not, I'll arrange for your travel home. I'll have Fairchild place you in one of the guest rooms for the night."

"I wouldn't want to put you out, *Your Lordship*," James taunted.

"I may not like it, but you were once my father, if only in name. I'll have Fairchild place you upstairs."

James stood in silence for a few moments before I called, "Fairchild!"

Fairchild rushed in and asked, "Yes, sir?"

"See to placing Mr. MacIntyre in the east wing," I instructed.

"Very good, sir. If you'll follow me, Mr. MacIntyre."

I threw the empty glass on the fire as they left the room. Then, threw the chair across the room in a fit of rage. I clenched my fist and wanted to chase after him to beat him for everything he had done to me over the years. But, I especially hated him for skipping Benton's funeral. Perhaps it was partly out of my own guilt for missing the funeral, or maybe it was the sum realization of how little James' own blood meant to him. Benton was important so long as he served James' twisted idea of social climbing. So long as he was the champion fencer and the social climber James had always wanted, he was fine. Dead, he was just another liability. James couldn't be connected to such scandal.

"Sarah!" I screamed, my blood afire.

I heard Gus comment to Sarah as they approached, "That went better than I thought." Then addressed me, "What's the matter, boy?"

"Not now, Gus!" I raved. "Sarah and I need to talk!"

"Fine," Gus voiced as he backed from the room.

Sarah's frightened eyes followed him, but was reassured when he mouthed, "I'll be by the door," to her.

When the door had closed I raged on, "What the hell were you thinking!"

"What do you mean?" she timidly asked.

"What do I mean? *What do I mean!* I mean sending HIM here!"

"He's your father."

"I have no father! He's wanted nothing to do with me for fifteen years! Gus even told me he couldn't be bothered to attend Benton's funeral, for Christ's sake! And my brother was the one he liked!"

Sarah looked concerned as I began to gasp for breath. She began to cry, "Ian, please calm down…your heart."

"To hell with my heart!" She started for the door handle when I raged, "Where do you think you're going?"

"For a walk," she replied. Then, slammed the door behind her.

I stood in the dim light of the fire, my heart pounding a

samba in my chest; my head hung low in the mantle. A cadaverous air filled the room as *Dead Man's Party* played on the stereo.

"Fine mess o' things, lad," a Scottish voice reverberated behind me. I turned to see Deos standing at the end of the mantle, clad in black leather, and holding his fedora in his hands. "Ye need to calm down, lad."

"Why?" I hesitated to ask, scarcely able to believe what I was seeing.

"I can hear ye pounding clear o'er here," he explained.

He slowly approached and placed a cold hand to my chest. His ghostly eyes seemed to look through me as my breath turned cold and my eyes seemed to burn with a cold fire. A tingle spread through my body and caused my arms and legs to go numb, leaving them to buckle beneath me. Finally, a mortal quiver filled my chest as my heart slowed and returned unsteadily to normal.

"There, now that's better," he stated, satisfied as I crumpled to the floor. I slowly rose back to my feet and braced myself against the mantle. "Now we can talk. Ye know, I've got a wee bit of information for ye. Ye may not be so lucky next time." He gently tapped my chest with the fedora then strode to the other end of the mantle. His black fedora twirled in his hand as he leaned against the wall and spoke. "I like what ye've done with the place…and I love the statue at the cemetery." He paused to listen to the wafting echo of the stereo. His grey hand tapped the brim of his fedora in time with the beat. "God, I miss this album! Hendrix is good, but honestly I can't wait until Danny Elfman kicks. Then we can party!"

"How did you live knowing?" I asked, my voice trembling.

"Don't sweat the small shit!" Deos poshed.

"All I ever wanted was a normal life."

Deos choked as he laughed, his grey eyes glowing ominously. "There's nae such thing as a normal life," he explained, "just life. You take it one day at a time and live each as if it twere yer last. Some men are never destined to have boring lives. We weren't." He glanced at the silver fob watch, emblazoned with the Jolly Roger, which he pulled from his hip pocket. "Shit! I'm late for my weekly poker match with Doc. The bastard is hell to play cards with, but he's got a wicked sense of humour."

    "Are you in heaven?" I ventured to ask, unsure.

    Deos laughed at the premise of heaven, always had.

    "Nah, close though…Tombstone."   Then, he vanished, leaving my heart to once again pound against my ribs and steal my breath as I collapsed to the floor with the lyrics, "…everybody's coming leave your body at the door…" wafting through my mind.

# Chapter Thirty-Two
## The Warpath

"Life is a gamble, at terrible odds-
If it was a bet, you wouldn't take it."
{Tom Stoppard, 1967}

"He's stable," the doctor addressed as he approached the group that had assembled at the hospital in wait. My mother sat holding the Admiral's hand as she sighed in relief. Sarah sat next to Gus who sat at the Admiral's right. To everyone's surprise, James sat beside mother on her left. The doctor pulled a chair over and took a seat across from the group.

"His blood pressure has come back up and his heart rate has returned to normal. There's still a little arrhythmia, but nothing I'd be too concerned about at this point. The good news is there is no evidence that he's had another heart attack."

"Thank you, Grandfather," Gus whispered to the Great Spirit.

"You still practicing that heathen religion of yours?" James hissed as Gus rose to confront him.

"Back off, white eye, before I scalp your dumb ass!" he hissed. "You're the reason the boy's here!"

"Gus! James! Enough!" mother shouted as she pushed between the pair, a hand on each, just like old times. "This is neither the time nor the place! You were saying, doctor?"

"I'm satisfied that if he stays stable, he'll be able to go home in the morning," the doctor finished. "He's asleep now. I've given him a sedative, but you're welcome to see him if you wish."

"Thank you, doctor," the Admiral addressed as they shook hands, then turned to mother, "Maggie?"

The Admiral led mother and Sarah into the emergency room bed where I laid. Mother gently brushed the hair from my cold eyes as Sarah stood entranced by the flickering of the monitor above, tears welling deep in her eyes. The Admiral set a reassuring hand on his wife's shoulder as he whispered, "There's nothing more to be done tonight, darling. He needs his rest."

Sarah ran crying from the room. Mother paused a moment longer then followed arm in arm with her husband. Outside the sliding doors of the entrance, a sobbing Sarah met Gus as he smoked his pipe in the cool night air.

"You all right, girl?" he asked, concerned.

"I've been thinking," she stated, "maybe I should call off the wedding."

Gus fumbled with his pipe, stared wide eyed, and then bent over to pick it up. Shaking the remaining embers, ash, and tobacco from the bowl, he prodded, "Why?"

"I'm too much stress on him. He was so angry…I almost killed him tonight," she explained.

"Now you listen to me," Gus snapped as he held her arm. "You're not the one killing him, his memories are! He's killing himself."

Sarah collapsed to the curb, crying uncontrollably. "I don't know what to do anymore, Gus."

"There's nothing you can do." Gus sat next to her and pulled a handkerchief from his pocket. "Always keep one for showing and one for blowing." He then placed his arm around her shoulders and held her in his arms. "He's got to work this one out for himself."

The next morning, I was pulling my tee shirt over my head as the doctor entered. I was surprised to be waking in a hospital room. In fact, with the previous night's events, I was surprised to be waking up at all. My throat was sore and my energy drained, otherwise I felt fine except for the persistent burning of my eyes.

"I'm glad to see you're feeling better, Lord Kingston," he chimed. "You're a very lucky man."

"So I'm told," I replied as I sat slumped over the side of the bed and fumbled with my boots.

"I've prescribed an anti-anxiety medication and am recommending adjusting the doses on your heart medications, just for a while until things settle. I'd like to see you in my office on Monday to see how you're doing."

"I'll make sure he's there," Gus voiced from behind the doctor as he entered the room.

I let out a disgruntled sigh and said, "Smore…"

"Smore, huh?" Gus laughed.

"Yeah, smore your damned business!"

Gus leaned in the doorway with his arms folded, looking at me curiously. "Good morning to you, too."

The doctor started for the doorway then addressed, "Monday it is then. And congratulations on the wedding."

"Thank you, doctor," I stated half-heartedly as he left.

Gus addressed the doctor as he passed by him, "Can I talk to you for a moment?"

The two of them moved to the side where they could talk privately. I rose from the bed and grabbed my jacket from the chair to the right. Gus returned a few moments later, grabbed the stack of release instructions, and smiled, "Shall we, Your Lordship?"

"Piss on you, Gus!" I taunted.

"I'm glad to see you're back to your cynical self."

Our footsteps echoed through the silent hallways. As we passed the nurse's station, a young nurse smiled from behind the group of monitors. The top of her blouse was unbuttoned to mid-bust, revealing the crease of her cleavage and a considerable amount of meat. I looked - hell, I was engaged, not dead…yet. Gus on the other hand, was panting like a dog in heat.

"Good luck, Lord John," she chimed as we walked by.

I leaned over and whispered to Gus, "You care for a handkerchief?"

"Why?" he asked.

"You're drooling all over yourself."

Gus shoved me as he snapped, "Go to hell, Ian!"

I laughed, "Got kicked out of there last night for passing out air conditioners. Why else do you think I'm still here?"

Gus paused by the entrance doors. The cool breeze ruffled his dark hair as he pulled his pipe and tobacco from his jacket and began to pack the bowl thoughtfully. I pulled the engraved gold cigarette case from my hip pocket and lit a Turk.

"Who's Deos?" Gus asked as he struck a match to light his pipe. I choked on the words. I had never told any of the family about Deos. "You were calling out to him when I found you unconscious on the floor last night. At first, I thought you were praying, then you opened your eyes for just a moment, looked up at me and said, 'Deos, help me'."

"Why would you think I was praying?" I questioned. He knew I was far from religious.

"Deus is Latin for God." No wonder Deos wasn't in heaven, there was only room for one god.

I fumbled with the contents of my pockets as I paused, wondering what to say. "You know that large portrait at the top of the stairwell?" Gus nodded. "That was him."

"That friend of yours that died."

I half-heartedly laughed, "Of a heart attack, no less. Twenty-eight years old and dies of a bloody heart attack. Ironic isn't it? Anyway, I saw him last night in the study." Gus looked astonished as he sucked on his pipe. "He was as real as you standing there now, Gus. Call me crazy or whatever, but he was there."

"I believe you," Gus solemnly admitted. He pulled the sunglasses away from my eyes as he stared bewildered at me.

"What?" I demanded.

"Have you looked in the mirror lately?" he asked.

"No, why?"

"I really think you should."

We rushed to the far side of the parking lot where Gus had parked the Mercedes. I knelt down beside the side-view mirror and looked at my face. I jumped back in shock at the image that left my chest tingling. Overnight, my once dark eyes had changed to a glowing golden. Not just light brown, but reminiscent of Deos' grey. Something had happened the night before, something neither of us could explain.

# Chapter Thirty-Three
## One Last Roll

"Never eat at a place called Mom's.
Never play cards with a man called Doc.
Never go to bed with a woman whose
Troubles are greater than your own."
{Nelson Algren, 1956}

I returned to Kingston Hall filled with dread. There was a pit in my stomach and my legs weakened beneath me. What would everyone have to say when they saw the change? How could I explain what I didn't even understand myself? I left my dark glasses on, just in case, as Fairchild met us at the door with a look of relief on his face.

"Welcome home, Lord John," he stated cheerily. "I am so glad to see that you are feeling better."

"Thank you, Fairchild," I dismissed. "By the way, it's good to see you, too."

He looked at me shocked, then smiled as he walked away. I had never been particularly warm to Fairchild. We always seemed to have a vinegar and oil relationship. We didn't mix well, but one without the other always seemed lacking. I wandered solemnly to the study and approached the liquor cabinet out of habit. As I reached for the crystal flask of Scotch, I stopped. *Ten in the morning, still pretty early,* I pondered to my own amazement. I was not in the habit of turning down a Scotch, regardless the time. After all, it was Happy Hour somewhere. Something certainly had happened to me and I wasn't entirely sure that I liked it.

Sarah raced into the room and threw her arms around my back. I gave a startled jump as she giggled.

"Sorry," she apologized. "I didn't mean to startle you."

I stood a moment longer before turning to face her. I pulled the sunglasses from my eyes and prepared to hear her scream.

"Don't ask me what happened," I warned. "I don't even know. All I know is I woke up this morning and my eyes were like this."

"Can you see all right?" she asked as she waved a hand before my eyes.

"Better than before." I paused and let everything sink in with Sarah before asking the million-dollar question, "So, how soon do you want to leave?"

She looked puzzled at me as she said, "Never. What would make you think otherwise?"

I shrugged before admitting, "I've been kind of an asshole lately and then this, this morning…"

"Don't be ridiculous!" She reached up and pulled my head forward. I leaned in expecting a long, passionate kiss, but was met by a sharp slap to the cheek, "But if you ever scare me like that again, I'll snap you in two like a twig!" then, turned and walked away. "By the way, the last of the arrangements have been made. The caterer will arrive at nine tomorrow and the landscaper will begin setting up some time this evening in the garden."

Just what I needed – more people stomping around the house. Over the course of the day, people were coming and going so routinely that I doubted I would get anything done and out of frustration, left for town. After seeing to a few last minute details of my own, I returned to the Hall in time for the rehearsal at three.

Everyone had assembled in the garden as I sauntered in. Gus looked at his watch then winked, "About time, boy!"

"We were beginning to wonder if we'd have a groom," the Admiral joked.

Dan leaned next to the fountain, smoking a cigarette as he spoke, "Shall we, your Lordship! It's your funeral."

I walked over and gently jabbed him in the ribs, "Go to hell, Danny-boy!" I razzed. "You could have talked me out of it!"

I began to look around only to realize that we were missing someone. "Where's Mouse?"

Fairchild emerged from the estate. There was a rush in his gate as he approached. In his black suit and slicked back hair, he looked like an overgrown penguin racing towards me. "Greatest apologies, your Lordship!" he stated. "A Mr. Jones just called to say his flight has been delayed and he'll be arriving in London late tonight. He sends his most sincerest of apologies."

"No worries," I voiced. "Thank you, Fairchild. All right, everyone! Looks as though we're one groomsman short until tomorrow. Mouse is stuck in transit."

"What about the best man?" the reverend asked.

I looked at Dan and winked. "Talked to him last night," I alluded. "He'll be here tomorrow."

The rehearsal and dinner went better than I expected. Gus and Dan joked their way through the proceedings to my utter delight and the vicar's chagrin. After dinner, I excused myself to the study to sit in silence. I sat before the fireplace watching the flame flicker and sparks float and dance their way up the chimney and let my mind become numb. So much was happening, far too much to deal with all at once. All I wanted to do was disappear into the shadows until morning. I was working on my third Scotch when I heard footsteps approach from behind.

"Hell of a place to be on your last night as a free man!" Gus scolded.

"And where should I be?" I asked.

"You're coming with us," the Admiral ordered.

Gus and the Admiral may have been an odd couple, but for a lifelong swab jockey fly-boy and a retired grunt, they did get along exceptionally well, especially if it had to do with plotting against me. The odd couple had planned a regular bachelor's night extravaganza, complete with the three "Bs," "booze, buds, and broads." Of course, they threw in a gratuitous amount of "tits and ass" tossed in for good measure. With a great-uncle and stepfather like that, who needed enemies? Sarah was going to kill me.

The "buds" in question were thrust upon me at our first stop, Deos' favourite pub on Pall Mall. Dan sat down in a corner booth surrounded by a group of men that I hadn't seen or spoken to in close to a decade. Symon sat next to Dan with Colin and Nigel (the Twins) and a far more dignified Devo (though now he was known as Reginald).

"You don't think we'd let our old Sergeant-at-arms get hitched without us did you?" a voice asked from behind as a hand lay upon my shoulder. I turned to see Mouse behind me. "I just got in. Trust the wake went well."

"The wake?" I asked to be met with flippant brows.

"Your funeral, mate," he explained with a hearty slap on the arm.

I introduced Gus and the Admiral as we got to the serious business at hand, drinking ourselves into oblivion. The night went well, but by the time we hit old haunt number five, I began to feel as though something were missing. Then, Dan hit me over the head with it.

"This would have been the perfect Ian's last hurrah, except for one thing," he lamented. "I believe I speak for all the lads when I say tonight could never be the same without Deos."

The joyous mood that had dominated the night's festivities suddenly sobered as a cold veil was lowered over the group from the empty void of Deos' absence.

"Hey, Ian," Symon called. "You remember the night that bloke...what the hell was his name...you know, the idiot that ploughed headlong into Harrods's...well, anyway, the night this bloke came into the club with five of his mates starting trouble."

"You're talking about Burnout!" Colin exclaimed.

"Yeah, that's the one," Symon continued.

"This bloke fried more brain cells than *KFC*," I commented.

"Anyway," Symon spoke. "These six blokes came in giving our mate, Ian here, a hard time. Deos knocked the lot on their arses a time or two before. They were just too stupid to learn. One of them knocked Ian in the jaw and from there it was all-out war. Deos went nuts. He had two blokes by the throat, one in each hand and still managed to kick one over a table, then head butt a fourth before bouncers arrived. It took three bouncers and seven blokes to hold him back!"

"They were just lucky Black Betty wasn't with him that night," Nigel laughed.

Gus and the Admiral looked dazed at each other, then Gus shrugged. "I give. Who's Black Betty?"

I ran a hand through my hair, grasped the handle of Deos' equalizer, lifted the handle as I brought it out of the sheathe at the base of my neck, and twirled it down until I stuck the blade in the scored table top.

"Shit!" Colin howled. "You've still got her!"

"And he's bloody near as good as Deos!" Nigel agreed. "You been practicing, mate?"

"Nah," I scoffed, "just had a good teacher."

"I remember when this bloke was a wimp," Mouse reminisced with a slap on my shoulder.

"I was the wimp?" I ribbed. "I remember having to save your sorry hide more than once."

"That didn't last long," Mouse explained. "Not with Deos around. Those two were joined at the hip."

"More like the arsehole," Dan corrected.

"Nobody could kick arse like Deos, mate!" Nigel voiced.

"To Deos!" Reginald called. "The best mate a bloke could ask for."

"To Deos!" we all cheered as we threw back our last shots.

Then, I rose unsteadily to my feet and prepared to leave.

"Well, mates," I addressed. "Its been real and its been fun…"

"…But its not been real fun!" Gus finished. "Can't pull the shit over your old great uncle's eyes, boy."

Mouse looked astounded. "You aren't that old, are you?"

"He's 110," I joked. "Them injins age gracefully."

"You and the horse you rode in on, boy!" Gus scolded. "I'm only 63. The swab jockey's the one that fits in the geezer category!"

"Go to hell, grunt!" the Admiral ribbed. "You got five years on me."

"Yeah, but you look older, pale face!"

# Chapter Thirty-Four
## The Wedding

"Don't panic."
{Douglas Adams (The Hitchhiker's Guide to the Galaxy, 1979)}

I awoke the next morning with a massive hangover and a stomach full of regret. I hadn't gotten that stupid in quite some time and my pounding head reminded me. Gus shook his head when I approached the table for breakfast in sunglasses, a fact the Admiral found just as amusing. Whether it was military training or years of experience that kept their composure, I cannot say. What I can say is their bright eyes and refreshed faces were an unwelcome accompaniment to the haggard and hung-over.

"Mission accomplished I'd say, Sarge," the Admiral gloated to Gus.

"Go to hell, Al," I replied.

I was relieved when my morning eggs came scrambled as opposed to the usual sunny side up. I don't think my stomach could have handled anything slimy and oozing. Sarah looked almost as miserable. Knowing mother, I could have imagined what the bachelorette party would have been like. Even Sarah's tea totter of a mother seemed as though she had enjoyed herself a little too much – a fact that infuriated her husband and made me laugh. No one ate much that morning, none of us had the stomach for it, with the exception of Gus and Al who purposely ate greedily and showed off their over easy eggs and dyed green oatmeal. They took delight in the suffering of the rest of us and each moan emitted from the languid faces only added to their joy.

By the time the wedding party began arriving at ten, I'd had enough *Tylenol*, caffeine, and nicotine in my system to begin feeling halfway normal. Mouse was the first to arrive, followed shortly after by Dan. Sarah's bridesmaids had been in the Hall for days. The incessant giggle of Sarah and her cousins at night was enough to drive anyone crazy. I think a couple of them took the whole valley girl thing a little too far. Their high-pitched squeals would carry and echo down the vast hallways.

My nerves were already worn like the breaks on a redneck's pickup. I had become accustomed to the quiet that solitude and isolation provides. The sounds of people had long lost its appeal for me. Instead of revelling in the chatter and hustle of fellow human beings, I was annoyed, irritable, and withdrawn.

A half an hour before the ceremony, I was alone in the study getting the finishing touches on my tux when Gus approached from behind. He looked regal in the black long tailed tux and top hat. His hand was fumbling with something in his right pocket. As he pulled out his hand, he revealed a white bone-bead choker with a phoenix carved from red stone. Around his own neck he wore a similar choker with a black wolf in place of the phoenix. He turned to face the mirror as he placed the chocker around my neck.

"I'm going to tell you something, boy," he said. "You can think what you will, but when I was just a boy, my grandfather Spotted Hawk told me before he died that he'd had a vision that one day his grandson would travel to a distant land to achieve great things…But, at a terrible cost to himself. For many years, I didn't think anything of it. Your grandfather and I never travelled much. I went to Europe a few times in the service, but that was all. I had forgotten entirely about the conversation until I found this the other day." He indicated to the choker around my neck. "Joseph Spotted Hawk made this before he died and entrusted it to me. He told me that I would know who it was for."

I was shocked. I didn't know what to say. So much had happened that could not be explained. I found myself blindly believing. I had stopped questioning why.

"It's beautiful," I stated in awe. "Thank you, Gus."

"Don't thank me, boy. Thank Ol' Joe. He was right. It just took a couple of generations. It was his great-great grandson he saw."

With that, he turned and walked for the door, leaving me once again, alone. I stood at the mirror, running my fingers over the beading of the choker. A lump in my throat formed as I swallowed hard to subside it. The beads were cold against my overheated skin. They glowed against my brown neck and left me feeling as though I were riding bareback across the plains. Then and there I vowed it would never be taken off.

"They are about ready for you," the Admiral informed from the doorway.

His eyes scanned the choker as he laughed, "Gus?" I raised my brow in reply. "Looks good on you...I mean it. It really seems to suit you. You definitely have the Lakota features."

When I arrived in the garden, I found row upon row of seated guests watch as the Admiral escorted me down the aisle, dressed in his finest Class A formal. Countless metals and bars dangled from his chest and reflected the bright sunlight. I pondered over what a mixed pair the Admiral and I made – he in his class A formal uniform and me with a bone bead choker around my neck. We had to look like the Lone Ranger and Tonto going to a black tie ball.

Gus, Mouse, and Dan were already assembled at the front of the procession. Next to Dan a coat rack stood, from it hung Deos' black trench coat and fedora over a large photograph of Deos. At the end of the groomsmen was an easel with a large photograph of my brother Benton. Gus gave me a large grin from between Mouse and Dan. To our left stood all five of Sarah's bridesmaids. I nodded to them as I took my place beside Deos' coat.

The Admiral shook my hand and stated, "Your mother and I are very proud of you, son." He then turned and made his way to the seat beside mother in the front row. Mother smiled widely at me as a tear fell down her cheek. She was stunning in a red formal. James sat to her right in a tuxedo. I was surprised that he even showed. We hadn't seen or spoken to each other since the night he arrived. I had assumed that he had gone home with his tail between his legs. I watched him lean over and whisper to mother. She nodded and said, "He's doing better. Don't ask about his eyes."

"I like the changes to the program," Gus whispered to me.

I had changed the groomsmen and best man at the last minute. After my encounter with Dan at the cemetery, I got the thinking. So what if my best man and a groomsman were dead. I'd heard of honorary pallbearers at funerals, so why not honorary groomsmen? I actually pulled it off better than I thought I would. No one was surprised by the eccentricity of it all. It was just the type of insanity that everyone had grown accustomed to from the past couple of Lord Kingstons.

I scanned the crowd to see Symon, Colin, Nigel, and Reggie. Symon gave a big thumbs-up as the bridal march began. Sarah emerged from the Hall looking stunning. She wore a flowing bridal gown that seemed to float around her and glow in the summer sun. Gold and silver beads dangled from her hair and echoed the glow of her shining eyes. I placed an open palm to my chest in awe as she took her place at my side.

"You all right?" she asked, concerned about the hand on my chest.

"You took my breath away, love," I explained. "You look stunning."

She blushed as the service began. It was a brief, un-religious ceremony. After a lengthy kiss, the vicar announced, "I am honoured to present to you, Lord and Lady John Holliday Phoenix."

As the wedding party stood in procession and greeted the numerous guests, I began to feel like a cordial hand shaking machine. That was until an unexpected guest came my way. Towards the end of the procession, an elderly Lakota greeted Sarah and I as Gus toted his frail form in arm.

"Ian, Sarah," Gus introduced, "this is Chief Sam Three Feathers from our Lakota nation."

"So, this is the one that Joseph Spotted Hawk envisioned as a firebird," the Chief said to Gus. "You were right, Night Wolf. If it weren't for the lighter skin and hair, I would have thought I was looking at Joe himself." I was shocked and complimented by the comment. "I have come to give you my and your people's blessing and best wishes. I would like for you to come to the Reservation, after the honeymoon, of course. We will feast and dance to your union."

"I…we, would be honoured, Chief," I humbly accepted.

We had a break between the ceremony and the reception for pictures, cutting of the cake, etc. When all the mid-festivities had ended, Sarah went inside to change out of her wedding gown. When she emerged, she was just as breath taking as before in a white sequined evening gown with a matching cape and mid-bicep length silk gloves. She was the epitome of elegance as she took my hand and I escorted her to the dance floor for the first dance. I had a little surprise in store. As the band began to play, I nodded to the Admiral who whispered in the bandleader's ear causing the music to suddenly change.

A tango?" she asked, a bit shocked and definitely scared.

"Just relax and follow my lead," I directed as I took her by the waist and arm.

As we danced, I felt as though we were making and falling in love for the first time. Sarah's long locks flowed as I twirled and dipped her with the music. Her long legs wrapped sensually around mine as I pressed close to her warm, soft body. With a final dramatic dip, the crowd exploded into applause.

"You sure you're not Italian?" the Admiral asked as Sarah and I took our places at the table reserved for the wedding party with her cheeks afire from embarrassment. The waiters brought around champagne as Dan rose from his seat, gently tapped his glass with a fork and cleared his throat.

"I suppose this is where I fulfil my duties as best man, in abstention, of course," he joked. "After all, the best man isn't able to speak for himself due to an unexpected departure." His mood sobered as his mind reflected on Deos, as did the minds of all that knew him. "As I sat awake last night preparing what I was going to say, I found something rather interesting." He pulled an aging, yellowed piece of paper from his pocket. "A decade ago when his Lordship first came to us, no one could have dreamed this day would come, or that such a key player would no longer be with us when it did. This wasn't necessarily written for this occasion, but I found it fitting none the less."

He went on to bring a tear to my eye with a long forgotten, but all too familiar, letter:

*If you're reading this it means two things have happened. One, the old kicker finally kicked me in the arse*

*and I'm worm food and two, you're
in trouble. From what or who I can
only speculate, but for one reason or
another, you need the security that
only I can bring. So, old friend,
congratulations. You are John
Holliday Phoenix, the new Lord of
Kingston Hall. I wish I were there to
see the look on Andrew's face.
Don't blame yourself for what
happened to me. I know you're
probably torturing yourself right
now. Just remember this, you were
my oldest, first and best friend, my
brother. There is no one else worthy
of my inheritance or respect. Take
care of yourself and may you live a
long and happy life, my friend, my
brother-Lord John Holliday Phoenix.
I am with you always.*

*-Deos*

Symon, Colin, Nigel, Mouse and Reggie rose and lifted
their glasses. They all looked at me and cheered one of Deos'
favourite toasts, "Be happy while y'er leevin', for y'er a lang time
deid!"

The rest of the group raised their glasses in toast. I lifted
my glass last as I looked towards the Hall in longing. Deos stood
leaning against the door, his coat and coal curls tousled by a gentle
breeze. His arms were crossed as he smiled in satisfaction. He
uncrossed his arms, raised a silver flask and disappeared as I
whispered, "To you, Deos." The ache in my heart told me that it
would be the last time I would see him. I struggled to keep my
composure. Long withheld tears of grief and longing tried to swell
from deep within my soul. I fought them back to have a solitary
tear run down my cheek. Sarah upon seeing this, reached under
the table and took my hand.

*******

I paused to regain my composure. My hand shook the full glass I held. I placed a cigarette to my lips and lit up as drew in a deep breath of smoke to calm my nerves, letting it trickle from my lips like a hookah smoking caterpillar. I took a sip of beer as I laid a cigarette-laden finger to my temple. The group sat in silence and waited for me to continue my tale.

*******

I wandered from guest table to guest table until I found myself at the bar. Sarah sat at a table with her family, talking and laughing. James sat with Dan, mother, the Admiral, and surprisingly, Gus.

"So, James," mother addressed. "You going to be in town long?"

"I'm leaving tomorrow for Washington," James stated.

"I thought you were still in Boston."

James' brow furled at the mention of Boston. "I was never so glad to be transferred in all my days. Damnable place, Boston; too many Irish. They should have sunk that infernal island centuries ago."

Dan's proud Celtic face turned red as he threw back his chair and stormed away. Gus' eyes burned like fire as he followed Dan. The pair instantly raced towards me.

"Bailey's on the rocks," Dan ordered the bartender.

"Bourbon," Gus asked.

"Is he always that cordial?" Dan asked.

"Who?" I enquired.

"Your father," Gus informed. "The asshole had the nerve to slam the Irish in front of Dan."

"I'm sorry, Ian...I don't want to ruin your day...Today is about you, I'm being petty," Dan lamented.

"No, you're not. Fact is, I never wanted him here," I informed.

"I can attest to that," Gus seconded.

"I think he should have been born German," I summarized. "At least then, he could have joined the Nazi party and gotten it out of his system. In a previous life he was Hitler."

"And you say he works for the British consulate?" Dan asked.

"My whole life. He's just drunk today. He doesn't have a new tart to flaunt in front of mother so he's wallowing in self pity."

Dan motioned me to wait. "I'll be back in a minute, hold on," he instructed.

Gus and I looked at each other in bewilderment as Dan raced to his car. He returned, panting, a few moments later, carrying a large, rectangular package wrapped in gold foil.

"I was saving this for a special occasion," he explained mysteriously. "Its just for you, so I didn't want to leave it with the other wedding gifts."

I pursed my lips in disbelief as I took the weighty package from his hands and set in on the bar. I peeled away the gold foil to reveal a large cardboard box. I was beginning to feel like I'd been there before. Then I opened it. Inside was my electric guitar. I had left it propped up against Deos' casket and swore to never play again. Dan had saved it all those years ago and had taken the liberty to wire it for a cordless amp. That left only one possibility.

"I kept it," Dan enlightened. "I knew you'd be needing it one day, when you came to your senses. You're good, mate. Best I've seen in a long time. You really should have taken those record deals. You could have gone far." Gus stared dazed at me. "You didn't know?" Dan continued. "He was offered a couple of different solo deals, but wouldn't take them if it didn't include the rest of us."

"I always knew you were a stupid son-of-a-bitch, but this takes the cake!" Gus expounded as he slapped me in the back of the head.

I stood there, my guitar in my hand. It had been so long. The looks of Gus and Dan seemed to egg me on. Then I heard my father voice, "At least he decided on some decent music. I remember that horrid rubbish he listened to as a child…"

"Lads," I called. "Maybe it's time…"

"I've already talked to the band, mate. We're just waiting on you."

"Give me a couple of minutes to change."

I took the guitar with me and raced to the Hall. I found a pair of Deos' leather pants, boots, and vest. As I stood clad in leather, with the exception of my bare chest, the guitar slung across my back, I looked at the mirror and thought, *You've really gone off the deep end this time, mate!* Then took a deep breath and walked back outside.

I gazed across the crowded yard and saw the band assembled on the stage in wait. Nothing had been said about what was going on and the guests were staring at the stage in wonderment. I cracked my neck and took in a deep breath to steel my nerves before I set the dials. Then, wiggled my shaking fingers and stared at the ground. As the shadow of a cloud passed overhead, I felt an invisible nudge at my back and knew it was time.

The opening guitar riff to *Dead Man's Party* echoed over and over as I marched to the stage. It was as if I had never quit playing. The notes flowed from my fingers flawlessly. Gus, mother and the Admiral smiled contently as I mounted the stage. Sarah ducked her face in her hands from embarrassment. Did I neglect to tell her that I was once the front man of a band? James just scowled in disapproval, adding to my delight.

We did a quick set with a lot of the old favourites. There were a few *Stray Cats* songs, which the Admiral seemed to especially enjoy, a couple of songs off *Oingo Boingo's "Dead Man's Party,"* and the *Kinks' "Destroyer."* I got a lot of laughs from *The Police's "On Any Other Day"* and *The Kinks' "Apeman."* The showstopper had to have been when I sang *The Police's "Does Everyone Stare."* I thought Sarah was going to find a hole to crawl down and die. An act she repeated when we played *"White Wedding," "All I Need,"* and *"Gypsy Jean."* She was so cute when embarrassed.

Afterwards, we turned the stage back over to the party band. I was intending to return to the business at hand, getting seriously drunk, when the guitarist of the band stopped me as he mounted the stage.

"Do you have a moment, Your Lordship?" he timidly asked.

"Of course," I replied as I swung the guitar from my shoulder.

"I was admiring your guitar," he commented as I raised the guitar to show him the signature.

"I don't believe it!" he gasped. "I thought it was just a rumour. No wonder you're so good."

"From one madman to another," I joked on the guitar's original owner being declared mentally ill.

"Wow."

I paused to place the guitar in the case before explaining, "She was a gift from a late friend. I left it next to his casket in '85. I never expected to see her again, that is until my mate with the bass over there gave it back to me today. I swore at the funeral I would never play again."

"You really haven't played since '85?"

"Not a bar, mate. Music was the farthest thing from my mind."

The man just shook his head in disbelief. "If that was rusty, I'd hate to hear you warmed up."

James stopped me as I stepped from the stage. I handed the case to Dan as he approached. The look of disapproval still evident on his aging face, leading me to expect the usual line of insults and taunts.

"Ian," he addressed. "I just wanted to say congratulations. Sarah seems like a lovely girl. For an American." My fists tensed. "I'm heading back to the hotel. I have an early flight in the morning. It's been...interesting, seeing you again."

I raised my brow before saying, "Goodbye, James."

"Until then," he replied sourly as he shook my hand. I cringed as his hand touched mine.

After James left, Dan addressed me sarcastically, as he handed me my guitar case, "That went well."

"I hate him," I hissed, "for what he did to mother, to me. This is only the fifth time I've seen him in almost two decades. He didn't even bother to go to Benton's funeral."

Dan's jaw dropped and his eyes were the size of saucers. "Surely, you're joking."

"I wish I were, mate."

"Real candidate for father of the year. So then why come to the wedding?"

I strummed my fingers nervously along the neck of the guitar case before answering, "Money. He didn't know who's wedding it was. He thought it would be an opportunity to brown nose with nobility. That's all he's ever cared about." I looked over my shoulder to mother's table as the Admiral was leading her to the dance floor and lamented, "Why couldn't the Admiral have been my father?"

"That would have been a mix, wouldn't it?" Dan observed.

"What do you mean?"

"Cajun, Indian, AND Italian…aren't you enough of a loaded gun already!"

# Chapter Thirty-Five
## After Hours

"For double the vision my Eyes do see
And a double vision is always with me.
With my inward Eye 'tis an old Man grey,
With my outward a Thistle across my way."
{William Blake, 1802}

A small group of us left for the country house after the reception. There was Sarah and I, along with Gus, the Chief, mother, and the Admiral. We sat around a blazing bonfire until late into the night. At around two in the morning, Sarah and I excused ourselves and returned to the house, leaving everyone else still basking in the light of the fire.

I stepped into the bathroom that adjoined the master bedroom to prepare for bed. Sarah entered from behind and grabbed me around the waist. Slowly, her hands descended the length of my shirt, opening buttons as she went. When she reached my jeans, she turned me around, unfastened the fly and slid them down my legs. My body tingled as she rose, her hot breath dancing on my skin. She then took my hand and led me to bed.

She trembled as I slowly removed the ribbon that held her lingerie, allowing it to gently fall to the floor. I held her close as I laid her upon the bed. Her warm body one with mine, our hands intertwined, the smell of her skin, the steam rising from our bodies, her staggered breathing and gentle sighs, the pounding of her heart against my chest. If my own had stopped that night, I would have died the luckiest man on earth.

I awoke from a deep sleep. Sarah was still cradled in my arms. If it was all a wonderful dream, I didn't want to wake. The song of the crickets drifted through the open window like a siren's call, drawing me outside as I pulled on my jeans. I could hear the faint crackle of the fire lure me into the cool, misty night. The country house sat in a valley surrounded by forest, causing the mist and smoke to mingle as it hovered along the valley floor.

Gus and the Chief still sat next to the dying embers, a smoking clay pot set between them. The smell of cedar and sage wafted through the air and incensed me. The Chief smiled as I approached and motioned me to sit.

"How did you know my great-great grandfather?" I asked.

"Joe was our medicine man when I was a very young man," the Chief explained. "And he was my father's best friend. You and Night Wolf are a lot like him. Gus doesn't have the sight, though. That's what happens when you're a mushroom…"

"Kept in the dark and fed full of shit!" Gus laughed with the Chief.

"But you do," the Chief finished, seriously. "I can see it in your eyes."

I began to then realize what had happened. I suspected the changing colour of my eyes was not so much a result of some vascular cause like the doctors had claimed, but rather a result of my contact with Deos. It was the physical mark of the gift he had given me – a result of contact with the other side.

As this realization cemented itself in acceptance, I felt myself drift away in the cool night, the crackle of the fire dancing through my mind, the smell of cedar and sage slowly separating spirit from body. A great cry filled the night as the last flickers of the fire burst to life to reveal a bird of fire from the embers. It looked at me with flickering golden eyes, then spread its vast, glowing wings and flew through me, causing me to grasp my chest and throw my head back in silent cry.

I awoke to find myself lying on my back before the fire, Gus' ear to my bare chest. He let out a sigh of relief as I began to sit up.

"Thank you, Grandfather," he praised. "You scared the shit out of me, boy! I couldn't wake you and I could barely hear your heart. I thought you might have had another heart attack."

"No, I'm fine," I replied uncertainly.

"He had a vision, Gus," the Chief stated in awe. "What did

you see?"

I hesitantly explained, "There was this giant flaming bird. It just looked at me strangely before flying straight through me." I began to wonder if this had been planned by Deos. Then, I questioned my own sanity. I knew what had happened was illogical, even absurd. Was I unconsciously taking this whole Phoenix concept a bit too seriously? Was I trying to make the metaphorical, physical?

I looked at Gus and the Chief as I ran a shaking hand through my hair. There was a comfort and acceptance that hovered in the thick air around us that forced all doubt from my mind. It compelled me to trust in what I felt, not what I could touch. I had to trust the wisdom that emerged from within, not without. I had to accept what I had been forced to ignore for so long. I had to embrace the ancient knowledge that had sought me and welcome it as a part of my being.

"I think now is a good time to give you your Lakota name," the Chief concluded. "We shall call you Firebird."

"It's a good name, a bit predictable though…John Phoenix, Firebird," Gus taunted and received a scowl from the Chief.

Curiosity welled in me as I felt compelled to ask, "How did you get your name, Gus?"

"When Gus was born, Joe saw a wolf as black as night peeing on a tree," the Chief explained, much to Gus' dismay.

I involuntarily laughed hysterically. "I guess you're lucky Grandpa Joe didn't call you 'Black Dog Pissing'."

"Go to hell, Ian!" Gus snapped sourly.

The Chief laughed and slapped Gus on the shoulder. "Lighten up, Gus! He's right though, I'm surprised Joe didn't just to be spiteful," he stated.

"This is serious," Gus sulked.

"No one knows better than me how serious this is, but you have to admit it was funny. He's got Joe's sense of humour, that's for sure. Joe once got kicked out of a pow wow. I'm not saying he didn't take sacred things seriously. I've never known a more spiritual man – he just had this awful childish streak that didn't allow him to take things too seriously."

"Sounds like someone else I know," Gus moped as he stared me.

# Chapter Thirty-Six
## Epilogue

"Faith may be defined as an illogical belief
In the occurrence of the improbable."
{H.L. Mencken, 1919}

As I finished, the group let out a collective sigh. Jim, the bartender, looked at me and asked, "Why Tombstone if you have all that?"

It was partly for Deos. I could feel his presence when I walked the streets late at night, saw his image in the shadows. Moreover, for the first time in years, I felt as though I belonged somewhere. So much of my life I had spent wandering and in want of a place to belong. I had found acceptance through Deos and was tied to him even in death.

"The ranch is an investment," I lied. "I'm entrusting it to Gus and the Admiral. Besides, it gives me somewhere to visit. Luxury can be so boring."

"Yeah, I bet, Chief!" Jim stated sarcastically. "I'd get tired of being waited on hand and foot, too."

The group exploded into laughter. They hadn't believed a word of my story. Gus laid a reassuring hand on my shoulder as a pit formed in my stomach at the notion that I was thought a fool.

"Hey, Pete!" Jim addressed the Tombstone marshal that stood in the doorway. "Something I can help you with?"

The marshal looked at the notepad in his hand before stating, "I'm looking for the Englishman...Lord John Holliday Phoenix?"

My stomach churned as I spoke, "I'm John Phoenix."

The marshal approached Gus, the Admiral, and I before

continuing. "There's been an accident…" I felt my heart begin to pound against my ribs. "The car your wife and mother were in had a blowout and rolled down an embankment just this side of Huachuca City." Cold sweat began to drench my brow as I was overcome with weakness.

"Ian!" Gus cried as I gripped my chest and sank from the seat. "Do you need your pills?"

"Pills?" the marshal asked.

"He has a heart condition!" the Admiral snapped.

I slid to the floor with Gus cradling my shoulders. My chest felt like it was swarming with angry wasps; the searing pain and the flutter combined to overcome me. My glasses slid from my eyes and fell to the floor next to me as Gus fished through my pockets and pulled a small pill container. I turned the top and poured one of the small nitroglycerin pills from the side of the round container. With a shaking hand, I placed it under my tongue and laid back.

"Dispatch," the marshal radioed. "I need an ambulance at the *saloon*. We have a possible coronary in progress."

"Just tell me what happened!" I demanded, breathless. "Are they all right?"

"They're fine. A stranger pulled them to safety."

"Stranger?" the Admiral asked.

"Strangest thing…some guy in black leather with dark curly hair and weird eyes." The marshal looked oddly at me before finishing, "Kind of like his."

My strength began to slowly return as I smiled and laughed at Gus.

"What's so funny?" Gus asked, shocked that I could find the near fatal crash of my mother and wife so amusing.

I trembled as I explained, "It was Deos. I told you he was here."

The ambulance didn't take long to arrive with the paramedics in full force. After being wired for sound, an oxygen mask over my face and an IV line inserted, I was placed in the ambulance on my way to the hospital in Sierra Vista. My tachycardia had returned and once again, I made a bad situation worse. The only reprieve came from the fact that I was going where my mother and wife already were.

Like clockwork, mother and Sarah were waiting in the Emergency Department. Sarah had a couple of stitches above her brow and mother's arm was in a sling, but otherwise they were fine. Sarah was wiping tears from her eyes as I was wheeled by. She leaned over and kissed my forehead. "Hell of a way to find a ride," she joked. "They never should have told you. I was afraid this would happen."

"I'm fine," I reassured, though I weakened by the moment.

The paramedics looked more and more concerned. As we arrived behind the curtained partition, Sarah and mother were ushered away by a nurse as the doctor raced over, a distinct rush in his gate. The whole experience seemed detached. I was once again becoming a stranger to my own body as I watched the movements of the medical staff.

"What do we have?" the doctor asked.

"Thirty five year old male, history of restrictive myopathy. Three doses of nitro given on route…He's been tachy with recurrent PVC's since we arrived on the scene…" one of the paramedics trailed off.

Everything suddenly appeared distant like I was watching from the bottom of a pool. My chest was overcome with an unearthly tingle as distant voices began to call, "He's arresting!"

My head rolled to the side and my gaze fixed on the doorway. I watched as Deos sauntered slowly in, his fedora in his hands before him in reverence. He was singing, "You take the high road/and I'll take the low road/and I'll be in Tombstone before ye…" His head was shaking in disbelief as the hospital staff worked to revive me.

"It's not time, lad," he stated as he walked towards me. "You canna give up, yet."

He placed a cold hand to my chest as I heard the doctor cry, "Clear!" My body arced as I was overwhelmed by the electric charge.

Deos just stood there gazing down at me, concern in his ghostly eyes, a cockeyed half-grin adorning his face. I could feel the pressure on my chest as they continued the compressions, the fire coursing through my veins as they injected medicines, but it was all like some disjointed dream.

Then, I was overwhelmed by a feeling of floating. A

strange fear engulfed me as I fought to keep spirit and body together. Yet, all I could think of was Gus' words, "You both try to be the first to drive the other away, like you're doing the other a favour." The past washed over me like a breaker as I stood at my head and watched a male nurse violently compress my chest. There was a disconnected fascination that engulfed me as Deos grabbed me by the collar and shoved me back to my body.

"As much as I've missed me best mate," he lamented a strange look of anger in his eyes. "You canna join me yet."

# Chapter Thirty-Seven
## The Unexpected

"In every marriage more than a week old, there are grounds for divorce. The trick is to find, and continue to find, grounds for marriage."
(Robert Anderson, 1861-1939)

My body arced, as I was shocked yet again. The cold, electric fire filled my chest with an odd tingle followed by a large thump against my ribs as my heart once again began to beat on its own. My mind was still cloudy and disjointed. Images came to me in clumps like I was watching a DVD on fast forward.

With a sense of relief, I heard the nurse exclaim, "We have a rhythm." I watched as Deos' cockeyed smile returned as he placed his fedora on his head and tapped the brim as he vanished from sight.

"Right!" the doctor decided. "Let's get this guy prepped and transferred to ICU. And will someone find out where the hell cardiology is!"

The cardiologist met me when I arrived in ICU. I was groggy and somewhat disoriented, but coherent enough to understand the options that were being posed to me. There were the same options I had been given before. The answer was always, and always would be, the same.

"I have reviewed your case," he explained.

I shook my head *no*. The doctor looked at me curiously, as if he wasn't used to being questioned. I knew he would try to convince my family to sign off, but my wishes were clear. Everyone knew I did not want anything surgical. It didn't stem from a fear of being carved like a Thanksgiving turkey. (I'd already been there and done that, thanks to Price.) What it did stem from was what I knew, or rather what I had already seen. Over the past two and a half years, my visions had become more frequent and a lot clearer. I had seen the consequences if I had either a cath or defibrillator installed. I had a 0% chance for survival on the table.

I never remembered Sarah, Mom, the Admiral, and Gus visiting in a revolving door pattern over the next couple of hours, but when I regained full consciousness, I found a stranger gazed down at me.

"Morning, Mr. Phoenix," the strange man smiled. "My name is Mark Ferris. I'm the hospital counsellor. Doctor Warner thought…"

"You could talk me into the surgery," I sighed irritantly.

"Mind if we have a chat?" he queried.

I motioned to a chair at my right as I informed, "It's a free country."

Mark pulled the chair over and sat down. He took a moment to glance me over before he ventured to speak again. All I could think was, *here we go again…*

"Why don't you want the procedure?" he asked conversationally.

"My reasons are strictly personal," I replied.

"Is it because you're Lakota?" I looked at him shocked and mildly perturbed. "I know of many Native Americans that have accepted modern medicine and all the wonders it has to offer."

I could scarcely believe what I was hearing. Had I been transported to the 1850's? A mild irritation rose in me at the presumption of the man. I tried to overcome the base urge to reach over and crack his redneck face.

"My heritage has nothing to do with it," I snapped. "As a matter of fact, I see my primary physician in Missouri every three months, a specialist in London every year, not to mention have a stress test, EKG and cardiac MRI every six months to a year. I have absolutely no problem with modern medicine. What I do have a problem with is the surgery and people that think that I'm an illiterate imbecile simply because I'm Lakota. And before you ask, yes, I have thought this through, many times and there is no way you're changing my mind."

"It sounds as though you're mind is set on this…"

"In concrete, mate."

Many have said that I'm a cold man. I suppose I had to be. All those years of wearing my heart on my sleeve, of being the charming, naïve type only brought me sorrow. It got me taken advantage of; not to mention, cost me not only my best friend, but my sanity as well. I swore years ago to never be put in that situation again. So as a result, I built a wall to barricade myself behind and isolated my broken heart from the world.

It was that heart whose limits were tested in more ways than one over the next few days. I spent two days in ICU before being transferred to the Cardiac Care Unit. Mark still popped in on a daily basis to check up on me, but the issue of implanted devices and minor surgery was never mentioned again. And neither was my heritage.

The day I was transferred out of ICU, I called Gus to have him bring *Blue* from the house. I had begun to go stir crazy and I figured at least my acoustic six-string would give me something to do other than stare at the blank walls. It was as I plucked lazily at the chords to limber my digits, that a man entered my room. He held a look of cold determination as he eyed me like yesterday's trash.

"John Holliday Phoenix?" he asked.

"Yes, can I help you?" I replied as he pulled an envelope from his breast pocket and I sarcastically gibed, "I was just transferred from ICU and I'm getting the bill. That's efficiency."

"Consider yourself served," was all the man would say as he turned and left the room.

I stared at the envelope in my hand, debating whether to break the seal when Mark stepped in for his daily visit. He looked at me strangely as he knocked on the door frame.

"Afternoon, John," he chimed.

"Come on in, Mark," I answered.

"What do you have there?" he asked as I waved the envelope in the air, a staggered exhale exiting my lips.

"Oh, well, here goes nothing," I decided as I ran my thumb through the flap. I slowly pulled the papers from the envelope, shook them open, and stared with unbelieving eyes at the document before me. "Well, it's from the Pueblo County Court in

Colorado. My wife filed for divorce two weeks ago… and I thought we were working things out."

Gus walked in, saw the look on my face and snatched the papers from my hands. He looked at them and then snapped at me, "When did you get these?"

"Just a couple of minutes ago," I replied.

"I'll take care of this!" he growled as the papers lazily fell onto the bed when he stormed from the room, his ear on his cell phone before he was even down the hallway.

My hands trembled as I tried to catch my breath. Terms such as *Emotional Abandonment, Anger Issues, Alcoholism, Paranoia,* and *Mental and Physical Instability* leapt from the page and tried to steal my breath. I felt betrayed, angry and alone.

"How long have you been separated?" Mark prodded.

"Six months. She's been living at the ranch in Colorado while I've been here setting up the Tombstone ranch."

I knew the question to follow. *Would I contest it?* Of that, I wasn't sure. I should have been hurt that she left to return to Colorado while I was in the hospital, I should have been furious that I was served the papers after just getting out of Intensive Care, but instead was numb with shock.

Gus returned a few minutes later with the Admiral in tow. Al looked as shocked as the rest of us about what had happened. The lot of them had last seen Sarah the day before when she left for Tucson with the insurance check to pick up a new BMW convertible. She never came back. Mother was at home, on the phone to my solicitor in London, planning our course of attack.

"How you doing, kid?" Al asked.

Mark took the opportunity to step from the room to leave Al, Gus, and I to the business at hand. Gus was still fuming and Al appeared to have spent the meanwhile trying to calm him down. Gus' dark neck was red with fury and his eyes were cold and distant from rage. I hadn't seem him that angry since I was a kid and he came home early to find his girlfriend in bed with another man.

"What kind of scum serves a guy that just had a heart attack papers?" Gus raved. "The bastard should be strung up by his…"

"Now is really not the time," Al soothed. "Maggie is dealing with that and as for these…" He grabbed the papers and shook them violently in the air, "we'll fight tooth and nail. This is wrong, especially now."

I grabbed my guitar and slowly began to pluck the strings. I had to do something to take my mind off things. Many of the songs that came to mind, seemed to only bring pain. Then, one emerged from somewhere in the back of my consciousness and transported me to before any of this had happened: before Deos, before London, but more importantly, before Sarah.

My voice was soft as I sang *Great Southern Land*.

Just as I finished my momentary lapse into the vast Outback desert, via *Icehouse,* was interrupted by the entrance of the cardiologist. He just stood in the doorway, a slight grin on his face.

"Seems as though you're feeling better," he commented. "Sorry to interrupt."

"Tell me you've got good news," I begged. "I could certainly use some today."

He walked in the room and stood at the foot of my bed.

"You should be able to go home tomorrow," he informed. "I would like to have you run another stress test, just to be safe." I rolled my eyes at the thought of running like a hamster in a wheel again. After all, I had just completed a stress echo the day before. "So far you're tests are coming back fine. There's a little bruising on your heart from the resuscitation, but it seems to be healing nicely and there doesn't appear to be any blockages. However, I would advise you to seriously consider giving up both your smoking and drinking. With your condition both have catastrophic effects…"

"Save it," I replied. "I've heard it before. So, how soon can I play hamster?"

"Play hamster?" the doctor asked.

I gave a cockeyed smile as I set my guitar aside, "Run on the wheel. If that's what it's going to take to get out of here, I'd just as soon get it over with."

"I'll set it up for this afternoon. If all goes well, you could be discharged as soon as tonight," he concluded.

# Chapter Thirty-Eight
## What Do You Do After You Fall…

"No failure in America, whether of love or money, is ever simple; it is always a kind of betrayal, of a mass of shadowy, shared hopes."
(Greil Marcus, b. 1945)

By the time I had my turn playing hamster, my mother, Al, and Gus had raised such a stink with the solicitors that a formal complaint, followed by a hefty civil suit, were being raised against the process server and Sarah's divorce attorneys. Mother and Gus had even tried to convince the state's attorney to file attempted murder charges because given my condition and recent setback, the shock could have killed me. My family embellished the tale a bit, however.

Other than an occasional blip, I passed the treadmill test with flying colours and was released late that afternoon after buying myself a side note on my permanent file of "high risk for sudden cardiac death" for refusing an implanted defibrillator. Little did they know how well I knew my limits. The doctor still thought I was mad for not agreeing to the procedure, but reluctantly accepted my decision after making it well known, he expected the next time he saw me would be in a body bag. I, however, had proved them wrong before.

When mother greeted me in the parking lot, she was on the phone. Al complained that since the papers arrived, mother's ear had been permanently attached to her cell phone. I don't think he was as irritated as he was feeling neglected. The pair had a very passionate relationship that was quickly finding its way to the back burner in light of recent events.

"The good news is Colorado is not a community property state," mother informed. "She can only potentially get half of marital assets. So, everything is safe. She can't get anything that was yours before you were married."

"Can we not discuss this now?" I decided as I got into mother's Cadillac.

I was just glad that Al had decided to leave the Ferrari at home. It seems as soon as the Admiral got behind the wheel, he thought he was a test pilot again and I really didn't feel like fighting G-forces the whole way to Tombstone. Mother's driving was much more sensible, if not borderline snailesque in nature.

The Sunday drive made a welcome diversion to the myriad of rampant thoughts and fears that plagued my mind. I found myself questioning every action I had ever made. Questioning what I could have done to cause this and who was to blame. As much as I wanted to hate Sarah for what she had done, I couldn't. Deep down, I knew I'd driven her away. Even when we were together, I was never really there. For in many ways, I was forever trapped in October of '85. Part of me never left that cold, upturned earth and was still prone on the ground with that gun at my head.

When I arrived home, I found Gus waiting at the ranch with BBQ, but as good as everything looked and smelled, I couldn't eat. This only seemed to irritate mother who scowled sourly at me as I put off eating in lieu of a tall glass of sweet tea.

"Are you trying to end up back in the hospital?" she snapped. "You need to eat. You need to keep your strength up now more than ever."

The one thing my mother never seemed to grasp was that I realized long ago, dying is easy. It's finding a reason to live that's hard. And it seemed since I first saw the stranger in the doorway, any reason was inching farther and farther from my grasp. Then again, I was never one to take the easy route.

We built a large bonfire at the back of the bunkhouse. Gus knew a good fire was always the one thing that could bring me comfort when all else failed. I found myself mesmerized by the flickering flames, the crackle of the wood and the floating nymphs of ash that glistened and danced in the curtain of smoke that rose high into the heavens.

I lazily spun *Blue* as I drifted in and out of planet reality.

My mind grasped at interrelated images, thoughts, and feelings. From this hodgepodge of obscurity, a coherent form began to take shape. Instinctively, I reached for the paper at the bottom of the guitar case and began to absently scribble.

## Heartbreak Ridge

Chocolate eyes beckon my wanton spirit
from the abyss. Fired by an electric charge
to bring continuity to the out of synch.
From the mountains between us,
the chasm looms, will beckons me go.
I stand on the razor's edge, the wall
forever shattered by mortars of paper,
my heart shattered like glass

on Heartbreak Ridge, the lure too much.
Heartbreak Ridge, oh, how I long to jump.

When will was gone, the fight
exhausted, adoration remained
The past, the past. The future,
if let be, full of potential.
Dying is easy; it's finding a reason to live
that's hard. Lost is the ultimate abstraction as
now here I stand on Heartbreak Ridge.
swayed by a cold, iron bed.
A voice in my mind beckons me to jump

from Heartbreak Ridge, the lure too much
Heartbreak Ridge, how I long to jump.

Muffled voices echo the direness
of a worsened situation. I know
the sleeper must awaken. Limbo denied
by a cold electric fire and the want
of what was lost to time.
As I stand on Heartbreak Ridge.

Knowing the sleeper must awaken,
from the balance so easily swayed
by your cold, iron bed.

Heartbreak Ridge, the lure too much.
Heartbreak Ridge, how I long to jump.

My fingers caressed *Blue 's* chords as I placed tune to emotion to create the ultimate expression of my sorrow. I found I was always most creative when faced with ultimate agony. I suppose in some demented, antiquated concept, I believed that I would forever have to suffer for my art. That through it I would find some ultimate catharsis, my absolute truth.

It was at that moment that I decided that I wasn't going to contest the divorce. I knew that I had done so much wrong, that it was time I did something right. She hadn't asked for much: the Colorado Ranch and everything it entailed; her three cars and a million for each year of marriage, which amounted to $2.5 million in cash plus another 5 million in assets.

In many ways, I was getting off easy. Her lawyers had wanted more, much more. They knew I was worth about $250 million at that time, but when faced with high-end London solicitors, Al's Washington law connections, and the opinion of a New York appellate court judge (who just happened to be one of Al's oldest friends) things changed drastically. We could have dragged things out, waited to take our chances in front of a judge, but I was shocked at how easily relenting Sarah was to the counter offer. She took the deal and ran.

# Chapter Thirty-Nine
## A New Beginning

"A kiss makes the heart young again and wipes
out the years."
(Rupert Brooke, 1887-1915)

That morning began much the same as any other morning. I rose at six for my two mile run. Gus was asleep in his wooden rocker on the porch of the bunkhouse as I emerged from the main house and made my way up the long drive. As I had done more times than I liked to remember, I made my way down the gravel road, but what differed that morning wasn't the run itself. It was the company.

A quarter mile into the run, I was approached by a tall, thin woman in her early to mid thirties with long, black hair pulled tight into a pony tail, spandex shorts, and a matching tank top. I was shocked by the presence of another person on the road. I would be occasionally passed by a pickup from one of the neighbouring ranches or someone on their way to work in Scary Vista, but never in two years had I seen another jogger.

"Use some company?" she asked as she kept pace next to me.

"Sure," I replied. "The name's John, but everyone calls me 'Doc'."

"Erin Connolly," she chimed as I offered my hand, still on the run.

Noticing the distinct Boston brogue in her voice I commented, "Nice German name. You're not from around here, are you?"

As she laughed, her eyes sparkled in the dawn sun.

"Certainly doesn't sound like you are either," she retorted on my mix of redneck and London boarding school. "Boston born and raised, you?"

"A little bit of everywhere…" She cast me looks of confusion as I went on to explain, "Born in New York, raised between Missouri and Vermont, schooled in London and Sydney."

"You do get around."

As she increased her pace, I hid the fact that I struggled to keep up, but talking was getting more and more difficult. She pulled ahead two paces, turned and said, "Let's race!" as she tore off down the road.

I shook my head in disbelief before chasing off after her. I caught her easily enough, but the burning of my throat and the pounding in my chest reminded me I wasn't as young or strong as I used to be. Common sense was pleading, *Are you trying to give yourself another heart attack, mate?* But my libido wasn't listening and my male pride was screaming, *You can't let a girl beat you!* We pounded down the road for the better part of a mile. Soon, we were neck and neck on approach to the gates of the ranch. When the drive was in sight, I tapped Erin on the shoulder and motioned with my right hand "cut" at my neck as I slowed, painfully to a stroll.

I stopped, briefly, bent over at the waist, then rose to arch my back, shook out my legs, and began to walk as I struggled to catch my breath. Erin laughed as she stood with her hands on her hips.

"Giving up, already?" she snickered.

I pointed to the ranch as I stifled the gasp that formed with the skip of my heart, "My stop. Care to join me?"

I opened the gates with the remote hanging from my hip and disarmed the security system. As we passed the bunkhouse, Gus raised a mug of coffee at us, a cockeyed grin on his face. I unlocked the heavy oak door to my house and motioned Erin to enter first. She shivered as her wet skin met the chilled, air-conditioned foyer. I led her into the kitchen that sat off of the living room. She wandered lazily into the living room, scanning the leather furniture and memorabilia on the walls.

"Coffee or mimosa?" I asked as I began to fish through the refrigerator, thankful for the chance to hide behind the door to take a long, deep breath to steady my nerve and check my pulse.

"I suppose a mimosa won't hurt," she decided. "I'm not going on duty today."

"On duty?" I asked as I poured champagne into a large flute and topped it with orange juice.

"I'm a deputy with the sheriff's department."

I handed her the glass, raised my own and watched her smile turn to shock as her eyes fell on the framed NASA flight badge that hung over the fireplace above the picture of Al and mother on the mantle.

"Is that real?" she asked, then noticed Al's picture. "You know Commander Cavelli?"

"Admiral now, actually," I corrected. "I should. He married my mother."

"Really? Wow. I mean, my father was kind of a NASA nut when I was growing up. We watched every shuttle launch."

"Al and mother should be passing through in another week or so. They're on one of their amorous getaways to Vegas, but he never misses Fleet Week in New York. I can introduce you, if you want."

Erin shook her head. "That's not necessary. My father's the space freak. Now, if you can get me *Peter Murphy* tickets…"

A woman after my own heart and I was intrigued from moment one. There was something about Erin that I easily associated with. I got the sense that we were both running away from something. She came off as carefree and wild, but I suspected there was something deeper, darker, and more obtrusive to her that I instantly connected with. She seemed to float through the room, making her way from one object to the next. She stopped at the stereo and glanced curiously at me.

"Think we could use some music?" she asked.

I shrugged, grabbed the remote from the shelf on the island above me and started the CD in the player. Almost immediately, the room was filled with the Brandos *Gettysburg*. Erin looked at me curiously before closing her eyes to listen closer.

"If you don't like *the Brandos*, you can pick something else out," I informed as I pushed the remote to open the wall behind the stereo, revealing my extensive album collection.

"No, this is fine," she relented. "They're pretty good.

What are they Southern Rock?"

"They're from New York. I guess they could be classified as more Roots Rock."

I refilled her glass before moving my guitars so she could sit. It had been so long since I'd had any real company that my manners seemed to have gone out the window.

"Do you play?" she asked.

"I've got a recording studio out back. It seemed a lot easier than hopping on a plane for London every time I wanted to record something. I started an Indi record label in London a few years ago. I doubt you've heard of it...*God of War Records.*" She shook her head *no*. Not that it surprised me. We had yet to release a major name.

"So, you got a band?" she asked.

"I play with a couple of guys from Sierra Vista. We're playing a benefit this weekend for the American Heart Association, if you're interested."

The next two hours passed much the same as those first minutes. There was something familiar, unimposing, and comfortable about Erin, a connection that I never really felt with Kat or Sarah, a sense of knowing the other without really speaking. It seemed the less we spoke, the deeper it became. There was an almost primal nature to the attraction. But beyond, an intellectual one as well – we shared many of the same interests, the same taste in music, the same innate desire to not be hurt again. Though, neither of us could ever really express why.

We were certainly a mixed pair; the cop and the rocker. We kept things casual. We went jogging together every morning, hung out in the evening at the ranch. She lived two miles down the road in a rented fifth wheel on two acres. She would sit and listen to me play my guitar well into the wee hours of the morning. The next step emerged as a natural progression into the occasional all-nighters.

I avoided discussing too much of my past and if I was having a bad day or a doctor's appointment, I avoided that issue as well. I didn't want to do anything to jeopardize what we had built. Part of me was afraid of what was developing and a bigger part was afraid of losing it. I would get nervous each time she would lay her head on my bare chest out of fear of what she might hear or how she would react if she knew. Eventually the fear waned, replaced by familiarity, but I still couldn't bring myself to explain what had happened to her. She had to find out on her own.

It was a Friday afternoon and I had stepped into the back to fire up the BBQ when the phone rang. Erin answered and asked to take a message. It was the hospital wanting to reschedule my latest stress test. When I walked back into the house, she was hanging up the phone, a look of shock on her face.

"Everything all right?" I asked.

"That was the hospital," she stated. I let out a staggered exhale as my head dropped. "They need to reschedule your stress test. Are you ok?"

"I'm fine," I replied. "It's just a routine test. But if this changes things…"

"Why would it change things?"

"Because, love, it always does."

Made in the USA
Columbia, SC
11 April 2023

14764546R00150